She knew that somewhere she'd crossed the line...

The photos spread out in front of her had at first been simply a legitimate attempt to gather information about the bomber's only surviving victim.... But now...

She knew them by heart. The dark eyes laughing down at his mother's. In a tux at somebody's wedding. Always taller than the people around him. Dominating. *Too good-looking for his own good,* her grandmother would have said. He was surrounded in one shot by smiling debutantes, who looked up at his smiling face with something like her own fascination.

Crazy, Kate thought to herself. *This is crazy. Like a teenager putting pictures of a rock star on the wall.* She was thirty-two years old. Way too old for this kind of crush. *So childish. Crazy.*

Tonight she had met him. Twice. She had even sat beside him in his car. She closed her eyes and remembered. How he'd smelled. Not cologne. Just clean. Soap. Male.

His voice had wrapped around her in the dark. Soft and very deep. Southern slow. He had been near enough that she could have reached out and touched him...if only she had.

Dear Reader,

Thank you so much for choosing *Heart of the Night*. Like most of my Intrigue titles, this story was inspired by events that paraded across my television screen. I began to wonder about the effect of a mail bomb on a victim—one who was lucky enough to survive. Then I began to wonder about the other invasion of that victim's life that was sure to follow—the presence of the media, who serve "the public's right to know."

The reporter in this story, Kate August, becomes very much aware of the impact of media attention when she tries to interview reclusive Judge Thorne Barrington. Barrington is the only surviving victim of a notorious serial bomber, nicknamed Jack the Tripper by the press. Thorne hates the press, with good reason, and yet he feels duty bound to do anything he can to help Kate catch the killer before Jack can strike again.

I must confess that another inspiration for this book is a more personal and, I suspect, more common experience. It concerns fantasizing about those beautiful guys who seem to be forever out of our reach. If you've ever daydreamed about getting stuck in an elevator with Brad Pitt or about licking that tantalizing trickle of lemonade off Harrison Ford's throat, then I promise you, this one's for you. Hope you enjoy!

Love,

Gayle Wilson

P.S. I love to hear from readers. Feel free to write me at P.O. Box 342, Birmingham, Alabama 35201-0342.

Heart of the Night
Gayle Wilson

Harlequin Books

TORONTO • NEW YORK • LONDON
AMSTERDAM • PARIS • SYDNEY • HAMBURG
STOCKHOLM • ATHENS • TOKYO • MILAN
MADRID • WARSAW • BUDAPEST • AUCKLAND

For Mona Kathrine, my heart's daughter,
who was supposed to be called Mona Kate,
and who instead, somehow, became our beloved
Katsy, and for her daughter Katelyn Joy.

ISBN 0-373-22442-7

HEART OF THE NIGHT

Copyright © 1997 by Mona Gay Thomas

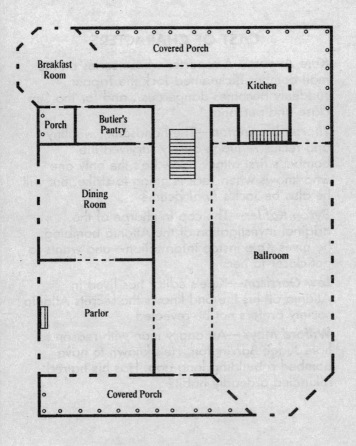

THE BARRINGTON MANSION
ATLANTA, GEORGIA

CAST OF CHARACTERS

Kate August—A reporter whose series on the mail bomber nicknamed Jack the Tripper suddenly becomes dangerous...and far too "up close and personal."

Thorne Barrington—The handsome, wealthy and reclusive judge barely survived the bomber's first attack. Now he's the only one who knows when Jack is going to strike. But will he also be Jack's *final* victim?

Byron Kahler—The cop in charge of the original investigation of the Atlanta bombing, he gives Kate inside information—and wants to get closer to her.

Lew Garrison—Kate's editor has lived in Atlanta all his life and knows the secrets Atlanta society prefers not be revealed.

Wilford Mays—An angry man with reason to hate Judge Barrington. He's known to have bombed a building long ago. Has his hatred rekindled a deadly habit?

Prologue

In a darkened room in Atlanta, Georgia, Thorne Barrington put the phone back in its cradle. It took a conscious effort to force his fingers to unclench from around the receiver. He raised his left hand to run it tiredly through thick black hair, a habit left from childhood, used then to subdue its stubborn tendency to curl. He became aware that he still wore the latex gloves with which he had handled the letter.

He stripped them off and laid them on the table beside the telephone. He shivered suddenly, although, even with the efficiency of central air, the brutal heat of the Georgia summer had invaded the house. Finally he closed his eyes. There was nothing to do now except wait. He had had a lot of experience waiting during the last three years. As he had endured the rest, he would endure this, but the waiting was always so hard.

IN AN OFFICE a thousand miles away, Hall Draper also put a phone back in its cradle and sat for a moment reliving the triumph of last night's game. They were in the play-offs, and Trent had gone two for three and then made a diving grab of a shot down the middle that no one had any right to expect a ten-year-old to catch. Tonight would be the test. The Sox were the best in the league, and everyone knew it.

Trent was pitching, and although Hall was nervous as a cat, he knew the boy wouldn't be. Trent would be keyed up, looking forward to the game, the challenge, but he'd be okay with a loss. It would give him more time for other things. It was a long season, and the kids were always glad when it was over. It was the adults who suffered the letdown, who cared how it all turned out, who held the bitterness of defeat into the coolness of fall.

Hall had often vowed he'd never be one of those Little-League parents, but that was before it had been his kid up at bat, *his* son on the mound. The adrenaline started flooding, no matter what he told himself. Jackie wouldn't even go to the games anymore. It made her too nervous. He just hoped for a win so he could sleep tonight.

"Mail," Claudia sang out as she came through the door that separated his office from the small reception area. An eternally cheerful woman, a little heavy and beyond middle age, his secretary had previously worked for an attorney who had just retired. Hall sometimes thought she knew more about running a practice than he did.

He had come to it late, had postponed the dream because of a lack of money and an early marriage. Trent had arrived before they were on their feet financially, and Hall had worked days and attended classes at night. It had taken far longer than it should have before he had his degree and had passed the bar, and it had been a struggle since. He hadn't attracted the interest of any of the big firms, his résumé unimpressive by his own standards. Even now, they were just barely getting by. Jackie was still working, but she didn't seem to mind.

Life was good, he thought, a little surprised by the introspection. He was not by nature an introspective man.

"A couple of remittances, a bill and a package. You want me to open it?" Claudia asked, a matter of form, they both knew. It was always slow enough that even the mail was an event in his day.

"Who's it from?" he asked, using his thumbnail to split one of the envelopes. It was a check from a client. A dollar-down-and-a-dollar-a-week law practice—he knew that's all he had. But at least this one was still sending his dollar.

Claudia turned the package, pretending that she hadn't already read the return address.

"Thornedyke Barrington," she told him. "It's marked personal. You know him?"

"If I do, I can't remember where. It sounds familiar. Just leave it, and I'll get to it later."

"You remember I'm taking Mother to the doctor? I'm taking the rest of the day off. I swear I dread it. That woman wears me out. You'll be okay, won't you?"

"Unless we get a rush. What are the chances of that, Claudia, do you think?"

They smiled at each other.

"Good luck tonight," the secretary said, turning to retrace her steps to the door. "Tell Trent I said to knock 'em dead."

"I don't think that's what you tell a pitcher—especially in Little League, but I'll try to convey the thought. Be careful on the way home from the doctor's."

"I will. See you tomorrow."

The door closed behind her, and Hall's thoughts moved back to the game. He thought about calling Jackie and asking her to run out and pick up some Gatorade. He decided finally that he could stop on the way home and then she wouldn't have to get out of the house in this heat.

He got up and walked to the windows behind his desk. He lifted one slat of the blind that was closed against the summer sun and looked out on the deserted street in front of his office. It was too hot for anyone to be out if they didn't have to.

He turned back, and the package caught his eye. Thornedyke Barrington, he remembered, but he turned it around so the address faced him and read it for himself. He had heard the name before, but for the life of him he couldn't remember where. He'd never been to Atlanta. Probably something to do with a client.

He took his old Boy Scout knife out of his top drawer and slipped it under the string that bound the brown-paper-wrapped box. He pulled the blade up sharply against the twine and cut through, the string releasing with a small twang. He turned the package over, his mind again slipping away to the familiar scene under the lights of the ballpark. He slid his thumb under the taped triangular flaps on the back and lifted the paper away from the box.

He had wadded the wrappings in one hand before he thought better of it. He probably should save the return address, he decided. He straightened out the crumpled sheet and laid it carefully on his desk. He put both hands on the box, one on each side, and the lid slid upward in one smooth motion.

As soon as the top had cleared the upright sides, just as the maker of the bomb had intended, the world exploded before Hall Draper's eyes. He was dead before his body slammed into the chair behind the desk and then fell heavily to lie on the blood-splattered floor of his office.

Chapter One

"Your boy did it again."

"My boy?" Kate August questioned, her blue eyes flicking up to meet her editor's as she opened the bottom drawer of her desk to put her purse back in its accustomed place. She'd just returned from a long and pleasant lunch with a college friend, and she had not yet refocused her mind on the newsroom. She didn't understand the reference. At the moment she could not, in any context, be accused of having a "boy."

She bent to fumble awkwardly under the desk, one-handed, trying to locate the comfortable shoes she'd worn this morning. The black heels she was now wearing, which she had put on for her luncheon appointment, had been carried in to work in a Rich's bag. There was something about meeting a friend you hadn't seen in a while, no matter how old or how good a friend, which demanded a little extra effort, a conscious decision to mask the evidence of years passing and the concessions that had inevitably been made to their passage.

So Kate had put her long, sun-streaked chestnut hair up today, had worn a little more makeup than usual and her best suit, but all the way back from the restaurant she had thought only that she couldn't wait to get the shoes off, no matter what they did for her ankles.

"Jack," Lew Garrison said, his usually smiling brown eyes serious. His thinning gray hair was disordered as if, distracted, he'd run his fingers through it. "Jack hit again."

Kate's hand, which had been searching in the black hole

where her flats had apparently disappeared, froze. Her cheek still resting on the metal surface of the desktop, she allowed herself a deep breath and then straightened to meet Lew's eyes.

"Damn," she said softly. "It's not near time…" The comment trailed. There was no point in voicing the obvious. The consensus had been that the mail bomber, whom the press had begun calling Jack the Tripper almost two years ago, was working according to a careful schedule. Twice a year some unsuspecting victim opened his mail and died.

Doctor, lawyer, Indian chief. Ridiculously, the children's rhyme ran through Kate's mind, which was still trying to deal with the shock of Lew's announcement. That was one of the many puzzles of this story she'd been working on the last four months. There seemed to be no connection between the recipients of Jack's mail bombs, at least none anyone had yet figured out. Only his timing had been consistent. Until now.

Shoes forgotten, her fingers quickly lifted above the edge of the desk to flip backward through the revolving calendar. She was right. It had been late March, a little more than three months ago. She didn't need the notation to remember where. Austin, Texas. She had gone there. With the help of Detective Byron Kahler, her "in" with the Atlanta police, she even had been allowed to view the carnage in the boarding house where the device had exploded, killing an old man. Such a *nice* old man, everyone had told her. She closed her mind to the images from that devastated room, denying their impact.

"Who?" she asked.

"A small-time lawyer in Tucson. A guy named Hall Draper."

Kate felt a small surge of excitement. "A lawyer? Like Barrington."

She couldn't remember exactly when the press had made the connection between the first bombing here in Atlanta and the others. The police had not originally discussed the Barrington case in conjunction with the rest—because, of course, there was one obvious and very important difference. Jack the

Tripper had screwed up. One intended target, an Atlanta judge named Thornedyke Barrington, had survived.

The Barringtons had always been prominent in civic affairs, cultured, educated at private Southern schools or the Ivy League. In Thorne Barrington's case it had been Tulane and then on to Harvard Law, followed by a return to Atlanta where he'd gone to work in the DA's office. And why not? Kate thought. Heir to one of Georgia's largest fortunes, he didn't need the income from some Peachtree partnership.

The surprising thing had been how good he was. A lot of people in Atlanta had waited for Thorne Barrington to fall flat on his face, believing his academic successes had resulted from his father's generous contributions to the schools he'd attended. Smart, dedicated, and realistic, he had proved the doubters wrong, and the most remarkable thing was that he hadn't even seemed to be aware he needed to.

Barrington had risen quickly through a stream of successful convictions, and when a judgeship had come open, his record and family name had secured it. If his daddy had used his influence, no one thought at that point to question the rightness of its use. Thorne Barrington was already being mentioned for the state Supreme Court when Jack's package arrived.

"There's no justification in linking this guy and Barrington," Lew said. "Maybe if all Jack's victims were involved with the law—"

"Barrington was a judge; this guy in Tucson's a lawyer. It seems a pretty obvious connection to me. Don't try to tell me that you didn't at least think about it."

"What about the six in between? Besides, the law those two practiced was poles apart. Apparently Draper had a hole-in-the-wall practice, mostly wills and simple divorces. And he wasn't born with a silver spoon in his mouth."

"Just because we haven't *found* the link between Jack's victims doesn't mean there isn't one," Kate said. This wasn't a new argument. The cops' idea that the bomber ran his finger down the pages of a phone book to choose the next recipient of his package had never made much sense to her. Other serial killers might be forced to depend on opportunity. Because of his method, Jack wasn't limited by that. He chose his own victims, and Kate was convinced they were chosen for a reason.

"Random selection," Lew said. "You know that's the usual rule. You just think your theory makes for a better story."

"Makes more sense, you mean. You think he'll talk to me?" she asked, keeping her voice casual. It took a second for Lew to sort through the possible *he's,* but he was bright, and of course, he knew Kate very well.

"Barrington? You think Barrington's going to talk to a reporter?"

"Yeah. Maybe," she amended. "Under the right conditions. Maybe the bombing today brought something back, triggered some feelings. Maybe I'll get lucky and catch him in a moment of weakness. You never know until you ask."

"Trust me," Lew said, "Barrington's not going to talk to the press. Today is only going to drive him a little further into that shell he crawled into. He doesn't see anybody. Not since the bomb. He didn't even go to his father's funeral last year."

"Was he disfigured?" It was a question that had bothered her since she'd begun the series, one there had been no information about. There was not a whisper about Barrington's injuries in the published reports. Only a lot of money could buy *that* kind of privacy.

"He'd have access to the finest plastic surgeons in the world, and it's been three years. Surely by now, *whatever* injuries he sustained..." Lew shrugged.

"Then why? Why disappear?"

"How would you react to someone trying to blow you up? Especially someone who has succeeded in blowing up everybody else he's targeted."

"Jack's only failure. You think he's afraid the bomber will try again?" Kate asked. She had become fascinated with the Tripper case and the cast of characters she'd studied so carefully during the past four months. And, she admitted, especially fascinated with Thorne Barrington.

"He hasn't changed his address. He hasn't run." Lew shrugged. "He's just…"

"Stopped living," she said. "More than three years ago."

"How would you react?" Lew asked again. "How can any of us know how we'd react to something like what happened to Barrington?"

The same thing that had happened again today in Tucson, Kate thought. Another human tragedy, its humanity lost, somehow, in the familiarity of its violence. By the national telecasts tonight, she knew and accepted, the coverage of the bombing would have been reduced to a four-minute segment, complete, if possible, with a glimpse of members of the grieving family, the real cost of today's events etched starkly in their faces—providing, of course, that the local affiliate came through with the tape.

AFTER SHE LEFT the office that night, Kate was reluctant to go home, too keyed up by the events of the day, by thinking about Jack and the series she was doing on the bombings. So she found herself heading once more in a now familiar direction. During the last three months she must have driven by the Barrington mansion a thousand times.

It was in a section of Atlanta that had been the city's most exclusive before the turn of the century. Only the Barringtons had never moved out, refusing to give in to the urban decay that had slowly surrounded the house during the last fifty years. This is where the Barringtons had chosen to live, and to hell with anyone who believed they had made a bad decision. The irony was that the area was coming back. The homes that were left, huge and hard to maintain, expensive to heat and cool, were being snapped up and renovated into exclusive apartments.

She slowed as she approached the house, only its shape and size visible, the distinctive Victorian tower and irregular roof lines jutting against the night sky. The one concession to the changing neighborhood that the family had made some time in the last thirty years was the high, wrought iron fence that surrounded its narrow grounds, the gate always securely locked against intruders. There were lights visible deep within the house, their glow diffuse and distant.

As she held the Mazda to a crawl along the street that paralleled the grounds, she saw that the front gate was standing open. That was unprecedented, and on today of all days, it seemed almost bizarre. Kate pulled the car up to the curb.

A golden retriever sat forlornly near the open gate. She could see the light-colored lead securing him to one of the tall spikes of the fence. There seemed to be no one around, and as Kate watched, the dog lifted his head and howled. The aching misery of the cry raised the small hairs on the back of her neck. She cut off the engine, but it took another plaintive wail before she opened the door and stepped out onto the street in front of the mansion.

The dog strained toward her, whimpering in his frenzy to free himself and to once again secure the safety of human companionship. It was obvious that he had not been placed here to serve as a watchdog. He was far too glad to see her, a stranger appearing out of the night, to be effective at that.

The retriever was almost beside himself by the time she knelt down to smooth her hands over his head, scratching behind the silky ears and eventually cuddling the reaching nose against her chest. Despite his size, she could tell he was still young, just an overgrown puppy.

Apparently someone had begun the dog's evening walk and then returned to the mansion, leaving the gate open. The only problem with that reasonable scenario was what she knew about Thorne Barrington's obsession for privacy.

Was it possible that the retriever had been brought out here deliberately to get him out of the way? she wondered suddenly. That idea was melodramatic, perhaps, but why was the gate standing open? Today of all days. Against her will, Kate again remembered the room in Austin and before she could talk herself out of it, she reached to release the puppy's lead from the fence.

As soon as it was loosened, the leather loop was pulled out of her fingers, and the dog, trailing the lead, disappeared into the darkness inside the fence, far more eager to escape her company than she could have imagined based on his previous delight. Kate hesitated a moment, and then, following the retriever, she entered the grounds through the gate she had not ever, in all her trips by the house, seen standing open.

Trespassing, she reminded herself, climbing the stairs to the front porch. *This is trespassing.* She had no right to be here, no logical explanation for the compulsion she felt to investigate.

The front door stood ajar. There was a faint light from inside, dimly visible through its heavy beveled glass panels. She put her palm against it and the door swung inward, almost inviting her to enter. *Breaking and entering* flashed into her head, but she ignored the mental warning because her sense that something was very wrong, a feeling that had begun before she'd ever gotten out of her car, was now too strong to deny.

The crystal tears in the chandelier overhead tinkled softly in the draft from the open door, and hearing them, she automatically stepped inside, closing the door behind her.

The faint light she had seen from the porch seemed to be coming from the back of the house, from behind the massive staircase that climbed to the upper stories. She walked to the foot of the stairs, and looked up, her gaze following their rise. Four stories of railings spiraled upward, like some Escher drawing, into the darkness at the top of the house.

It was as still as death except for the faintest strain of music drifting into the foyer like fog. Even the sounds from the street had disappeared behind the thickness of the materials that had been used in the mansion's construction.

"Hello," she called, her voice too tentative to reach the back of the house or upstairs, the most likely places to find the inhabitants. Still she waited, listening. Even the crystal teardrops were silent now.

"Is there anyone here?" she called again, holding her breath. She had wanted to meet Thorne Barrington, but somehow, despite her legitimate concerns about the deserted puppy and the open door, she knew this was a bad idea. She had invaded his privacy on the flimsiest of excuses: his front gate was open on a day that Jack the Tripper had claimed another victim, more than a thousand miles away.

It would be better to leave and call 911 from her car phone. The police could come and check. An anonymous call from a concerned citizen who had seen the dog and the opened gate. She wondered if they'd send a car if she refused to give her name. Or better than that, she should call Detective Kahler, who would certainly understand the strangeness of the situation. Kahler had been the officer in charge on the Barrington case, long before anyone had realized they were dealing with a madman.

Instead of following any of those sensible avenues, she found herself surveying her surroundings. There were four sets of closed double doors, two on each side of the long entrance hall. She crossed the foyer to stand before the first set on the right. She fumbled for a knob in the dimness, realizing finally there was none. What her fingers discovered was an indentation by which the door could be pushed open. The half of the door that she touched slid almost noiselessly to disappear into the wall beside it.

Through the opening created by the sliding door, she saw an empty ballroom, lights from the cross street behind the tall sweep of windows providing enough illumination to allow her to determine, without any doubt, the room's purpose. Both sets of doors on this side led into this ballroom. In the stillness, she could almost visualize couples swaying on the floor that still gleamed softly, as if awaiting their return.

She stood a moment, caught by the ghosts her mind had created, and eventually she realized that the faint echo of melody was not part of the fantasy. The music was very real and had been there from the first, softly whispering into the darkness. Leaving the ballroom doors open, she moved back across the foyer to those on the opposite side.

The doors there operated the same way, sliding just as noiselessly to hide themselves in the wall. The design was such, she realized, that all four sets could be opened at once to create an enormous space, encompassing the wide foyer and the rooms on both sides, suitable for the lavish entertainments the Barringtons had been famous for. Now the house itself was as lonely as the man who inhabited it. So different from its past. So different now from his.

The music originated from this room, much louder now than the eerie whisper it had been before. She stepped into what had obviously been the downstairs parlor, the familiar shapes of the Victorian furniture indicating that it had stayed unchanged from the century before. In the dimness she couldn't see the fabrics that covered the scattered chairs and couches, but she could imagine their richness.

Despite her fear, despite the sense of urgency that had compelled her to enter tonight, she had been caught by the house's timelessness. Thinking only about the slow, deliberate gentility of the life that had been lived in these rooms, she was totally unprepared for the voice which spoke from the shadows gathered thickly to the left of the fireplace.

"What the hell are you doing in my house?" Thorne Barrington demanded.

Kate could see nothing of his features. Her eyes had not adjusted to the gloom after the faint light of the hallway. She doubted, even when they did, that she would be able to distinguish details about the man who sat in the darkest part of the room. There were no streetlights on this side of the mansion to provide even the faint glow that had unveiled the splendor of the long-deserted ballroom.

There was something, however, in the deep voice, an authority bred from generations of privilege, that made her very sure the questioner was Barrington himself.

"The gate was open," Kate said. It was why she'd stopped, but as she said it, she knew it didn't begin to answer his question.

"Obviously," Thorne Barrington said. "I asked why you're in my house."

"I saw the dog. He was tied to the fence, but he was upset, and then I found the front door wasn't closed. I thought something was wrong. I was worried..." She hesitated, considering all the things she couldn't tell him. All the real reasons she was here. *Because I know the gate shouldn't have been open, that it never is. Because...because I know all about you.*

"Where's Elliot?" asked the voice from the shadows.

"I don't know," she said. Who was Elliot? Did he expect her to know that? "There was no one here. I called, but no one answered, so I thought something must have happened."

"Because the gate was open?" The question was derisive.

"Because of the dog. The front door," she added, trying to sound convincing. It was the truth, and she wondered why it sounded so specious.

"Who are you?" Thorne asked.

Kate hesitated, but she knew she had no choice but to tell him. He might ask to see an ID and besides, she doubted he'd recognize her name. People read a thousand stories without ever looking at the byline.

"My name is Kathrine August."

"August. I should have known," Barrington said, his soft laughter sardonic. "Don't you ghouls ever give up? Feeding off other people's pain like vampires. Doesn't what you do keep you awake at night?"

There wasn't much doubt after *that*, Kate thought, that he had recognized her name. So much for playing a long shot. "People have a right to the news, Judge Barrington," she argued, fighting to keep emotion out of her explanation—one she truly believed. "You know that. It's one of the most fundamental rights in this democracy."

"A fundamental right," the dark voice repeated, still mocking. "Does seeking to provide them with that 'news' give you the right to break into my home. I'm not 'news,' Ms. August. Not anymore. Get out."

"I'm afraid I can't agree with that. I'd like to talk to you about what happened in Tucson today. About—"

"Get out," he ordered softly, but there was no denying the threat. For the first time, Kate felt more than a sense of unease. More than embarrassment for having done something which she knew was wrong. For the first time, she was afraid. There was so much anger in the quiet command.

"You can't hide forever," she said. It was something she

had thought since she'd realized what his life had become. How empty. Hiding. That was the truth, and maybe one he needed to hear, but as she said it she knew *she* had no right to tell him what he should do. Lew had been right. Who could know how they would react if faced with the lack of trust Thorne Barrington must deal with every day for the rest of his life? She couldn't imagine how opening a seemingly innocuous package and having it blow up in your face would color your view of the world.

"Hide?" he repeated. His voice was louder now, stronger in the darkness, apparently furious with what she had suggested.

The puppy whimpered at his tone, and Kate realized the retriever was sitting beside Barrington's chair. Her eyes gradually adjusting to the darkness now, she could make out their shapes, a darkness against the surrounding shadows. Barrington's hand rested on the dog's neck, the animal pressed as closely as possible against the chair in which the judge was sitting.

"Is that what you think I'm doing, Ms. August? Hiding?" Barrington asked again.

It was what everyone thought, Kate knew, but given the anger in the dark voice and her situation, she hesitated. Apparently he had never realized what people believed about his disappearance.

"I don't think anyone blames you for that. I can't begin to imagine…" She hesitated. "I don't know how I'd react to—"

"I'm not *hiding,* Ms. August. Now get the hell out of my house before I call the police and have you arrested for breaking and entering."

"I didn't *break* in. The door's open. The gate. And your dog…" she paused, wondering for the first time how the dog had gotten in here. Obviously, there was another entrance.

"Elliot was supposed to…" He stopped whatever explanation he had begun when the retriever whimpered again. The puppy shifted position, uncomfortable with the anger, pushing his head against his master's hand. "Look, none of that's your concern," Barrington said. "Just get the hell out of my house."

"I would really like to talk to you. It doesn't have to be tonight, but you have a different perspective on the bombings than anyone else. I'll meet with you anytime you say. I'm doing a series. You may have read—"

"No," the voice from the shadows said. "I won't talk to you, Ms. August. Not tonight. Not ever."

"It's understandable, after all that's happened, if you're afraid, but surely you must realize—"

She never finished whatever idiotic advice she was about to offer. In the darkness she didn't see him press the button of the speaker phone which was on the table beside him, conveniently near at hand. By the time she'd realized that he had, he was speaking to whoever had responded.

"This is Thorne Barrington. I have an intruder. She doesn't appear to be dangerous, but I want her out of my house. Please send a patrol car."

"You're going to have me arrested?" Kate asked, stunned. She had played the good Samaritan because she was concerned about his safety, about breached security, and he was calling the cops.

"*Afraid*, Ms. August?" he asked mockingly.

Unable to believe it was really happening, she heard in the distance the siren of the patrol car. Apparently when Thorne Barrington asked for the police, he got them. Immediately.

Son of a bitch, she thought resignedly, wondering what in the world Kahler was going to do to her for pulling this stunt.

WHEN THE OFFICERS had gone and silence again reigned in the familiar darkness that surrounded him, Thorne Barrington closed his eyes. He recognized the perfume the woman had worn, floating to him from across the room. His mother had worn Shalimar, and the fragrance haunted the room now, reminding him. Smell was the most evocative of the senses, and he wondered how the reporter could have known what to wear to create the images that were moving through his mind. Images of life as it had once been lived in this house. Images of what his own life had once been. Angered again, he pulled his thoughts away from the past and back to the reporter who had invaded his well-guarded privacy.

Kate August. She was the one who had written the series of articles on the bombings. He should have known. God, he should be better prepared by now. After what had happened today in Tucson, someone was bound to try. Usually the fence was enough to deter the curious. Either she was very determined or she had somehow convinced Elliot to let her in.

Where the hell is Elliot? he wondered for the first time. He hadn't escorted the policemen into the parlor. They must have entered through the door she had claimed was standing open. In his fury at her intrusion, he had totally ignored what Kate August had said, discounting her explanations as lies. Was it possible that something *had* happened to Elliot?

He stood up suddenly to stride across the dark parlor. He knew these rooms by heart. Not a piece of furniture was ever moved. Nothing ever changed in the house.

Except tonight, he thought. Tonight the house was different, its aura subtly disturbed, because the elusive fragrance she had worn moved before him now through the once again silent, deserted rooms.

Chapter Two

The cops had been businesslike and impersonal. They acted as if escorting a female reporter out of Judge Barrington's mansion was part of their nightly routine. By the time they'd arrived at their precinct house, Kate was completely humiliated by her own stupidity, but she made the call to Detective Kahler, praying he would be in and at the same time dreading the possibility. And Kahler didn't let her down.

He looked long-day tired, slightly rumpled, with the collar of his oxford-cloth shirt unbuttoned, rep tie loosened as a concession to the heat. Kahler was pushing forty, but his face was good, the lines around the eyes and tonight's slight shadow of beard not detracting from its attractiveness.

It was, however, his voice Kate liked best. The transplanted Yankee speech patterns had softened just enough to take the edge off. He was a good-looking man, and she had begun to think of him as a friend, but it was obvious he wasn't feeling friendly tonight and his usually pleasant voice was coldly furious.

"What the hell made you think you had the right to walk into the man's house at night?" he asked. "You're damn lucky he didn't shoot you. I would have. What the hell were you thinking, August?"

"I've already told the cops all this. I saw the dog tied outside and the open gate. It's never open, so—"

"How do you know Barrington's gate is 'never open'?" he interrupted the reasons she'd attempted to offer before. "You take a survey of his neighbors? They tell you that if the gate's open, there's a crime in progress? The bomber always leaves it open when he visits? If you really believe something's wrong, August, you call the police. You don't waltz in on your own. It won't wash. You just wanted to talk to Barrington about what happened today, and so you break into his home and—''

"I didn't break in. The damn door was open. How many times do I have to tell you that?''

What she didn't tell him, would never tell him of course, was how she knew the gate was always closed. She wouldn't admit the number of times she'd driven by Barrington's home. Kahler's reaction was making her question what she had done. Not tonight—she knew what she'd done tonight was beyond the bounds—but before. To question her growing fascination with the central character of the story she was working on.

She even had a file folder of material she'd collected on Thorne Barrington. But if she didn't admit the number of times she'd driven by his mansion, she certainly wouldn't confess the number of times she'd studied the black-and-white photographs that folder contained.

Maybe Kahler was right. Maybe she needed to back off, maybe even get Lew to assign someone else to finish the series. She had broken the first commandment, the prime directive. She had become personally involved with this story. She was no longer objective. Not about Barrington. And not about the bomber.

"You broke a trust, August," Kahler went on. "I agreed to talk to you, against my better judgment, I have to tell you. And then you go and pull something like this.''

Kahler had been up-front from the first about his and the department's motives in agreeing to help her with the series of articles she was writing about Jack. *"Anything that will draw this joker out is okay with me,"* he had said. *"Just remember that we're using you, August. Not the other way around."*

So they had shared some dinners, all of which she'd put on her credit card, a legitimate business expense since they had talked about the bombings, with only an occasional foray into how the Braves were doing. And he took her calls, patiently answering her questions and guiding her series into something that might, they both hoped, spark a response in someone who had information about the bomber that they didn't realize might be important. And in the process, she had come to consider Kahler a friend. Only gradually had Kate begun to wonder if the look she had occasionally surprised in his hazel eyes was rooted in the growing personal interest she'd been attributing it to.

"I didn't mention your name," she said defensively. "Barrington doesn't know you've talked to me. He won't ever know. All he knows is I'm a reporter. He called us vampires."

That comment had bothered her. *Feeding off other people's pain.* She knew there was a lot of truth to the accusation. It just wasn't the way she usually thought about her job.

"The media frenzy might be one of the reasons Barrington chose to disappear. Somebody sneaked into his hospital room and took pictures a couple of days after the bombing."

She hadn't known that. Those photographs weren't part of the collection in her file, of course. Those were all pre-Jack, from the social pages or stories about his courtroom, his family.

"What happened to them?" she asked.

"You want to publish them?" Kahler asked sarcastically. "They'd be spectacular, all right, released now, given the timing with the one in Tucson."

"You know better than that," Kate denied hotly. "You know I'd never do anything like that. Lew wouldn't."

"How could Barrington know? *Somebody* took those pictures. A reporter for some scum of a paper. At a time when he was…"

Kahler paused to gather control, but Kate wouldn't let her eyes fall from the accusation in his. She knew how people felt about journalists. None of this was new to her, but it hurt to find out this was what Kahler thought. The same things Barrington believed.

"Did Barrington call you today?" she asked. A change of

subject seemed prudent since, after tonight's escapade, she wasn't exactly in a position to argue the ethics of her profession.

"As soon as his mail was delivered."

"Minutes before Draper got the package," she guessed. The bomber's revenge for his one failure had been a subtle torture. Before each bombing a warning of what was about to happen was delivered to the one man who had escaped, but never in time to allow the authorities to prevent the bombing.

"He's added a new refinement. The return address on the package sent to Draper was the judge's."

"Barrington's address?" she repeated in surprise. "Why would he do that?"

"You're asking me why Jack does the things he does? I don't have any answer, August. Maybe to put the press back onto Barrington. More punishment. Like the warnings. Interest in the judge has died down, and Jack probably doesn't like that. Maybe he knows how much Barrington hates publicity, and the news of the return address is bound to generate a lot if the authorities decide to release it."

"What did Barrington tell you when he called?" she asked.

"Same as always. That Jack was going to kill again. That it would be in Tucson. And that he had sent Barrington his best wishes for another pleasant day."

Kate tried to imagine receiving such a message, and knowing, better than anyone else, exactly what was about to happen to the next victim. Being unable to do anything to prevent it. Seven warnings, all delivered to the one man who survived.

"Did you ever wonder if he deliberately spared Barrington to be his messenger?" she asked. "To taunt the police."

"Maybe Jack was still learning," Kahler said. "He screwed up, and Barrington didn't die. If anything, that mistake caused him to move on to overkill. He's making sure now there's no chance anyone will survive."

"Have you ever seen Barrington, Kahler?"

"He calls me. He sends me Jack's letters. He's meticulous about protecting whatever evidence they might provide, but I don't meet him, August. Nobody sees him. Not since the bomb.''

''But he always calls you.''

''He thinks he's obligated to reveal the contents of the notes. They created a pretty strong sense of duty in their boy.''

The Barringtons and their golden boy, their only son and heir. There had been a younger child, she remembered, but something tragic had happened. An accident involving the family swimming pool. Then there had been only one son, the focus of all the Barrington ambitions, and all that very old money.

''Did you ever wonder what it was like growing up as Harlan Thornedyke Barrington IV?'' she asked.

''I don't have that big an imagination.''

She didn't know much about Kahler's background, but enough to know there was no old money there. In answer to her question about how he'd gotten into law enforcement, he had told her he'd joined the Marines at seventeen and ended up an MP, but other than that single piece of personal information, Kahler had been as reticent about his own past as about the case he had worked on for the last three years.

''The Barringtons are way out of my league, too,'' Kate agreed. ''They used to make the papers a lot. Only it was on the social pages then. I guess they didn't hate reporters so much in those days.'' There was a trace of bitterness in the comment. She had finally met Thorne Barrington, the man in the pictures she'd collected, but it hadn't gone exactly like her daydreams about it.

''The guy's been through hell, August, and people like you want him to relive it, to satisfy the public's lust for all the gory details. 'How did it feel, Judge Barrington, to have a bomb explode in your hands? Can you tell our viewers how that's affected your life?' ''

''I told him he was hiding,'' Kate admitted. Put it all on the table, all the *mea culpas*. If Kahler wanted to despise her, she'd give him the right reasons.

''Maybe he is,'' Kahler said. ''Maybe I would. Maybe you.

Who knows? But it isn't your right to question how Barrington reacts to what happened to him."

"You know better than that," Kate said. "He's news, Kahler, and he will be until Jack's caught."

"You're as bad as the rest of them," Kahler said in disgust. "Leave him alone, Kate."

There wasn't much left to say. No high moral ground to take in what she'd done. Neither of them credited her claim that her actions had been motivated by real concern for what she'd seen when she'd driven by. She didn't particularly want to explain that driving by had become a normal part of her routine. Kahler thought she'd gone there to question Barrington about today's bombing. The judge thought she was there because she was just like whoever had sneaked into his hospital room to take those pictures. A ghoul. A vampire.

"Can I go now?" she asked when the silence between them grew beyond comfort.

"You can go. I'll try to get Barrington to drop the charges."

She thought about telling him not to bother, but she wasn't sure enough about the consequences if the judge wanted to pursue it. Between being taken in by the patrol car and Kahler's fury, she was beaten down enough to be afraid. Of what Lew would say. Of eventually ending up in jail.

"Thanks," she said. She waited a moment to see if Kahler's anger would allow him to relent enough to say good-night.

"Your car's in the north lot. I had them bring it in."

"Thanks," she said again, glad he seemed willing to allow her to escape. To run home and hide. *To hide*. That's what she'd accused Barrington of doing, she suddenly realized, and all that had happened to her—

"Don't bother him again, August. Stay away from Barrington. I want your word on that."

"You've got it," she said. "But it wasn't what you thought. It wasn't what *he* thought. I swear to you I wasn't there because I wanted an interview." She didn't wait for a reply. She walked out of the small room with its revealing glass walls where she'd waited for Byron Kahler's arrival and endured his

fury and disgust. Then she went out through the Saturday-
night confusion of the station house.

The heat hit her when she opened the heavy outside door,
but she stopped a moment before she started down the shallow
steps. She'd tell Lew tomorrow to give the series to someone
else. She wasn't sure she'd tell him all the reasons. It was
enough that she'd lost Kahler's trust. She knew she would
have to endure a similar lecture from her boss when he heard
what she'd done. She'd blown it, big-time, and maybe it was
just as well. But she wouldn't pass on the file, she thought,
embarrassed by the pictures she'd acquired. Like some kind
of groupie. *That* she'd throw away. No one would ever know
about that secret collection.

She almost bumped into the man who came hurrying up the
steps, briefcase in hand. Despite the haste with which he
brushed past her, she had no trouble recognizing Barton Phillips. She wondered what one of Atlanta's highest-priced attorneys was doing in a neighborhood precinct house this late
at night.

She glanced at her watch, surprised to find that it was almost
eleven. She fought the automatic urge to follow Phillips inside,
her instincts telling her that if he was here, something was
going on, but for some reason she didn't even want to know
what. It could be the biggest story of the year, and all she
wanted to do right now was go home. She started down the
shallow stone steps, feeling more depressed than she could
remember.

When she reached the street, she had to stop and think what
Kahler had told her about her car. North lot. She turned right
and had taken several steps before she became aware of the
black Mercedes paralleling her movement down the sidewalk.
The windows, closed against the heat, were so heavily tinted
that she couldn't catch even a glimpse of the occupants.

She didn't become concerned until the Mercedes turned into
the parking lot, pulling to a stop before her, blocking the path
to her car. Her heartbeat began to accelerate, her mind dredg-
ing up all the stories of carjackings and kidnappings she'd

heard in the last few months. This was a police station. Surely...

The rear window glided down smoothly, but she jumped at the unexpectedness of its motion.

"Ms. August." It was the same voice that had spoken out of the shadows tonight—Thorne Barrington. "I'd like to talk to you," he said. "Would you get into the car, please?"

The invitation was the last thing she'd expected. In view of what she'd just promised Kahler, it couldn't have come at a worse time. Except she hadn't sought Barrington out. He had found her. However, considering the fool she'd made of herself tonight, she knew it was better that she apologize now and then do what Kahler had told her.

Reluctantly, she put her hands on the top of the glass, bending her knees to look into the car. She could barely see Barrington, a silhouette against the blackness of the glass behind him, its tint dark enough to prevent the parking lot security lights, almost as bright as day, from really penetrating the car. He would be able to see her clearly enough, she knew, with one of the powerful lights just above her head.

"Judge Barrington, I can't tell you how sorry I am for what happened tonight," she began. "I know it's no excuse for entering your home, but I really thought—"

"Ms. August, I would be deeply grateful if you'd just get into the car," Thorne Barrington interrupted.

Kate hesitated a moment longer.

"Please," he offered finally.

There was something compelling in that single syllable. She suspected that Barrington seldom asked favors. That *please* had sounded as if it had been wrung from him against his will.

While she was trying to decide what to do, Barrington reached across the wide back seat and, releasing the latch of the door, pushed it slightly open. He leaned back against the opposite door, waiting.

Kate knew somehow that he wouldn't ask her again. *This is what you wanted,* some inner voice reminded her, but it wasn't, of course. Not this way. Not under these circumstances. Kahler had supplied all the abuse her frayed conscience could handle for one night. She didn't want another lecture, so she was a little surprised to find herself crawling awkwardly into the back seat.

Despite the size of the car and the width of that seat, she felt very close to Barrington. He was a big man—six-four, she remembered from her notes—and she was very aware of his size. In the diffuse light that filtered into the car from the lot's security light, his features were revealed for the first time. He looked just as he did in the pictures taken before the bomb. If there had been facial injuries, they were no longer apparent—at least not in the dimness of the car's interior.

"Would you close the door, please?" he asked.

She took a deep breath before she complied, and then listened to the window slip up again as soon as she'd done what he'd asked. The tinted Plexiglas panel between the driver and the back seat was already closed.

"It appears that I owe you an apology," Thorne Barrington said. His voice was soft in the enforced intimacy, holding now none of the anger it had held before. The accent was still there, familiar and comforting, caught below the overlay of years he'd spent up North. A Southern gentleman.

Kate's lips lifted suddenly in relief. He was apologizing to her. "The gate was open," she said.

"Elliot had fallen. He had left the dog and had come back inside, but then he fainted. The dog's too much for him. I should never have…"

Kate waited, but he didn't complete the explanation.

"Elliot?" she asked.

"My butler. He's a little…beyond caring for a puppy. Especially one that size. I should have realized it before now."

"Beyond?" she repeated.

"He's almost ninety. A vigorous ninety, but still…"

Again the soft voice faded. Guilt and regret for what had happened to the old man was clear in his voice. Yet despite his concern, Judge Barrington had taken the time to find her, to apologize to her. Only…she wasn't sure she deserved an apology. Had her motives in going inside his house been as straightforward as she'd indicated to Kahler? Or had her judgment been clouded by other emotions? Even now she wasn't completely clear about that.

"Is he all right?" she asked finally.

"Just a small cut on his forehead. He's been treated and released. I took him home."

"So...I was right. Something was wrong."

"Yes," he admitted.

"You don't intend to press charges."

"No."

"Thank you," Kate said.

"It seemed the least I could do. To apologize. I'm afraid I didn't even listen to what you tried to tell me. When I heard your name..." Again he hesitated, and Kate remembered what Kahler had told her about the hospital photographs. "When I realized you were a reporter, I prejudged your motives. I simply wanted to tell you that I'm sorry. I was wrong."

Leave it alone, her head argued. Accept his apology, be gracious and forgiving. Let him take the blame. *I was wrong,* he had just confessed, letting her off the hook.

"Not about everything," her mouth whispered instead.

"I beg your pardon?"

"You weren't wrong about...everything."

The silence lengthened. "I see," he said finally.

"No, you probably don't," Kate said, knowing she could never really explain, "but it doesn't matter. I'm not as guilty as you thought, but I'm also not as innocent as I would like to believe. Some of what you said tonight..."

She had intended to say that some of what he'd accused her of was true, but she couldn't seem to bring herself to admit it. Not to him. He had been through hell, just as Kahler said, and she *had* wanted to stick a tape recorder under his nose and ask, if not the mocking questions the detective had suggested, others just as hurtful. Just as invasive.

"I'm sorry," she said. "For everything."

There was no answer from the man on the other side of the car. She found the handle of the door and stepped out. The Mercedes didn't move until after she had backed the Mazda out of its parking place and was driving across the lot. She

turned south and in her rearview mirror, she watched the tail-
lights of the big car, which had headed in the opposite direction, disappear behind her into the night.

SHE MANAGED TO UNDRESS down to her bra and panties before
the phone rang. A little apprehensive, not only because of the
lateness of the hour but also because of all that had happened
since she'd left her desk, she let it ring a couple of times. Had
Barrington called Lew at home or had Kahler thought of another sarcastic remark that couldn't wait until he saw her
again? She finally picked up just before the sixth ring, which
would trigger the answering machine.

"Hello," she said, trying to sound as normal as possible.

"I just thought you'd sleep better if you knew there won't
be any charges," Byron Kahler said. There seemed to be no
residual anger in the deep voice.

"That's wonderful," Kate assured him. Apparently, the
judge hadn't admitted he'd already talked to her when Kahler
had, as he'd promised, asked him to drop the charges. Letting
Kahler think he'd arranged for her rescue might put her back
into his good graces, and she needed all the help she could
get.

"Thanks, Kahler. And thanks for letting me know."

"As much as I'd like to, I can't take credit for the dropped
charges. Barrington had a change of heart. It seems…"

When Kahler hesitated, Kate's lips involuntarily curved into
a small smile. It seemed the detective was also having a hard
time admitting that he now knew her story to be true.

"There *was* a problem at the house. The gate and the door
were open and, under the circumstances, he decided to give
you the benefit of the doubt," he finished.

She fought the urge to say "I told you so," and awarded
herself a few character points for finding the willpower.

"Whatever the reason, I'm grateful. I'd already decided to
tell Lew to put somebody else on the story. I didn't think I
could be too effective having been arrested for breaking and
entering one of the victim's houses, no matter how innocently
that happened."

Kahler's laugh expressed his disbelief. "I can't see you giving up that easily, August. Once you've got hold of a story, you're not going to let go. You'll be there at the bitter end."

"Which for this one is soon I hope. You going to Tucson?"

"Yes," Kahler said.

The voice had become official, putting distance between himself and that unpleasant task. Kahler had visited all the scenes, talked to all the victims' families, all the business associates. He had been the officer in charge on the Barrington case, and the Atlanta bombing, like all the others, was still open, the investigation ongoing.

"I hope you find something," Kate said softly. "I hope this time he screwed up. I hope you catch him, Kahler."

There was a silence on the other end. She knew she'd said something so obvious it didn't require an answer. Kahler lived with that hope daily. It probably intruded even while he worked on his other cases. Then every six months—except this time, it hadn't been six months.

"Why do you think he hit early?" she asked.

"Who knows? Who knows how he thinks or why he does what he does? I don't have any answers for you, Kate."

"I know. It was just a thought. I'll talk to you when you get back?" It was a question. *Will our arrangement still hold despite your anger, despite what you revealed tonight about your opinion of what I do, of my profession?*

Again there was a brief hesitation, and she held her breath.

"You must have made a big impression on him, August."

It threw her. It made no sense in the context of the conversation. He couldn't mean Jack, so that left... *Barrington?* He thought she'd made an impression on Barrington? Maybe, she conceded, but not the one she would have liked to make. She couldn't even keep her mouth shut about her motives in entering his home. She just blurted that out with all the other confessions she been forced to make tonight. Too many years of Sunday school. Confession's good for the soul. Yeah, right.

"Impression?" she said aloud.

"He sent Phillips to take care of you."

"Barton Phillips?" she asked, remembering the hurrying

figure on the stairs. Apparently, like the Atlanta police, when Barrington said, "Jump," Phillips simply asked, "How high?"

"Esquire," Kahler agreed. "Quite an impression," he repeated, some nuance in his tone she had never heard before.

She wondered what she was supposed to say. Was he jealous because Barrington had come to apologize? *My God, Kahler's jealous,* she thought in wonder.

"He just realized he was wrong," she said. "Southern gentlemen always apologize. Their mamas teach them how in the cradle. You should try it sometimes," she suggested.

"There're only two things wrong with that plan, August. I'm not Southern..." He paused to allow her to finish.

"And you're not a gentleman. What a shame."

"*You've* just known too many of both. You might consider broadening your field of knowledge. That's what an education is all about. I'll see you when I get back from Arizona."

He had hung up before she could think of anything witty—or even halfway witty—to say. That had definitely sounded like an invitation, and not one to continue the strictly professional relationship they had shared up to this point. She wasn't sure how she felt about that. She had avoided thinking about Kahler in that light. For a lot of very good reasons.

She took a quick shower and put on her nightgown. She walked back to the kitchen and poured herself a glass of milk. She stood by the refrigerator drinking it, feeling the pleasant coolness of the tile floor under her tired feet. Unbidden, under the fluorescent brightness of her kitchen light, came the remembrance of the man who had sat alone listening to music tonight in the darkness of that dead mansion.

She carried her milk with her into the living room. She set the glass down on the table beside the couch while she opened its drawer and took out her collection of pictures. She sat cross-legged on the sofa. She forced herself to finish the milk, slowly, before she would allow her fingers to open the folder and spread out the contents on the coffee table in front of her.

She knew them by heart. The dark eyes laughing down into his mother's. In a tux at somebody's wedding. Always taller than the people around him. Dominating. *Too good-looking for his own good,* her grandmother would have said. He was surrounded in one shot by smiling debutantes, who looked up into that handsome face with something approaching her own fascination. *You must have made quite an impression,* Kahler had said. Not exactly the one she had daydreamed about making.

She knew there was something weird about looking at pictures of some guy she didn't know. Like a teenager putting posters of a rock star on the wall. She was thirty-two years old. Way too old for this kind of crush. *Crush,* she repeated. That's exactly what this felt like, and it was so stupid. So childish. Crazy.

Tonight she had met him. Twice. She had even sat beside him in his car. She closed her eyes and allowed herself to remember. To think past the embarrassment and the fear to remember what it was like to sit beside him. To remember how he had smelled. Not cologne. Just clean. Soap. Male.

His voice had wrapped around her in the dark. Soft and very deep. Southern slow. He had been near enough that she could have reached out and touched him. *Crazy,* she thought again, deliberately breaking the spell of the memories.

Finally she pushed all the pictures back on one side of the folder and closed it. She hid it again in the drawer and turned off the light on the table. The apartment was dark except for the lamp she'd turned on in her bedroom, its soft glow inviting her down the hall. Even when she crawled into bed and switched off the lamp, creating total darkness, the images from the pictures, superimposed over the reality of the man she had met today, were still there. It took her a long time to go to sleep.

Chapter Three

Kate overslept on Monday, arriving in the office a little late, feeling pressured and behind schedule. She hated to have to rush in the morning. It made her feel disorganized and out of sorts the whole day.

Lew greeted her with his usual mind-on-something-else lack of awareness, and she was relieved. Apparently no one had called him to complain about the incident on Friday night. She listened to his suggestions about the things she was working on, jotting down quick notes she'd have trouble deciphering later. A typical day, and after Friday, normality was a relief.

She worked a while on the Tucson bombing, which had pushed up the deadline for the next victim profile. Since she had started, the series had contained other types of articles: the FBI's psychological profile of Jack, a brief overview on the other well-known mail bombers, and some carefully screened information about the technical aspects of Jack's explosives. She was also planning to do a segment about the agencies and officers involved in the hunt. Lew had arranged to have a stringer contact each local police department which, like Atlanta, had open cases on the bomber's victims to gather information on the officers in charge of those investigations.

Working on that would have been far more pleasant than doing a profile of another victim. They were the hardest to write, chronicling the poignant details of the seemingly ordinary lives. But it was from Kate's profiles that the police were hoping some reader might make a connection, might provide a reason, a new direction for them to pursue. Hoping for anything.

The story on Barrington had started her obsession with him, what had become her secret collection of the newspaper's photos at first simply a legitimate attempt to gather information about the only survivor. She had carried the pictures home after she'd finished the article, and that, of course, had been her mistake.

She cleared Thorne Barrington from her mind and tried to pull all the available information on Hall Draper together. On the surface there didn't seem to be anything in this guy's life that should result in his becoming a target for a killer. Too ordinary. Like the old guy in Austin. She couldn't imagine any skeletons in those closets to attract Jack's attention.

Maybe the cops were right. Maybe the bomber just found an address in a phone book. Maybe the victims weren't related, and if that were true, they might never find Jack.

Most serial killers were caught only by happenstance or if they made a mistake, an action that went against the routine that had worked in the past. They were usually bright, at least the ones who succeeded for any length of time. A couple had been on the inside, knowing how the system worked. That had allowed them to escape detection longer than the guy on the street might.

Others had been "interested observers," seemingly fascinated with the case. *Why shouldn't they be?* she thought. They were at the center of it. Often that's what gave them away— the desire to let someone know they had the starring role. The urge to take credit and to have their brilliance admired eventually became overwhelming. Or maybe it was the urge to get caught. Maybe something inside said they had caused enough carnage. Maybe those things the police labeled mistakes or happenstances were really pleas for someone to stop them.

Kate realized she'd been staring at her screen for a long time, not composing and not editing. Just thinking about Jack, wondering when he'd reach his saturation point. Distanced from the reality of what he did, would he ever give them the means to identify him, ever become overwhelmed by what he was doing?

"You got some mail, Ms. August," Lew's nephew announced. Trey was this summer's office gofer. A nice kid. Polite.

"Thanks, Trey. Put it down anywhere you can find a clean spot," she instructed, glancing up to smile at him while putting her fingers back on the keys.

Trey surveyed the clutter on her desk. Finally he grinned at her, handing a package and some letters over her computer. Automatically, Kate reached up to take them.

"I don't think you've *got* a clean spot," he said truthfully.

"I think you're right," she acknowledged, smiling at him.

"You working on the bomber?" he asked, watching her pile the mail he'd given her on top of the wire releases.

"Trying to. I think I've run out of things to write."

"Cops don't have anything, do they?"

"So they say," Kate agreed. She sometimes wondered if Kahler knew as little as he said he did. Occasionally there was something at the back of his eyes that made her question his claim to have come clean on everything they had. People like Kahler always knew more than they told you.

"You think they'll catch him?" Trey asked, his face serious.

The public's right to know, Kate thought again. "Eventually. He'll make a mistake or somebody will remember something. Or somebody will see a link between the victims that will trace back to Jack. They'll catch him."

"I guess you're right," he said, sounding relieved.

After he'd moved on to deliver the rest of the morning's mail, Kate allowed herself a small smile. She supposed she was some kind of authority figure to Trey, someone in the know. If she thought they'd catch Jack, that was good enough for him.

Fingers still resting on the keys, she glanced at the package he'd given her. It was wrapped in brown paper and tied with white twine. She turned it around to be sure that the return address said what she thought it did. Thorne Barrington.

What in the world would Thorne Barrington be sending her?

she wondered. Even as she thought it, she knew. He was a man who had been reared in the old school. *Well brought up* was the phrase. A Southern gentleman, as she had thought Friday night, and there was a code that went along with that training.

She would have thought he'd send flowers—roses, maybe. But he didn't have to be caught in the Dark Ages. Just because he lived in that mausoleum didn't mean he wouldn't know something beyond the traditional dozen roses. Maybe candy. Godiva chocolates. In a box this size that would be a hell of a gesture.

Which he could well afford, she thought, opening her center drawer to take out to her scissors. She couldn't find them, so she pushed her chair backwards on its plastic pad, putting the package in her lap. That gave her more room to open the drawer, and she found her scissors at the very back. She snipped the cord and put it on her desk. She turned the box over and slid her fingers under the taped, triangular flaps, lifting them free. The paper had not been taped together where it met at the center back, so it slipped off easily. The box was not the distinctive gold foil she'd half expected. It was plain white cardboard, a little heavier than the kind you bought at Christmas from Wal-Mart, five for a dollar ninety-nine. She turned it over and eased the top off.

The explosion wasn't that loud. No more startling than a backfire or a distant gunshot, she thought later—when she was capable again of coherent thought. Only it had gone off in her lap, literally under her nose. Whatever exploded had enough force to propel the lid out of her hands and across the room. And enough force to carry the metallic red confetti the box had contained almost ceiling high, so that it rained down on her desk, showering her hair and the surrounding area like some kind of crimson fallout.

Kate didn't realize she had moved, but the chair she'd been sitting in banged into the desk behind her, and suddenly she was standing, knees trembling, the remains of the package scattered over her feet and the plastic square she was standing on.

"What the hell was that!"

She was aware that the comment came from Trey. She even knew when someone pulled the chair back and helped her sit down in it. She thought she responded to the questions about whether she was all right. Someone handed her a small cup of water from the cooler, but she couldn't hold it. She was embarrassed by how much her hand was shaking. Finally Lew was there to take the paper cup away, to stop the icy drops from sloshing out to mark the pink linen dress she was wearing.

She wanted to put her head down on her desk and cry, to scream, to do something. Instead she kept saying to the gathering crowd that she was all right. "I'm all right," she said over and over, wondering if she would ever really be again.

"It was with the other mail. I couldn't remember where I'd heard the name before. I didn't make the connection."

Trey's voice, explaining. Some part of her mind was still working, still functioning on a rational level. The other part was looking for a cave to hide in. A hole to crawl into. Who could know how they'd react, Lew had asked. Now she knew what it felt like. At least on some minimal level she knew.

"I didn't recognize the name," Trey went on, enjoying the limelight, maybe, now that it was obvious no one was hurt. When he'd come charging up to her desk, his face had been as blanched as Kate supposed hers was. "Thorne Barrington. I knew I'd heard it, you know, but I couldn't exactly remember where."

I didn't put it together either, Kate thought, *and I had a lot more reason to than you, Trey. Only I never suspected…*

What did she suspect? she wondered suddenly. That Jack had sent her a fake bomb? A warning because her insightful series had hit too near home? Yeah, right. She and about a thousand other journalists who were cooking up stories based on the bits and pieces which were all they had on Jack.

The bomber was *real* worried about what she was revealing in her articles, which, when you got down to it was *nada*, nothing, zilch. Jack the Tripper wasn't worried about Kate August. Which meant, of course, that he hadn't sent the package. She knew who had filled a box with red confetti and some kind of explosive and had it delivered to her office. *You want to know how it feels to have a bomb go off in your hands, Ms. August?*

The bastard had even put his return address on the package. He had called her a vampire, feeding off the pain of other people, and he had apparently decided to arrange a taste of what it was like to be those other people. She had been lulled into believing his apology. She wondered if she would have been fool enough to have opened the package if he hadn't apologized Friday night. She would like to think she wouldn't have been this stupid if she hadn't had that personal contact.

After all, she was one of the few people who knew about the return address on Jack's last package, something the police hadn't made public. So Barrington couldn't know, of course, that she'd been told. The return address wasn't supposed to trigger any red flags. He had even asked her Friday night, mockingly, *"Afraid, Ms. August?"* He had wanted her to feel as terrified as she'd accused him of being, and so he'd arranged a demonstration of exactly how that terror felt.

She opened her bottom drawer and took out her purse. She was aware of the confusion of voices around her, but her head was remarkably clear, her mental processes functioning very well, she thought. Considering.

"Excuse me," she said to whoever was standing over her chair. *Lew,* she realized, looking up. "I have to go now."

"Relax, Kate. The police will be here in a few minutes. I've already called Detective Kahler. They'll want to talk—"

"I have to go *now*," she interrupted, insistent. She pulled her arm away from his hand. "I *have* to go. Please, Lew, I really have to go."

Maybe he could read the building hysteria. Not just fear any longer. Anger. She was so furious she could strangle Thorne Barrington with her bare hands for making her feel this way. Especially when she remembered how she'd daydreamed about him, practically drooled over his damn pictures, for heaven's sake.

"At least let me drive you home. Kahler can meet us at

your apartment. You're in no condition to drive,'' Lew argued. His voice was quiet and reasonable, like someone talking to a child who was afraid of the monsters under her bed.

"I'm *fine*,'' she said again, walking past him. She was relieved no one else attempted to stop her. The room was perfectly quiet now, a silence unnatural to its usual frantic atmosphere. With every step she took, pieces of red confetti fell out of her hair, off her shoulders.

When she reached the hallway, away from the watching eyes of the people in the newsroom, she stopped. She shook her head, aware of the resulting shower of metallic bits. She glanced down at them, scattered over the flat charcoal of the commercial carpet. Several caught the light from the ceiling track, glittering like freshly spilled droplets of blood. She picked off a couple that had clung to the damp spots on her dress.

A newsreel picture of Mrs. Kennedy climbing the stairs of the airplane that day in Dallas, still wearing that blood-splattered pink suit flickered into her head. Blood. That's why he'd made them red. Like the room in the boardinghouse in Austin, she thought, and then she was forced to block the image.

Did he think this was some kind of joke? Even given the fact that she'd entered his home, invaded his damned privacy, did he believe she deserved this? How sick could you get?

Pretty sick, her subconscious jeered. From the mail she'd gotten since she'd started the series, she certainly had cause to know that there were a lot of very sick people out there. Only she had never before believed Thorne Barrington was one of them.

SHE SHOULD HAVE KNOWN the gate would be locked. She had pulled up to the curb exactly as she had on Friday night, but today the security system was clearly back in place. She wondered briefly if Barrington had been expecting her.

She opened the car door and stepped out, the heat rising around her from the street and the sidewalk. There had to be a bell or a buzzer, something to let the inhabitants of the house know they had a caller. She found it beside the gate, almost directly above where the dog had been tied Friday night.

As she waited for some response to her jab on the button, she looked over the wide, tree-lined street to watch the construction crew working on the ruined house that stood directly across from the Barrington mansion. It had been the victim of a recent fire, windows charred and the glass blown out. In some places the damage was enough that she could see into the exposed rooms, their walls literally burned away.

Heat waves shimmered off the pavement between the two old mansions, despite the scattered shade of the oaks, and she wondered how the workers could continue to labor in the sweltering heat.

"May I help you?"

Apparently there was no intercom. An old man stood inside the fence, waiting for her response to his question. He was thin and stooped, wearing…what butlers wear, Kate realized with a trace of amusement, despite her anger. Like something out of a thirties movie, those old black-and-white society comedies. He looked like Carole Lombard's butler.

The sparse white hair was neatly combed, but clearly visible under its sweep was the flesh-colored bandage on his forehead. Elliot, she thought. This was Elliot. And Barrington was right. That big lummox of a puppy would certainly be too much for this fragile old man.

"I'd like to see Judge Barrington, please," she said, smiling at him. She hid her anger, but it took a great deal of effort. First she had to get in; then she'd tell that bastard exactly what she thought about his sick prank.

"I'm sorry, but Judge Barrington is not receiving guests," the butler said. He placed a trembling, liver-spotted hand on the crossbar of the gate, as if to steady himself.

It bordered on criminal to send this old man outside into today's inferno, Kate thought. Why didn't Barrington answer his own door, or at least hire staff that didn't appear to be at the point of death? "Are you all right?" she asked. She wondered what she'd do if he fell again. She wouldn't even be able to get inside to help him.

"Oh, indeed, miss. I'm fine, thank you."

"Would you please tell the Judge that Kate August is here? I'd like to...thank him. Would you tell him that, please?"

"Of course, but I must warn you, miss, that he doesn't see visitors. He hasn't for years."

"Please," Kate begged, smiling at him again, "just ask."

She wondered why she was bothering. Barrington wasn't going to let her in. Why should he? He had to know how angry she would be. Her only hope was that he might personally want to gloat over the results of what he'd done.

"Do you have a card, Miss August?" the old man asked.

"Of course." She fumbled in her purse and then handed him her card through the wrought iron bars. His hand trembled so much she was afraid he'd drop it in the transfer, and she knew if he did, he'd never manage to bend over to pick it up. However, he finally grasped it and turned to totter up the walk. She held her breath as he climbed the steps to disappear into the house, shutting the glass-paneled door firmly behind him.

Kate took a breath, letting it out almost in a sigh. She was still angry, but the flight or fight adrenaline that had brought her here was beginning to fade, and she wondered if she'd be able to get up enough steam to say all the things she wanted to express to Thorne Barrington. *If* she got in, and that appeared to be a very big if.

KATE AUGUST, he thought again, looking down at the card Elliot had handed him. She'd come to thank him for dropping the charges, he supposed. At least he thought the old man had said something about thanking him.

He hadn't listened too carefully after he'd heard her name. He had surprised himself by agreeing to see her, but his responses to being told she was here had surprised him even more. Anticipation. And something else, stirring deep and hot in his body. A feeling that he had almost forgotten.

Despite the situation Friday night, he hadn't been able to forget her. He had especially liked her voice. Low and husky. A "whiskey-voiced" woman was the old expression. And he had remembered her perfume. Released by her skin's warmth, its sweetness had invaded the room. As it had later in the car. All the way home, he'd savored the lost pleasure of being surrounded by a woman's perfume.

When he woke last night, it had not been the familiar nightmares, not those scenes of devastation that the media celebrated, which had pulled him from sleep. Instead, her softness had been under his lips, the familiar fragrance, the smooth texture of her skin tantalizing. His body had responded to the dream. A hard, aching response. It had taken him a long time to go back to sleep, and he had remembered it all this morning. He had lain in bed, remembering the dream. Remembering Kate August. And now she was here again.

IT WAS PROBABLY ten minutes before the front door reopened, and Kate watched the old man retrace his slow journey down the walkway. This time he carried a black umbrella, still furled. Kate found herself wishing he'd use it as a walking stick, but he carried it with the crook over his forearm. Her card seemed to have disappeared, but she was gearing herself up for another polite Southern argument if he refused her admittance.

"I'm so sorry to have kept you waiting," Elliot said, releasing the latch on the inside of the gate, "especially in this terrible heat."

Unbelievingly, Kate watched as he pulled the gate inward, inviting her to step inside. Then the butler carefully reclosed the gate and checked the lock. He turned to her with a smile, opening the umbrella to hold over her head.

"I thought that a little shade might be welcome," he said.

"Thank you. That was very kind of you," Kate responded, biting the inside of her cheek to prevent a smile.

"My pleasure. Judge Barrington sees so few visitors. I must confess," he said, "that I was a little surprised when he agreed to see you. Please don't misunderstand. I was very pleased, of course, but surprised. Since that terrible, terrible explosion, you know." He paused and glanced at her face.

"I know," Kate said.

She was trying to slow her pace enough to match his and

to stay under the umbrella he carried. Anything else would have been rude, and no matter how angry she might be at Barrington, she could never be unpleasant to this old man. Since the butler was at least two inches shorter than she, Kate was finding it difficult to accommodate his umbrella.

"I worry about him being so alone," Elliot confessed.

So did I, Kate thought bitterly, *until he pulled his little stunt today.*

"I'm so glad you've come, Miss August," Elliot said, as he opened the door for her, inviting her into the coolness of the dark interior. He carefully closed and refurled the umbrella and then placed it in the stand by the door. "Mr. Thorne is in the parlor. He said you would know the way. If you'll excuse me, I think I'll fix some iced tea. That would go nicely on a day like this, don't you think?"

Kate's own training was too strong. She knew all the things she was supposed to say, and she found herself saying them without effort. "Tea would be wonderful, but please don't go to any trouble."

"No trouble at all. I'm delighted you're here. You go right in, Miss August. Mr. Thorne is waiting for you."

Somehow in the enforced intimacy of the shared umbrella, Barrington had become Mr. Thorne. She had been accepted. By Elliot, at least, who was now going to make them some iced tea.

And then they could have a tea party. Just Thorne Barrington and her. That was okay. She probably would, she thought on reflection, work up quite a thirst telling him exactly what she thought about the way his mind worked. Surprisingly, she found she was dreading this confrontation. She was still angry, but somewhere in the back of her mind, she remembered all the things she'd said to this man. She'd accused him of hiding, and maybe he was, but who had given her the right to judge?

What gave him the right to do what he did today? To make a fool of me in front of everyone. To scare me to death.

She pushed the sliding door open. The room was dim, an artificial twilight, the heavy shades all pulled to keep out the afternoon sun and its heat. It reminded her of her grandmother's house in Tupelo, always darkened against the oppressive invasion of the summer heat. People had kept cool that way in her grandmother's day, but here she could hear the air conditioner's efficient hum in the background. Apparently the darkened parlor was simply another anachronism, clinging to the dead past.

"Ms. August," Barrington said from across the room. "You asked to see me?"

He was standing. The perfect gentleman. She was a little surprised to see that he was wearing jeans and a dark knit shirt. Somehow she had expected a suit. Because of the butler's formality, she supposed. But there was no reason, of course, for Thorne Barrington to be formally dressed in his own home.

His shoulders were broader than she'd expected, and his chest filled the cotton shirt, its muscled width tapering to a flat belly and slim hips. She'd seen his physique often enough in the photographs, but as he had last night, he seemed a little larger than life in person. A little overwhelming.

His eyes were very dark, surrounded by that sweep of long lashes. His coal-black hair was longer than in the pictures and maybe touched with gray at the temples. Something new, but what was he now? Thirty-seven? Thirty-eight, she thought. Old enough to be graying. The same strong nose and square chin. The individual features weren't that remarkable, but taken together—

"Ms. August?" he interrupted her inventory, questioning.

"Why would you do that to me, you bastard?" Kate asked.

That wasn't what she'd intended to say, but it was the crux of the matter. Why would anyone, no matter what he thought about what she did for a living, do what he had done today?

"I beg your pardon," Barrington said.

"Did you want to make me afraid? Is that what it was all about? Because if you did, I think you should know how well you succeeded," Kate said.

She moved closer to him, almost across the width of the room, to hold out her hands. Despite the time that had passed, they were still shaking. Seeing that, she could feel the anger

Elliot's kindness had tempered beginning to rebuild. The dark eyes left hers to move downward to her trembling fingers.

"I couldn't even hold the cup of water they gave me," she told him, wanting him to understand what he'd done. Suddenly she clenched her hands into fists and brought them back to her sides. She regretted showing him her trembling fingers, regretted giving him that satisfaction.

Furious, more with her own fear than with what he'd done, she forced herself to look up. His dark eyes were slightly narrowed. She was close enough that she could see the small lines around them. There was a whitened scar on his temple. And she had been right about the graying. Even that looked right. Perfect. *Too good-looking for his own good,* echoed in her head.

"I didn't deserve that," she said aloud. "No matter what you think about what I do for a living, I didn't deserve what you did to me today."

"Ms. August, forgive me, but I don't have any idea what you're talking about. I thought you were here because of—"

"Don't you *dare* pretend you don't know. Your name was on the package. Your return address. Don't you dare pretend. At least, admit that you—"

"The *package?*" he interrupted.

That had certainly gotten a response, Kate thought with satisfaction. Even his voice had changed, no longer polite. No longer pretending he didn't know what she was talking about.

"The package you sent me," she went on. "The exploding one. The red confetti. It worked just like you intended. It blew up in my face and shot that damn red crap all over the office, and I was *scared,* Judge Barrington. Real scared. I really thought for a second that I was dead. Is that how you wanted me to feel? Is that what you wanted? To make me understand what you felt?"

His face hadn't changed. He was still watching her with those too-dark eyes. Almost black, she thought. She'd never seen eyes that dark.

"I didn't send you a package, Ms. August. Not of any kind. Not today. Not ever."

"I accused you of hiding, of being afraid, and maybe that bothered some image you have of yourself. So you got even. Only that's really sick, you know. Especially for someone..." She paused, whether for breath to go on or because he was watching her so intently, she wasn't sure. He didn't speak into the sudden silence, so she tried to pick up the thread of her anger.

"Especially with Jack out there, *really* blowing people up. Sending death out with your return address—" She stopped abruptly. She shouldn't have told him that she knew his address was on the last bomb. It wasn't public knowledge, and he would wonder how she knew. "It was sick. For *anybody* it was a sick thing to do, but especially for you," she finished lamely.

She had run out of steam, faced with his lack of response. The lines of his face revealed no emotion. He was giving nothing away. The silence grew, stretching, filling up all the dark corners of the room. Finally he moved, blinked, something. Kate wasn't sure exactly how or why, but the stillness was broken, and then he spoke very distinctly.

"I didn't send you a package. If you're aware that the bomber used my return address on Friday, then you must also be aware of the implications of its use on any package you received. I suggest you discuss this with the police, Ms. August. And now if you'll excuse me," he said.

He was dismissing her. *Inviting* her to go to the police. Trying to make a bigger fool of her than he'd already made. Except they were both aware that Jack didn't send red confetti. Jack sent bombs. Explosives and shrapnel. Enough to kill. This son of a bitch was denying responsibility for what had happened today, talking to her as Lew had earlier, in the same soothing adult-to-hysterical-child tone.

"You're really something, you know. A real piece of work," she said, suddenly as angry as she'd been in the office. "I told you the truth about yourself, and you couldn't take it. The great Thorne Barrington couldn't face the fact that he's gone into hiding, so you had to have your revenge."

"Ms. August," he interrupted, but she went on, speaking

over whatever he intended to say. Because it didn't matter what he wanted to say. She didn't want to hear it.

"Apparently there's no one around to tell you the truth. I did, and you couldn't deal with it. I let a little light into all this darkness, and you didn't like the man who was revealed. But that's not my fault, Judge Barrington. I didn't make you a coward who stopped living three years ago. Jack did that. So why don't you send *Jack* a package and leave me the hell alone."

She saw and heard the depth of the breath he took before he answered her, but his face still revealed nothing.

"If you're finished, Elliot will show you out, but I strongly suggest you follow my advice."

He was angry. His features might not have changed, but his voice had. There was nothing like a blue-blooded Southern accent for expressing anger. She'd gotten to him all right. Since that had been her intent, she should be feeling a whole lot better than she was. Instead, she was disgusted with herself, ashamed of what she'd just said, and that made her mad at herself. What he'd done had been unforgivable, and so he deserved to hear everything she'd said if only because it *was* the truth.

"I'll follow yours if you follow mine," Kate said. "You called me a vampire, but *I'm* not the one who's afraid of the light. As a matter of fact, I think we ought to let a little more light in on this situation. The real kind. A little daylight into your mausoleum."

While she was talking, she walked around the velvet sofa to one of the long windows to the left of the fireplace. She jerked the bottom of the shade and released it, allowing it to fly up. She moved to the next one and sent it whirring to the top. She was a little shocked at how exhilarated she felt with the noise they made and with the flood of sunlight that invaded the room.

She moved behind Thorne Barrington, between his still figure and the fireplace, to the windows on the other side. She threw those shades upward with the same angry satisfaction.

It was as bright now inside the room as it had been on the heat-parched street outside.

When she turned back to face the man who had so infuriated her, she realized that Barrington hadn't moved. Despite the noise, he hadn't turned around to watch what she was doing. Apparently he intended to make no response to her childishness, but the muscles in his broad shoulders and his back were rigid beneath the dark knit shirt.

Somehow she wasn't quite satisfied with that. Not enough reaction, she supposed. She walked back to where she had stood before, back to face the man who had sent her the package this morning.

"I guess I was mistaken," she said, her tone revealing contempt. The black eyes were slightly narrowed, but they met hers unflinchingly. "All this light, and you still didn't melt. Maybe you're not a vampire after all."

Barrington said nothing, his face set and controlled. Obviously, he didn't intend to give her the satisfaction of a reaction, and now that her tantrum was over, she realized how childish she must have appeared, throwing up the shades of his windows and shouting at him about how he should live his life.

She had already headed toward the sliding doors when they opened unexpectedly. Elliot entered, silver tray, tall glasses of tea with fresh mint leaves garnishing the tops, linen napkins, the works. *The best of the South,* she thought, cynically. *Real Southern hospitality.*

"I don't think I'll be able to stay for the tea, but thank you anyway, Elliot," she said, brushing by him. She just needed to be out of this room, out of Thorne Barrington's house.

She heard the butler's agitated exclamation behind her and the sound of breaking glass. She wondered if Barrington had thrown something, and knew that if he had, that would at least be some indication that she had gotten under his skin, threatened that iron control.

By that time she had reached the glass-paneled front door, but she turned back before she stepped through it, guilt and regret crowding her throat. What she had said had been unforgivably cruel, and in saying it, she had been both loud and rude, the only crimes a woman could be found guilty of in the South. She knew by the changes in the quality of light filtering through to the foyer that Elliot or Barrington was in the process of pulling down the shades she'd raised, returning the house to its eternal darkness. *Hiding.*

Three years hadn't changed this situation, and her cruelty certainly wouldn't. She shook her head, ridiculing herself for thinking she could change anything here. A piece of the red confetti he'd sent her fluttered to lie on the hardwood floor. She left it there and walked outside into the sunshine.

Chapter Four

By the time Kate had driven home, whatever adrenaline rush had carried her through the confrontation with Barrington was fading. She wanted only to crawl back into the bed she had not had time to make and pull the covers over her head.

She had begun the process of extracting her keys from the bottom of her purse before she reached the door to her apartment, shuffling through the junk she had shoved into the black leather bag for safekeeping. When she found them, she looked up to insert the key into the lock and realized the door wasn't closed. There was an inch of space between it and the frame, and despite her hurry this morning, she knew she hadn't left it that way.

The terror that mushroomed in her stomach was almost as strong as her reaction to the fake bomb had been. Was it possible that whoever had sent the package was waiting inside? *Not* Barrington. Was it possible that the package had *not* been the sick prank she had accused him of, but something else? Someone else. Someone really dangerous.

But if someone *were* lying in wait in her apartment, she forced herself to reason, he wouldn't have left the door open. That would be a dead giveaway of his presence, unless he was trying to do exactly what he had just accomplished—still trying to frighten her. *And if that is the purpose, then damn it, he certainly is succeeding,* she thought, pushing the door open enough to see into her small living room. At what the widening doorway revealed, relief washed over her.

Byron Kahler was sitting on her couch, thumbing through one of the magazines she'd arranged on the coffee table. He had looked up when she pushed the door inward, hazel eyes assessing, but he didn't say anything.

"If I were Judge Barrington, I'd have you arrested for breaking and entering," she said. She walked into the apartment and put her purse down on the table to the left of the door.

"I picked up a few tricks of the trade through the years," Kahler said.

"And it seemed like a good idea to use them on my door?" She was relieved it was Kahler sitting on her couch, but a little surprised that he'd jimmied her lock to get in.

"I guess I owe you an apology," he said.

"I'll settle for an explanation."

"When I got to your office, Garrison told me you'd gone home. He was concerned about you."

"He sent you to check on me?"

"We have to talk about what happened anyway. Officially talk. I rang the bell, and when there was no answer..."

"You just broke in."

"I was afraid you might have—I don't know—gone off the deep end a little. When I couldn't get you to the door, I decided it might be wise to investigate. I even thought that whoever had sent the package might have tried something else."

She hesitated, weighing her feelings about the invasion of her privacy against the idea that he'd cared enough about her to come personally. "Thanks," she said finally, almost grudgingly.

"You're welcome," Kahler said, "and you need a better lock. All it took was a credit card and a few seconds."

"I'll keep that in mind."

She walked across the room and sat down on the love seat facing the couch. His eyes followed her, and knowing that questions were inevitable, given it was his job to ask them, she took a deep breath, trying to gather her control. When she thought she had found enough composure to talk, she looked up. The detective's usually penetrating gaze had softened, resting on her features with something that looked like compassion.

"You want to tell me your version of what happened?" he suggested. It took her a second to realize he meant what had happened at her office and not what she had done at Barrington's mansion. There was no way he could know about that. Not yet.

"There's not that much to tell. Trey brought the package in with the other mail. Plain brown paper wrappings. It was tied with string and had Barrington's return address. I thought it was a gift, maybe even some kind of apology for Friday night."

Kahler also couldn't know about the judge's appearance at the precinct house, but she decided not to get into all her reasons for opening the package, not unless he asked. "When I opened the box, it blew up in my face. It was filled with red confetti that went everywhere, all over the damn office."

"We don't think it was Jack, Kate, if that'll make you feel any better. I sent the package to the lab. We won't have the results for a couple of days, but I can tell you that in no way did it resemble what Jack sends. It worked through compressed air, just enough force to blow the lid and scatter the confetti."

He was reassuring her, she realized, trying to make her feel less afraid. Only he wasn't making her feel any better. He was only reinforcing the conclusion she'd already reached.

"I *did* have enough presence of mind to realize that Jack doesn't fool around with confetti, Kahler. The only thing my package had in common with the others was they all blew up." She paused, again fighting her anger against the man who had sent the package. "And that son of a bitch knows exactly how it feels," she added. "That's the one thing I can't get over. He knows, better than anyone, how I felt this morning."

"You think it was *Barrington?*" Kahler asked, his voice expressing his surprise.

"Who else could it have been? He had motive—to get back at me for what I'd said to him, for coming into his house. The timing seems a little too coincidental *not* to implicate him. Who else would get his jollies scaring me spitless?''

"Nothing I know about Barrington would lead me to believe that he would do something like that.''

"Nothing you know?'' she repeated, letting her sarcasm show. "Like the fact that he never leaves his house, not even to attend his father's funeral. That he lives in the dark like some kind of—'' She stopped abruptly, remembering all she had said to the man they were discussing. *Like some kind of vampire.* She remembered, too, Barrington sitting alone in the darkened room, the faint music floating out into the night like smoke. "Like some kind of creep,'' she finished instead. "Face it, Kahler. *He's* the one who's gone off the deep end.'' Her tone was bitter, but Kahler wouldn't understand. He didn't know about the folder with the pictures of the man she'd admired so long.

"Look, I know you're angry at Barrington for having you hauled off the other night, but there are…explanations for some of those things,'' Kahler said, his voice reasonable.

"He just sits there in the dark. What kind of explanation is there for that? What kind of explanation for the crap he pulled with the package? What *kind* of explanation?'' she demanded angrily.

"We don't know he sent the package, Kate.''

She laughed, a small, tight derision of sound. "Right,'' she agreed sarcastically. "*You* may not know. If not His Honor, then who? Who else *could* it be?''

"Someone who doesn't like your writing style? Hell, maybe somebody thinks you misused a semicolon,'' Kahler suggested. The hazel eyes were carefully controlled, but his tone had lightened. "There are a lot of crazies out there, August.''

He was certainly right about that, Kate thought. Several of the letters she'd received about the series had contained graphic illustrations of bomb blasts, dismemberments and the like—crudely drawn but effective. As a matter of course, she had pitched them into the round file, but now she wondered if she should have saved them, turned them over to whoever in the police department was in charge of checking out the crazies.

"Lucky for us," Kahler went on, "not all of them want to kill people. Some of them just like sending stuff through the mail. Dead rats or birds. Voodoo dolls complete with pins. All kinds of crap. Maybe even red confetti. This wasn't Jack, but that doesn't mean it has to be Barrington."

"Why send it to me?" she asked. "Seriously."

"Maybe someone's been following the series. Maybe they didn't like what you wrote. Who knows what sets people off."

"You admire him, don't you?" she asked. His eyes widened slightly at the comment, and she realized that her thoughts had outpaced the conversation. "Barrington," she explained.

"What makes you think I *admire* Barrington?"

"You tell me to leave him alone. That he's been through hell. You reject the obvious about the package—that Barrington was the crazy who sent it. You even defend the way he lives."

"I'm not defending him, and you seem to have forgotten who we're talking about. Barrington doesn't need me to defend him. He's got all the marbles. If he wants defending, he can afford to hire the best. That's something you might want to remember before you start accusing him of this morning's prank. That accusation would probably be grounds for some kind of suit."

"So you're telling me to ignore what happened today?"

"I'm telling you not to go off half-cocked. At least wait until the lab results come back. They might tell us something."

"And they might not," she said. She knew that the materials used in Jack's packages had been frustratingly unrevealing.

One corner of Kahler's mouth quirked, acknowledging that possibility. "It depends on how much the sender knows about how mail bombers are caught. They'll at least let us see whether we're dealing with an amateur. Until that time, I don't think you're in any real danger, Kate." He smiled, and she thought how rare an occurrence that was. "Not if you get yourself a new lock. A dead bolt. A good heavy one."

Kahler stood up, putting the magazine he'd been holding down on the coffee table between them. "Don't worry," he offered. "The last time I checked the statistics, nobody had ever been killed by confetti."

She laughed, feeling better for his sardonic reassurance. It *had* helped to have Kahler here. She was even willing to forgive him for letting himself in. His eyes held a moment, and she found his rough masculinity more appealing than it had ever been before. He was a good friend, and he'd shown up at a time when she'd really needed one.

She walked him to the door. There was a brief, awkward moment when they reached it. It felt a little like saying good-night after a first date, unsure what the next move should be and who should make it.

"Thanks," she said, trying to put an end to the awkwardness.

"I'll let you know what the lab finds out," he said.

She nodded, and he turned to go. "What kind of explanation?" she asked. The words had slipped out, not even in her consciousness before they were on her lips.

"What?" Kahler asked.

"You said there were explanations for some of the things Barrington does. I just wondered what you meant."

"Off the record?" he asked.

"Yeah," she agreed. "Just between you and me." She felt free to accept his condition. This wasn't information she wanted for the series. It was personal. What could possibly explain the change in Barrington from the assured, charismatic man in those pictures into the cold recluse she had met today?

"If you use any of this, August, if any of it ever gets into print..." Kahler paused.

"Off the record," she said. "I swear. I just need to understand why."

Again the hazel eyes studied her face, trying to read, maybe, the reason she needed to know. Feeling the intensity of that assessment, her own eyes dropped momentarily, and she forced them back up to meet his.

"Personal?" he asked.

She hesitated, and finally she nodded. The muscles around Kahler's mouth tightened, and then, with an effort she could see, he deliberately wiped the sudden tension from his face.

"Since the bombing, Barrington has suffered from migraines."

"Migraines?" Kate repeated. "Headaches? What does that have to do with—"

"Apparently they're…extremely severe, and they're triggered by exposure to light."

"Light?" she echoed, remembering the satisfying whir of the rising shades, the sudden blaze of summer sunshine she'd sent into the darkened parlor.

"I don't understand all the mechanics," Kahler went on, shrugging his shoulders. "From what I was told, they're probably not related to his eye injuries, but to head trauma. Maybe damaged nerves or scar tissue. Maybe the speed at which his pupils react to sudden light. Maybe they're even psychogenic. Nobody seemed willing to pin down a definitive cause, but nobody would deny the kind of trauma Barrington suffered could cause all sorts of problems. The headaches began as soon as the bandages came off, and they haven't lessened in severity."

"How severe?"

"The usual treatment for headaches as intense as the ones Barrington has is an injection of something powerful enough to knock the sufferer out until the migraine's over. That's what they did for the judge while he was in the hospital."

"How long do they last?"

"For some people migraines can last several days. Given his situation, it makes some sense out of Barrington's decision not to expose himself to that risk."

"Why didn't you tell me about this?" Kate asked. "We talked about Barrington. Why the hell didn't you tell me?" Damn Kahler and his reticence.

"The information came from a friend, somebody at the hospital where the judge was treated after the bombing. Not Barrington's physician, but somebody who knew about the case and owed me a favor. None of this is for public consumption, August. I told you. The guy's been through enough.''

"I just wish you'd told me," she said again, regret tightening her throat, regret for things she'd said and done that she certainly couldn't share with Kahler.

"I only told you now because you seemed convinced he'd sent the package, that the way he lives makes him more suspect. I wanted you to understand that there are some valid reasons for Barrington's seclusion. Maybe the headaches aren't reason enough for everything, but they help to explain the way he lives.''

She nodded.

"What's the fascination, August?" he asked. His voice had changed. No longer a clinical assessment, but deeper, more intimate. *Personal.*

"I don't even understand it myself. It's just there. It's been there from the beginning.''

"I guess all that money would be appealing. I can't speak for Barrington's supposed sex appeal," he said. "I never saw any of that." His lips had moved into a slight smile, but there was no matching amusement in his voice. "You know he may no longer even look the way he once did.''

She almost denied that Barrington had changed—physically changed. She almost revealed that she'd seen him much more clearly since that first night when she'd acted on impulse and entered his darkened house.

"I know," she said. "For some reason, he just…interests me. Maybe it's seeing the effect Jack had on the one man who survived, and it's not the money, Kahler, no matter what you think. I can't explain what I feel. I know it's unprofessional. More than that, it's a little…weird," she admitted. "I know all that. I almost asked Lew to take me off the story because of it, but…I just can't seem to leave it alone.''

"I think you ought to back off. For a lot of reasons. Let the series die a natural death. Maybe that's what the package this morning was intended to do—to tell you to back off.''

"Is that what you really think, Kahler? Is that a professional assessment?"

Again the hazel gaze held hers. "Personal," he said. "I don't want you hurt, Kate."

She smiled at him. "Trust me, I don't want to be hurt. That crap this morning made me very aware of how easy it is to get someone if you really want to. All you need is an address. I found out I'm not nearly as brave as I thought I was."

"Good," Kahler said, his tone ordinary again. "A little less brave is a lot safer. Get a dead bolt, August, and think about the other—about dropping the series."

"I will," she promised.

He stepped through the door, pulling it closed behind him. The apartment seemed suddenly very empty. She walked back into the living room where they'd been sitting. She stopped before the table beside the couch. She hesitated, trying to resist, but finally she opened the drawer and looked down at the folder containing the pictures of Thorne Barrington.

She put her hand down on top of the file, but she didn't take it out. Instead she stood, touching it, the tips of her fingers whitened against the manila surface, remembering the cruelly exposing slashes of sunlight and the stillness of the man who had never turned to face the windows she'd uncovered.

"You okay?" Lew asked the next day. He pitched his question low enough that their conversation would remain private.

She glanced up from the words on her screen. "Better than yesterday. Thanks for sending Kahler. Talking to him helped."

"I don't think I can accept responsibility for that," Lew said, smiling at her. "He seemed worried about you. I think he just wanted to see for himself you were all right. He didn't seem to think your package had anything to do with Jack."

"I know. He promised to let me know what the lab finds."

"Kahler also thought it might be a good idea if you back off the series. You want me to get someone else to do the feature on the guy in Tucson, or you want to just let it stand with the articles you've done? It's your story, Kate. It has been from the beginning, so it's your decision."

"You think Kahler's right? About the package not being from Jack?"

"He gathered up the remains, and he's seen all the others."

"He told me everything was different. The mechanics. Everything. But the return address was the same on this one and the Tucson bomb, and that information hadn't been released. How could someone know about that?"

Lew shrugged. "There are always leaks. Any information gets out, if enough people know about it. Maybe not to the general public, but out just the same. The fact that Barrington's address was on the Tucson bomb would be interesting to anyone with Atlanta connections."

"I thought he'd sent it," Kate said.

"I guess that's natural, considering that you've been working on the bombings, but Kahler said—"

"Not Jack," she corrected. "Barrington. I thought Barrington had sent it."

"Judge Barrington?" Lew said, the disbelief in his voice reminding Kate of Barrington's reputation.

"I know. Kahler thought it was ridiculous, too. It's just that we have some...background." She glanced up in time to catch the surprise in Lew's brown eyes.

"I didn't know you knew Barrington," he said.

"We've met," she hedged. It was the truth, but it didn't explain why those meetings would make her suspect him. She wished that she hadn't started this. "I just keep coming back to Thorne Barrington as the sender, despite what everyone else seems to believe about him."

"Why do you think Barrington would do something like that?"

"We had a run-in. I tried to talk to him about the bombings. I've always thought he was the key to understanding Jack's motives. There's got to be some significance to the fact that he was the first victim. But the judge made it pretty clear he didn't want to talk."

"Knowing you, I'd bet you didn't accept his refusal."

"Eventually. I didn't have a choice. But now I wonder if trying to talk to him made him angry enough that—"

"It wasn't Barrington," Lew interrupted with conviction. "There's no way someone like Thorne Barrington is going to pull a stunt like that. It's no secret he hates the press, and with reason, but still, I can't see him putting together the package you got yesterday. It's totally out of character."

"Maybe your character changes when someone tries to blow you up," Kate suggested. She realized suddenly that Lew would be the perfect person to verify what Kahler had told her. "Lew, you've lived here all your life. You move in some of the same circles as the judge, know the same people. What did you hear about Barrington's injuries?"

"Information for the series?" Lew asked.

"Not really. I just need to know. Kahler told me there was some trauma to his head. Brain damage can...change people. Personality changes. One of Kahler's sources mentioned the judge suffers from migraines, possibly psychogenic in nature."

"Psychogenic?" Lew questioned.

"I looked it up. It means having an emotional cause."

"Like having a bomb go off in your hands, maybe?" Lew asked, smiling. "That kind of emotional cause?"

Kate knew he was right. Even if the migraines were emotional in origin, that didn't mean Barrington had turned into the kind of crazy Kahler had talked about.

"I'll ask around," Lew surprised her by saying. "I know a few people who were close to Barrington at the time. They may not talk to me, but I'll see what I can find out."

"Thanks," Kate said.

"What about the series?"

"I'm not ready to give it up. Not yet. If it's possible, I'd really like to go to Tucson. I want to talk to Draper's widow. Personally, one-on-one. There's a connection between all these people, Lew. I know it in my gut. We just haven't found it yet. Somehow Draper and the others, Thornedyke Barrington included, are all connected. I don't care what the cops think, Jack's not working at random. And I think it's significant that the interval between victims has shortened. For some reason, suddenly Jack's in a hurry. Maybe we're closer than we think.

Maybe the Feds have something. Or maybe he just wants it
to be over. Maybe he wants to finish it.''

"And nobody knows how many more people are on his
list.''

"We know there's at least one more name on that list,''
Kate said. Lew shook his head, puzzled by her comment.
"One more name,'' she repeated. "The name at the top. The
name he started with three years ago. Thornedyke Barrington.''

HE OPENED HIS EYES slowly in the dimness of the massive
bedroom. Even the slight movement of his lids hurt. Not the
ice-pick-in-the-brain agony of the headaches, but the dull sore-
ness in every muscle that they always left behind. He knew
from experience that the effort of turning his head on the pillow would be a vivid reminder of the residual effects. He
swallowed carefully, his mouth dry from the drug Elliot had
administered.

He closed his eyes again. The dim, curtain-shrouded light
that seeped in from the windows should not be enough to set
off another attack, but it was sometimes hard to judge what
was enough. Of course, with the sudden flood of summer sunlight yesterday, there had been no doubt. Because he had refused to stand there with his eyes closed while she shouted at
him, he had known exactly what he faced from the moment
Kate August had released that first shade. He had been too
stubborn—or too stupid—to leave.

He opened his eyes again, raising the damaged right hand
in an unthinking gesture, automatically protecting himself
from even the faint light the draperies allowed into this sanc-
tuary.

Vampire, he thought again, repeating the word that haunted
him. *A damn vampire.* He usually had more success keeping
the bitterness at bay, but remembering the troubling dreams
he'd had about Kate August, he knew why that was now so
hard.

KATE SPENT most of Thursday's flight to Tucson worrying
about the letter she'd mailed before she left Atlanta. It had

taken her most of the previous evening to write, despite the fact that she'd spent all day thinking about what she wanted to say.

Not exactly *wanted* to say, she admitted. She had written a couple of letters of apology at the beginning of her career when she had overstepped her own ethical boundaries. Because doing that had been extremely painful, she had let nothing like those incidents happen in the years since.

At least not until she'd rushed into Judge Barrington's home and thrown up the shades with the same kind of hysterical indignation that had propelled the temperance ladies to chop up bars with axes. Despite the fact that she was genuinely sorry if she had triggered one of the migraines Kahler had described and despite the fact that she was a writer by profession, it had been a very difficult letter to compose. And it had been harder to drop it into a mail slot and let it go.

That's what she had to do, she thought. Let it all go—the guilt, the remorse *and* her fascination with Barrington. That was really what had gotten her into the situation in the first place. As soon as she got back to Atlanta, she intended to throw the folder and the pictures she'd collected into the trash. No more obsession with Thorne Barrington.

Chapter Five

Using Kahler's name and copies of the articles that had appeared in the series as her foot in the door, Kate had wrangled Jackie Draper's address and an introduction by phone from the Tucson Police Department. Although Hall Draper's widow had sounded a little confused about why she was being asked to talk to a reporter from an Atlanta paper, she agreed to the interview.

Mrs. Draper's eyes looked as if she hadn't slept since her husband's death, and Kate felt guilty about putting her through this. The comments the judge had made about her job crept into her head as she opened her notebook.

"I don't really understand what you want me to tell you, Ms. August. You said you were trying to help the authorities find a connection between the victims?"

"I don't believe Jack sends his packages at random. I think there's some link between the people the bomber targets, and if we can discover what that link is..."

"Then the police can catch him," Jackie Draper finished.

"Hopefully," Kate agreed, smiling at her.

"What kinds of things do you need to know?"

"Anything you're willing to tell me, really. The kind of man your husband was. His family. His background. Where he grew up. College. Career. Why don't you just talk, and I'll listen. Then I can ask you anything I've thought of that you might not have covered. How does that sound?"

"Okay," Jackie Draper said.

Her eyes had already lost their focus, moving back into memories that might even provide some kind of comfort. Permission to go back to happier times. Kate found herself hoping that if what she was doing didn't help, at least it wouldn't make the grieving harder.

The soft voice went on a long time. The shadows lengthened, and the narrow strips of light that filtered between the closed slats of the blinds slowly inched across the carpet. She had begun with Hall Draper's childhood, spent in a tiny coal-mining community in Pennsylvania. It had apparently been a life of almost endless deprivation, never enough money, food or warmth.

"I think that's why he ended up here," Jackie said, a brief smile touching her lips. "He finally felt warm. You don't forget the things you do without in childhood. Or the way that doing without made you feel. You may not ever tell anybody, but you're always careful to see that your own children—"

Her voice broke, the emotion that comment had evoked seeming to catch her unaware. "I just can't imagine what Trent's going to do without him. They were so close," she whispered. "Hall's own father wasn't much. Not like we think of daddies nowadays. Maybe he was just a different generation, but remembering his own childhood, Hall always bent over backwards to make sure Trent knew how much he loved him. He was a good man, Ms. August. I don't understand why someone would do this. It doesn't make any sense. Why Hall? That's what I can't understand."

"Nobody can, Mrs. Draper. None of them really seemed to deserve what happened."

"But you think the killer *chose* them?"

"I do. I'm sorry if that…" Kate paused.

"It's all right," Jackie Draper said. "If he did do that, I want him caught. Especially if he thought Hall deserved what happened to him. If he did it out of hatred or revenge."

"Can you think of anyone who disliked your husband, Mrs. Draper?"

"Enough to kill him?" Jackie asked, shaking her head. "Hall didn't have an enemy in the world. I know that's hard to believe, but he really was a good man. He did a lot of *pro bono* work. I used to tell him we were going to starve to death while he was defending somebody who didn't have a cent. He'd tell me that people who had money would always go to someone else, and that I should be grateful poor people needed lawyers, too. I think they reminded him of the people he grew up with."

Mrs. Draper smiled slightly. Remembering. It had probably really been an issue, her chiding him for his willingness to help those who needed legal advice, but couldn't afford to pay for it.

"I wish I could take back all those things I said. All the times I fussed on him for doing what he thought was right. I just wish I could tell him—" Her soft voice stopped again, and the tears that she had mastered until now flooded the shadowed eyes. "I'm sorry," she whispered, wiping the moisture away with the tips of her fingers. Embarrassed to cry before a stranger.

"It's all right," Kate said. "I understand."

"If that's all you want to know..." Hall Draper's widow said, letting the suggestion trail.

"One more question, and then I'll leave you alone, I promise. I'm so grateful you were willing to talk to me."

Jackie Draper nodded, still trying to remove the traces of forbidden tears.

"Was there anything in your husband's life he felt he...shouldn't have done, maybe?" Kate asked. All these people, all Jack's victims seemed so ordinary, but Kate had thought for a long time there must have been something that made them targets for a madman. Jackie Draper's eyes expressed her puzzlement, and Kate tried to clarify. "Something he shouldn't have gotten mixed up in? Or something he regretted later. I don't really know—"

"Hall wasn't ever mixed up in anything that wasn't good and decent, Ms. August."

Kate nodded, knowing she couldn't probe any deeper. For some reason she felt exactly like the kind of vampire Barrington had accused her of being. *Feeding off other people's pain.*

"Thank you so much for seeing me, Mrs. Draper," she said, standing up. "I hope some good comes out of the information you've given me."

Hall Draper's widow nodded, standing also. Kate stuck her notebook and pen back into the leather handbag. She held out her hand, and Jackie Draper put hers into it. Kate was surprised at how fragile it felt. She looked stronger than the frail delicacy of that hand. Unless you looked into her eyes, she thought. Kate had already turned toward the door when the woman spoke.

"There was…one thing," Jackie Draper said, her voice so quiet Kate had to strain to catch the words. "These days…" She hesitated again, her shoulders hunching slightly. "It doesn't seem like much today, but Hall was always sorry. There wasn't anything he could have done about it. He was just a kid, but he was sorry. Especially after we had Trent, after he found out how much…it means to have a child."

Kate held her breath, unwilling to slow the whispered words.

"The girl was just…trash. I know that sounds harsh, but she was. Hall never even knew for sure if it was his baby. She said it was, but she was…" Again, the slender shoulders moved upward. "Even Hall knew it could have been anybody's baby. He was sixteen. She was maybe a couple of years younger. But the thing was…it *could* have been his baby, you know. It was possible. Hall admitted that. He told me about it. Years later. After Trent was born."

The story died, and still Kate waited. The woman's eyes were focused again on the past, reliving the years that had moved so quickly, fluttering by with a sameness that always made you believe they would continue that way forever.

"What happened to the baby?" Kate asked, her careful question pitched as low as the halting narrative had been.

The dark eyes came back, focused briefly on her face, and then turned away to contemplate the glowing lines of late afternoon light seeping between the slats of the mini-blinds. "She had an abortion. That's all I know. That's all Hall knew. The family moved away after that, and he never saw her again." Her voice faded, and Kate thought it was the end of whatever she intended to tell her. Until she added, "*That's* the one thing my husband regretted in his life, Ms. August. That poor lost baby."

"They'll find the guy who did it," Kate said. "I promise."

Jackie Draper nodded, and her eyes returned to the windows.

KATE FOUND A MESSAGE from Kahler when she got back to her motel room. Apparently he had learned from Lew that Kate was coming out to interview Mrs. Draper. She sat down on the edge of the queen-size bed and dialed the local number he'd left.

"Kahler." The deep voice was pleasant, familiar, a welcome touch of home, despite the slight accent.

"August," she countered, smiling.

"Don't try to be cute," he said, his voice relaxing into something less official.

"What?" she teased. "You don't think I'm cute? I'm hurt."

There was no answer for a few seconds. Kahler wasn't usually slow with a comeback, and again there was something odd about the brief silence.

"I think you're cute," he said.

That had almost sounded sincere. Devoid of sarcasm.

"Thanks. I think you're cute, too—like a cobra or some other predator. So spill your guts. Tell me what you've found out since you've been here?"

"Meet me for dinner," he suggested.

"I don't know if my expense account will stretch that far. Unless you're game for McDonald's," she said, relieved they seemed to be back on a more normal footing.

"I'm inviting you."

"You get a raise?" she asked. "I thought cops were like reporters—in the business just for the sheer love of it all."

"I can afford to buy you dinner, August. You got a car?"

"Want me to pick you up?" she asked.

"No, I have a couple of things to finish up. Meet me at a place called Ellington's. Thirty minutes."

THE RESTAURANT was more upscale than the ones where they had eaten together in Atlanta. Kate briefly wished she had taken time to change her clothes and then shrugged away her concern. They didn't have the kind of relationship where you worried about how you looked. She had already been seated, looking over the restaurant's offerings when Kahler arrived. She glanced up when the hostess brought him to the table. He looked tired.

"Hard day?" she asked.

His eyes flicked up from their contemplation of the dinner selections. "A real bitch of a day."

"You go to Draper's office?"

He nodded, his gaze again deliberately focused on the menu. Obviously, he didn't want to talk about the bombing. She couldn't blame him. She wished she had never gone to Austin. It had taken her weeks to get that scene out of her head. Even now the images would reappear suddenly, out of nowhere, catching her unaware, no less vivid for the time she had put between.

She looked back down at the menu, although she had already decided what she was going to order. Kahler had asked her to meet him, which meant he didn't intend to stonewall. She'd just have to let him work his way around to talking in his own time.

"The salmon looks good," she offered.

"I don't think you ever get used to it," Kahler said. His voice was low, just above the background buzz of conversation. He hadn't looked up, eyes still directed at the menu. "You think you're ready for it, that you've developed some—I don't know—some kind of barrier between yourself and the reality of it."

She let the noises of the restaurant drift between them a few seconds. "I talked to Draper's widow today," she said, closing her menu and laying it beside her plate. When she looked up, the hazel eyes were focused on her face. Waiting.

"It seems the worst thing Hall Draper ever did was *maybe* knock some girl up when he was a kid. Apparently that possibility bothered him for the rest of his life."

"His wife tell you that?"

"That and about everything else that ever happened to him," she said. Despite her attempt, somehow she couldn't be objective or cynical about Hall Draper. Something about his wife's hesitant memories had touched a chord, too deeply felt to be glib about. So she told Kahler the truth.

"He was a good man who had worked hard to get where he was. He did a lot of charity cases. She regretted fussing on him about those." She paused, remembering the pain in those shadowed eyes. "He didn't deserve to be blown up."

Kahler's gaze shifted, seeming to focus on the people that were being seated a few tables away. "What makes you think the rest of them did?"

She shook her head. Kahler was right. Nothing they had uncovered about any of the victims seemed to warrant the horror of what had happened to them.

"Some of them just seemed less real to me. Draper was raised in some little coal-mining town. He pulled himself up by hard work and his own force of character. Then the American dream gets blown to smithereens by some maniac who doesn't even have the guts to do it personally. Murder by long distance."

"Sounds like you've got the lead paragraph of your story."

There had been nothing reproachful in Kahler's tone, but for some reason the comment hurt. It had sounded too much like Barrington's crack. As if she were only interested in these people for the increase in circulation their stories provided.

"Believe it or not, I hadn't even thought about writing the story. I'm not quite the vampire Barrington accused me of being."

"Look, I'm sorry. Maybe getting together tonight wasn't such a good idea. Seeing the scene always makes me edgy. I always feel like there must be more that we could be doing. Only I never know what. Nothing we do seems to work with this guy."

"It's not your fault. Let's forget Jack tonight. Let's talk about something besides murder and mayhem for a change."

"I'm a cop, August. A homicide cop. I'm not sure I *know* anything else. I'm not good at social stuff, and other than Jack, you and I don't seem to have a lot in common."

"I'm not complaining. We can talk about the weather. Baseball. I don't care. I'm just glad I'm not eating room service alone. You don't have to be entertaining."

He laughed, the sound pleasant and unfamiliar. Kahler didn't laugh nearly often enough, she thought, smiling at him.

HE WALKED HER to her rental car after the meal. "How long are you staying?" Kahler asked, as he unlocked the door and then handed her the keys.

"A few days. I guess I need to see what else I can turn up on Draper. His widow's not exactly an unbiased source. I'll stay until I think Lew's gotten his money's worth out of the trip. How about you?"

"I'm going back tomorrow."

"I'll call you when I get back to Atlanta," she said.

Kahler nodded. Suddenly, the tension that had been between them at her apartment door was back. He had bought her dinner. Maybe he thought that meant he was entitled to a goodnight kiss.

"Thanks for dinner," she said.

"Thank *you*. I needed the company."

"Me, too," she admitted.

The silence after that admission lasted too long, and she found herself looking for something to say. "I thought I might go to Draper's hometown," she offered. It was an idea that had been growing since she'd left Hall Draper's neat suburban house. She'd try it out on Kahler before she approached Lew.

"What for?" Kahler asked. They were still standing, the opened door between them.

"I don't know. Just to poke around. To see if anyone remembers anything about the story Mrs. Draper told me. See if I can find any trace of that girl."

"You think she's the bomber, August? Revenge for a preg-

nancy that happened years ago?'' Kahler asked. Obviously, he
wasn't impressed with the lead. Lew probably would be un-
derwhelmed also, especially when he thought about costs.

''I don't think she's the bomber. I just don't have anything
else to try. Dead end. Just like it's been all along with Jack.
Just a lot of dead ends.''

''I hope that wasn't supposed to be a pun,'' Kahler said.

''That's not funny.''

''It wasn't meant to be. A lot of dead ends. Dead people.''

''Who apparently didn't deserve to be dead. What kind of
person does something like that?''

A strictly rhetorical question. There was no answer, and
they both were aware of it. A group of diners leaving the
restaurant passed within a few feet, glancing at them curiously.

Kahler waited until the party had moved on before he asked,
''You remember a guy named Wilford Mays?''

''Mays?'' Kate repeated, trying to place the name. She
knew she had heard it, but she couldn't think in what context.
''It doesn't really ring a bell,'' she said.

''School bombing back in the sixties? Two little boys who
had gone back inside to get a forgotten book were killed.''

Kate nodded her head, remembering hearing the story, but
not details. The bombing was something that had happened
more than thirty years ago, during the height of opposition to
school integration in Georgia.

''Mays was probably the guy responsible, but he was never
convicted,'' Kahler went on. ''One of the men who had supposedly been in on the planning got religion in his old age.
He tried to implicate Mays, but his own credibility was ques-
tionable and his memory faulty after all those years. The state
could never put together a case they thought would convince
a jury. They did eventually haul Mays into court on some
charge that had resulted from a search of his house—possessing an illegal firearm, a short-barrelled shotgun, very minor
stuff compared to the murders they wanted to stick him for. I
don't remember everything, but the judge who heard the case
put him away for as long as he could.''

''And?'' Kate said, waiting for the punch line.

"The judge on that case, the illegal weapons charge or whatever it was, was Thorne Barrington."

"Then surely somebody has checked Mays out before now."

"Whoever ran the dockets of Barrington's old cases saw only a firearms charge. Since there was no connection to bombs, no alarm went off."

"So how did you come up with Mays?"

"You keep telling me these killings are related, so I went back over those cases myself. For some reason, the name triggered something. I pulled the informant's information and then the original police reports on the school bombing. The MO, the materials, everything is different, totally different, so logic says there's probably no connection. But Mays is someone who at one time may have killed at long distance, and Barrington came in contact with him."

"*And* put him away," Kate said.

"Barrington sentenced him to the max, but with time off for good behavior, Mays served less than a year."

"You think Mays is Jack?"

"Not based on things we usually use to tie cases together. Nothing Mays did was like what Jack does, but still it's hard to deny the significance—another bomber with ties to Barrington."

"Does Mays fit the FBI profile of the Tripper? A brilliant loner? Product of a dysfunctional family? Probably abused?"

"Jack's fooled us on everything else. Why wouldn't he be able to screw us on the profile?"

"Is Mays that smart? Smart enough to get away with mail bombs? That's a hell of a lot different from setting off dynamite in an empty building—a supposedly empty building."

"No way to know," Kahler acknowledged, shrugging. "He left school in the sixth grade. He's uneducated, but that doesn't mean he doesn't have enough intelligence to—"

"To keep everyone in the dark for three years?" she interrupted. "About where he gets his materials? How he gets the packages through the mail undetected? That smart? You don't really believe that, Kahler. You're grasping at straws."

"Straws are all I've got, August," he said, quick anger at her sarcasm coloring his voice. "I'm trying to catch a killer who's been blowing people up for three years."

"I know," she said softly, genuinely sorry for her ridicule.

"It just seemed too coincidental that Barrington had dealt with Mays. Another bomber," he said again.

She knew that was really all he had. Mays had possibly set off one bomb, a crime for which he'd never even been charged, so maybe he was implicated in the more recent series. They both knew what a stretch that was—even given the Barrington link.

"You really think there's some connection?"

"I thought I'd talk to Barrington about him. Maybe visit Mays. Talk to the guys who investigated the school bombing."

"If any of them are still alive," she reminded him.

His mouth tightened, and his eyes moved to focus on the darkness beyond the boundaries of the parking lot. His face reflected his frustration. That must be something he had fought for the last three years. Finally, he looked back at her, a smile lifting the tight line of his lips only fractionally. "Call me when you get back to Atlanta. And thanks," he said.

"For what?" she asked. "You paid for dinner."

"For listening."

"Thanks for talking. As always, thanks for being willing to talk to me. I'll call you."

She got into the car and closed the door. Kahler waited while she fastened her seat belt and started the engine. Before she put the car into gear, she lifted her hand to wave to him. He touched the top of the car with his fingers, almost like a benediction, and then turned, walking off into the shadows between the scattered pools of light.

THE PHONE WAS RINGING when Kate unlocked the door of her apartment in Atlanta the following Tuesday night. Despite her hurry to catch the call, she closed the door behind her and took a moment to slip the chain into place. She hadn't had time before she left town to do what Kahler had advised her to do—to install a good dead bolt. *Tomorrow,* she promised herself, setting her suitcase down and grabbing the phone.

"Hello," she said, her voice a little breathless. Probably Lew. No one else knew she was coming back tonight.

"Ms. August?" She had never heard this particular voice over the phone, but in spite of the electronic distortion, she recognized the caller immediately.

"Yes," she answered. All the possible explanations for a phone call from Thorne Barrington ran through her head.

"Did you take my advice, Ms. August?" he asked.

She could think of nothing he had said to her that might qualify as advice. "Advice?" she echoed.

"Did you tell the police about the package you received?"

Belatedly, she remembered that he *had* urged her to do that.

"Yes, I did, Judge Barrington." For some reason she seemed unable to manage anything beyond monosyllables. This was the last thing she had expected, given the situation between them.

"To whom did you speak, Ms. August?"

She hesitated briefly, wondering if she would be giving away her relationship with Kahler if she told the truth. However, it was well known in Atlanta that he was the detective in charge of the case relating to Jack. Barrington had enough contacts that he could easily check the veracity of whatever she told him. The last thing she needed was to be caught in a lie.

"I spoke to a Detective Kahler."

"What did he tell you?" Barrington asked.

She was beginning to wonder at his obvious interest in her package when the realization came that he was the one man in Atlanta who would be avidly interested in anything that might figure in the eventual apprehension of the bomber.

"He believes the package I received wasn't related to the Tripper bombings."

"On what grounds?"

"Everything was different. The packaging. The triggering device. Everything."

"Except my address," Barrington reminded her.

"Yes," she acknowledged.

"No matter what you believe, I didn't send that package."

She wondered how she should respond to that. Finally, she realized that she had already acknowledged his denial—before she ever left Atlanta.

"Did you get my letter, Judge Barrington?"

"Yes."

"I'm truly sorry for…what happened." Her voice was hesitant, lacking its usual confidence. Apologizing was something that didn't come easy to Kate August. She always hated having to admit that she'd made a fool of herself, and she knew that in this case she had done it with a vengeance. "I'm sorry for the way I acted and for accusing you of sending the package."

"Then you no longer believe I had anything to do with it."

"No. And I regret that I jumped to that conclusion. It just seemed…coincidental. Given our previous encounter."

"Then we're left with a real problem, Ms. August."

It seemed there were still a lot of problems, but she couldn't think of one she and Barrington shared. After a few seconds of silence, he went on.

"If you've accepted my denial and if Detective Kahler believes the package had nothing to do with Jack, then who sent it? And more importantly, why?"

The pertinent question. One for which she had no answer. Unless… Why not ask Barrington about what Kahler had suggested? During the days since the detective had mentioned the school bombing, she had thought a lot about the possibility that Mays was involved in this. The more she had thought about it, the more she had wondered what the odds were on two bombers being connected to Barrington. That *did* seem too coincidental.

"Do you remember a man named Wilford Mays, Judge Barrington? He came before you on an unrelated charge, but it's possible—"

"I remember Mays," he interrupted. "Where did you come up with his name?"

"Someone told me he was suspected of being the school bomber in the sixties. I know he was never convicted on that, but isn't it possible that he might have some involvement in this case?''

"Mays was still in prison when the bombings began.''

Kahler hadn't told her that. Maybe he didn't even know. Or maybe Barrington was wrong. Kahler had said Mays had gotten time off for good behavior, so perhaps he had been out when the bombings began. She considered the judge's choice of words—impersonal and distanced, considering that the bombings had begun with the package sent to Thorne Barrington.

"But not for the others?'' she asked. "It's likely he didn't act alone on the school bombing. Maybe he has an accomplice.''

"That's not the usual pattern with mail bombers,'' he said. There was a thread of interest in the denial. He was at least considering what she had said.

"Nothing about Jack's been *usual* from the start, and Mays is bright.'' There was a silence. She waited one heartbeat. Two. "Isn't he?'' she prodded. Fishing now. Hoping he'd talk to her.

"I'd say he's cunning,'' Barrington said. "Shrewd rather than smart.''

Her lips tilted. "I'd like to talk to you about what you remember about his case.''

"I'm sorry, Ms. August, but considering our previous—''

"This time I'll ring the bell,'' she offered, allowing a trace of self-directed mockery into her voice. "And I promise to leave the shades alone,'' she added.

When the silence stretched again, she knew she had gone too far. Damn her smart mouth. This wasn't Kahler, and it wasn't the time for sarcasm. There was nothing funny about what she'd done to Thorne Barrington.

"I interviewed Hall Draper's widow,'' she interjected into the suddenly frigid silence. She offered the change of subject to make him forget what she'd just said. "I'd like to run the things she told me about her husband by you.''

"Why?''

"To see if anything sounds familiar. I still believe there's a link between all the victims." *Wrong word,* she thought immediately. He was certainly a victim, but she shouldn't have called him that. At least he was still alive.

"What kind of link?"

"I don't have a clue," she admitted truthfully. "Something pretty obscure or somebody would already have picked up on it. I just thought I could tell you what Jackie Draper told me and see if any of it meant anything to you."

She waited, realizing that he hadn't said no, so he must be considering it. She closed her eyes, praying, wondering if she could possibly get lucky enough to have him agree to meet her. Despite all the ways she had screwed up, was it possible that he was even thinking about talking to her about this case?

"You'd have to come here, Ms. August."

She bit her lip to keep her gasp of elation from slipping out. Barrington was going to do it. Meet with her. Talk about Mays. Listen to Jackie Draper's story. All of it. And he wondered if she minded having to come to his house.

"Of course," she said. "That's no problem." She was pleased with how calm she sounded.

"Tomorrow?"

"The sooner the better."

"Four o'clock."

"You think Elliot will let me in?" she asked. Teasing again. Automatic. Only, what in the hell she was doing teasing Barrington, especially about her last visit?

"Try ringing the bell," he suggested, and then the connection was broken. There had been some nuance of amusement in his voice, and she realized she was smiling as she put her phone back on its stand. She couldn't believe he'd agreed.

"Yes!" she said softly, her voice full of triumph.

She glanced down at the small table on which the phone rested. Not even attempting to fight the urge this time, she opened the drawer and then realized it was empty. The folder containing Thorne Barrington's pictures was gone. It took a moment for the reality of that to hit her.

Although the drawer wasn't deep, she pulled it out further, running her fingers to the very back. There was no manila folder. She tried to think of the last time she had opened the drawer, tried to remember if she had taken the Barrington file out and had then forgotten to put it back. But despite the fact that she lived alone, the pictures were a forbidden pleasure. She knew she would never have left them out.

Still trying to remember what she could possibly have done with the folder, she switched off the lights in the living room, at the same time turning on the light in the short hallway that led to the bedroom and bath. She walked down the hall, unbuttoning her blouse as she went, becoming aware again for the first time since she'd heard the phone ringing of how exhausted she was.

By the time she reached the bedroom, the blouse was off and she held it loosely folded in her hands. Too tired to find a hanger, she laid the garment across the top of the bedroom chair. She stepped out of her low-heeled pumps as her fingers found the button on the waistband of her skirt. She unzipped it and let it fall, stooping to pick it up and throw it across the chair on top of the folded blouse. She continued to undress, piling her slip, bra and hose on the other garments. She'd straighten up in the morning. That was one advantage of living alone—no one else would see the clutter.

She took a cream-colored sleeveless gown out of her drawer and slipped it on, enjoying the fall of soft cotton over her body. She thought briefly about how good it felt to be home and how wonderful sleeping in her own bed was going to be.

She stacked the sham-covered pillows on the floor beside the chair that held her clothes and then removed the comforter, putting it on top of the pillows. She walked back to the bed, reaching under her pillow to find the top edge of the sheet, pulling it and the lightweight blanket down at the same time.

It took her a moment to realize what was in the bed, lying red and somehow obscene against the smooth white fabric of the bottom sheet. Her hand was still gripping the top sheet and blanket, but it was trembling now. Very slowly she drew them downward, exposing the vivid spill of glittering confetti. The same red confetti that had showered her office the day she'd received the package.

In her mind, unwanted, without logic or reason, out of nowhere a phrase echoed, just as obscene and just as terrifying.
Jack's back.

Chapter Six

She opened the door, leaving the chain in place until she could be sure it was Kahler. He was more casually dressed than she'd ever seen him, but she'd gotten him out of bed to answer her almost hysterical phone call. He had told her he'd be right over and had ordered her not to touch anything—to stay out of the bedroom and wait until he got there.

She released the chain, opened the door, and then surprised herself by stepping into Kahler's arms. They closed around her, almost automatically, despite the leather case he held in his right hand. She hadn't even thought about her action, about what effect it might have on their relationship. She had simply been so glad to see him, so relieved not to be in the apartment alone.

"You're all right," he said, his mouth moving against her hair. She could feel the warmth, and she took a deep breath. The first real breath she'd gotten since she'd pulled back the covers to reveal the prankster's calling card.

"He was here," she said.

The words were almost a whisper. She still felt sick. She had been since she'd realized all the implications of what she had found. She had read that people whose houses were burglarized felt like this—invaded, violated. She shivered, despite the heat of Kahler's body still holding her. She found herself wondering if she'd ever really feel safe again.

This was her home, and whoever had sent the package to her office had been here. He had opened drawers, touched her personal possessions. Maybe run his fingers over the soft cotton of the gown she had put on tonight—a hundred years ago—when she had been so glad to be back to the familiar pleasures of home.

"He was here, Kahler. In my *apartment,*" she said. She wondered if Kahler would understand or if he was too inured by the years he'd dealt with real violations. Suddenly embarrassed, she removed her body from the embrace she had sought.

"He's not here now, Kate. You're all right. That's all that's important right now."

She nodded, knowing he was right.

"Where's the bedroom?" he asked, and despite the situation, she felt her mouth react to the question, the corners lifting.

"What? No foreplay?" she asked, trying to pretend she wasn't devastated by this, trying to again be what she had always thought herself—a strong woman, able to joke about the sometimes dangerous or disturbing elements of her job.

Kahler wasn't buying the act. His eyes held hers a moment, and then, still unsmiling, he broke the contact, glancing around the apartment. He moved to the doorway of the hall which led to the bedroom and bath. She trailed him reluctantly.

He walked into the bedroom and stopped, looking at the spread of confetti, the metallic surfaces of the scattered pieces catching the reflections from the overhead light. From this angle, the metal bits looked exactly like the ones that had fallen onto the carpet that day. Like freshly spilled drops of blood.

Kate stood in the doorway, watching Kahler make his careful observations. He hadn't touched anything, and he had moved around the room as little as possible.

"The bed was made?" he asked.

"Yes."

"Notice anything different about the way it was made?"

"I wasn't looking for anything different, but... I don't think there was anything—"

"Anything missing?" he interrupted.

Just my collection of Barrington's pictures, she thought. *My fantasy. My secret life.* Somehow she couldn't imagine confessing that loss, that particular violation, to Kahler. There was nothing the intruder could learn about the case from the folder he'd taken. Nothing beyond the fact that she was hung up on looking at pre-Jack photographs of Thorne Barrington, she thought, mocking her own obsession.

"No," she lied. "At least nothing I know of."

"I'll dust a few of the likeliest areas for prints, although truthfully I'll be surprised if we find any. Thanks to the tube, everybody knows enough to wear latex gloves. Unless you want to wait for the lab boys to come out and do it tomorrow?"

He turned to look at her, his eyes carefully impersonal now, although they had touched quickly over the smooth skin exposed by the low neck of her gown before they had lifted to her face.

"No," she said. "You do it. If you will. I just want to clean that up. Just get it out of my bed."

"Give me another set of sheets, and I'll take care of it."

"I don't want you to have to—"

"I'd like to take this set in. Test them for any physical evidence. We might get lucky. While I'm at it, I'll put the clean sheets on the bed."

She nodded again, grateful for the offer, however he wanted to justify it. When she brought sheets back into the room, Kahler had already begun dusting for prints.

"You can put them on the foot of the bed," he instructed.

She deposited the small stack and then looked around the room. "Sorry about the mess," she said, gesturing toward the chair where she'd piled her clothes and the bedding on the floor.

Kahler glanced up from what he was doing, and he smiled at her for the first time. "I grew up in a three-room house with my mother and sister. You don't have to apologize for the feminine clutter, August. It just makes me feel at home."

She returned his smile, wondering what Kahler had been like as a boy, what his early life had been, before he'd joined the military. He had told her almost nothing beyond the fact that he couldn't imagine having grown up surrounded by luxury as Thorne Barrington had, that he had not been born with a silver spoon in his mouth. And, of course, neither had she.

"You don't have to stay," Kahler added.

Kate realized suddenly that she didn't want to. She wanted out of this room, away from the violation. Kahler seemed to be very perceptive tonight where her feelings were concerned.

"Thanks," she said, and she turned and left him alone.

IT TOOK KAHLER maybe twenty minutes to finish. Kate sat on the couch in the living room while she waited, images of someone rummaging through her belongings invading her mind. Occasionally she thought about the missing pictures, wondering why he would have taken those. It didn't make sense. Unless...

Resolutely, she banished that thought. Barrington wouldn't want his own pictures. No one had believed her idea that the judge was involved with the package that had been sent to her office. Both Kahler and Lew had discounted that scenario. It was somehow even more far-fetched to imagine a respected jurist breaking into her apartment to throw confetti between her sheets.

She hadn't told Kahler that Barrington had called her or that she had an appointment with him tomorrow, and she didn't intend to. She had already confessed that she wasn't completely unbiased when it came to the judge. It was all too complicated to explain, especially with everything else that was going on.

"All done," Kahler said. "You want me to stay a while?"

He was standing in the doorway of the hall. She had the sudden, inexplicable feeling that he might have been there a few minutes, silently watching her.

"I'm not quite that big a coward," she denied.

"Sometimes having company helps," Kahler suggested.

"It's just the thought that he was here." She had said that before, but somehow it was the one thing she couldn't get past. He had been in her home. He had touched her things, had run his hands over the sheets of her bed. Violation. She shivered.

"Put the chain on. And get that lock tomorrow. Then if he wants in again, he'll have to break the door down. You just made it easy for him, Kate."

"I know," she admitted. "Who do you think could have—"

"Whoever sent the package. We've already played this game. I don't have any answers for you. We'll let the lab see if they can find anything. There's nothing more I can do to-night."

"Thanks for coming," she said. She stood up, aware for the first time of the sheerness of her gown. Not that Kahler had revealed he'd noticed.

"I don't like this, August. I don't like the way it feels. Usually creeps who pull stunts like this are harmless. But oc-casionally…"

"Occasionally, they do more than terrorize," she finished for him. She was very well aware of the dangers of stalkers.

"You be careful," Kahler ordered. "You're smart. Don't take any chances. And forget the series. Let it drop. It's not worth the risk. Not for some stupid story." His voice was suddenly passionate. No longer the detached professional. Ap-parently, this felt personal to Kahler also.

"It's my job, Kahler. If I run at the first sign of trouble, at the first indication that someone doesn't like what I write, then I'm not much of a reporter."

"Maybe they'll put that in your obituary. She was a hell of a reporter, but she didn't have sense enough to know when to leave it alone."

"If you're trying to scare me, I want you to know that you're doing a hell of a fine job." Her voice was tight with anger. He was supposed to be comforting, protecting her from this maniac, and instead he was just making it worse.

"Good," he said. "Get the lock, August. First thing to-morrow. Be late for work if you have to. Remember what they say." His voice was just as hard as hers, his eyes challenging.

"What do they say, Kahler? I know you're dying to tell me."

"Better late than never," he said. He stalked across the room and opened the door, every motion indicating anger.

She watched him, her eyes glazed with sudden moisture. She hated it, but it always happened. She always cried when she got mad. Kahler was supposed to be her friend. He wasn't supposed to tell her it was too dangerous to keep doing her job. That wasn't what she wanted to hear from Detective Byron Kahler.

"By the way," he said, turning just before he stepped through the opened door. She blinked, determined not to let him have the satisfaction of seeing her cry, but still his features were slightly blurred. "To me, August, foreplay won't consist of putting confetti between your sheets."

He closed the door behind him, the noise sharp in the confines of the small room. She opened her mouth slightly, almost the comical dropped jaw of the sitcoms, and then realized she had nothing to say. Even if she had been able to think of a comeback, he had timed it so it was far too late to deliver it.

THE HEAT WAS SHIMMERING off the pavement again. The members of the construction crew across the street were at least pretending to work, but somehow all the jobs they had found to do today were in the shade. Kate didn't blame them. The bank clock she'd passed on her way to the Barrington mansion had read 102, and it was probably ten degrees higher than that in the exposed upper stories of the dilapidated house they were renovating.

She followed the judge's instructions, ringing the bell. Her lips curved as she remembered the comment on which he'd ended their conversation last night. She had thought a lot about his tone. There was no doubt it had contained amusement. It was the first time in her encounters with Barrington that she had been allowed a glimpse of the man reflected in those old photos.

Her smile faded when she remembered the fate of the pictures. She had also thought long and hard about taking Kahler's advice, but she could no more have cancelled this appointment today than she could have confessed to the detective what she had confirmed during the sleepless hours of last night—that the only thing missing from her apartment was her secret collection of Thorne Barrington's pictures.

"Miss August." The old man had arrived, his trembling hands already beginning to deal with the gate.

"Hello, Elliot," she answered, smiling at him. She knew the butler would not have forgiven her for what she had done the last time he'd let her in. Not given the degree of affection that had been in his voice for his beloved "Mr. Thorne."

"Judge Barrington is waiting in the parlor," Elliot said, pulling the gate inward. "If you'll follow me." She could tell from his tone there would be no protective umbrella today and no iced tea. She had definitely not been forgiven.

He said nothing else to her as he led the way up the now familiar walkway and through the glass-paneled front door. The crystal tears of the chandelier in the foyer proclaimed their entrance as they had the first night she'd come to this house. She had expected Elliot to announce her, but instead he disappeared into the darkness behind the central staircase, leaving her alone in the artificial twilight.

This was what she had wanted—an interview with Thorne Barrington, so she didn't know why she was hesitating. Her palms were clammy, and it had nothing to do with the humidity. Unconsciously, she straightened her shoulders, and taking a deep breath, she pushed aside the sliding wooden door to reveal the formal parlor, exactly as it had been before.

Its dimness was a contrast even to the unlighted hall. Enough light seeped in from the porch-shaded glass door there to offer some illumination, but Kate had to pause on the threshold of the parlor to allow her eyes to adjust to its lack of light.

"Ms. August." The deep voice came from the shadows on the opposite side of the fireplace, the spot where he had been sitting on the first night she'd come here. Gradually, his figure began to take shape, emerging again from the surrounding darkness. And again he was standing—the perfect gentleman.

"Judge Barrington," she acknowledged his greeting, walking toward him with her hand outstretched. Properly brought up Southern men never extended their hands unless a lady offered hers first. Business women down here knew the rule—a rule that hadn't changed as far as the old-money crowd, a group to which Barrington certainly belonged, was concerned.

His voice stopped her before she had halved the distance between them. "I no longer shake hands, Ms. August. Please forgive me." There was no inflection in the statement, no embarrassment, and despite the way it had been phrased, no apology. Simply a statement of fact.

There must have been injuries to his hands, she realized, remembering what Lew had said. Something about how it would change your character to have a bomb blow up in your hands. She hadn't picked up on the significance of that. The comment had undoubtedly stemmed from some bit of gossip her editor had heard.

Her gaze dropped to Barrington's hands, to verify that was the reason for the curt dismissal of her attempted handshake. His arms were at his sides, the big hands almost touching the faded denim of well-worn jeans. She could see no details other than the seemingly normal shape of the thumbs and the profile of the rest, palms relaxed, curving slightly inward.

Belatedly aware of the rudeness of what she was doing, she forced her eyes up. His were focused calmly on her face, waiting, his expression absolutely unrevealing. She allowed her own hand to drop to her side. Like an idiot, she had continued to hold it out, even after his comment. All her encounters with this man seemed destined to be mired in embarrassment.

"I'm sorry," she said. "I didn't know."

"Since you're not at fault, I see no need for you to apologize. Would you like to sit down?"

"Thank you," Kate said, finding that another chair had been conveniently situated directly across from the shadowed one the judge had chosen. She sat down in it, putting her bag on the floor and fumbling in it for her notebook and a pen, attempting to hide her nervousness. She was aware when Barrington sat down, still moving as gracefully as the athlete he once had been.

"You said on the phone that you'd learned some things about the Draper bombing which you wanted to discuss with me," he said.

That really wasn't what she had meant to suggest when she'd talked to him. She didn't know what might be significant about the minutiae of Hall Draper's very ordinary life. She had just hoped something would trigger a response from the judge.

"I don't know that I've *learned* anything. Not anything relevant. I just talked to Draper's widow. I thought if I read you some of the things she told me, you might make a connection."

"Did you see some connection, Ms. August?"

She smiled, thinking how far removed from the privileged life-style of the Barrington millions Hall Draper had been. How different his growing up. His career.

"You and Draper seem light-years apart to me, but…" She paused, trying to think what she wanted to say, and he waited patiently through the hesitation. "But there must be something. Somewhere in your lives—*something* in your lives— must connect. It's the only way to make sense out of all this."

"You're still trying to make sense out of what he does?"

"You think he strikes at random?" she asked. This was what she had come for. To finally talk to Thorne Barrington. To get his take on the whole insane situation.

"No," he said simply.

"Then…" Again she hesitated.

"I think he chooses his victims," Barrington went on. "But despite the three years I've spent thinking about who might hate me enough to…" The break was brief, but there was a tinge of emotion that had not been allowed before. "…want to kill me, I'm no closer to an answer than I was then."

"What about Mays?" Kate asked. "Did he hate you enough?"

"He hated us all. With all the mad-dog rabidness you'd expect from a man who would blow up a school because a black child had been allowed to enter it. But he didn't seem to single me out particularly. I was just part of the establishment that had been trying to destroy his mind-set, his way of life, for the past thirty years. He seemed to despise the fellow conspirator who had gone to the authorities far more than those who were attempting to impose a long-overdue justice for what he'd done."

"But that informant didn't receive a bomb through the mail."

"No," Barrington confirmed.

"Do you think Mays was responsible for the school bombing?"

"Yes," Barrington said, with a conviction she could hear.

"No doubt in your mind?"

"No."

"And that's why you gave him the maximum sentence?"

From out of the shadows came a brief whisper of laughter. Unamused. Self-mocking. "The maximum? A year. Less than a year out of his seventy to pay for the deaths of two children."

"That was all you could do." Surprisingly, Kate found herself wanting to comfort that bitterness.

There was no answer from the man in the shadows.

"But you don't believe he's Jack?" she asked when he seemed disinclined to pursue the justice, or injustice, of Mays's sentence.

"Based on everything I know, he doesn't fit. It bothered me enough—the fact that I'd had personal contact with another bomber—that I *did* mention Mays to the police. Apparently, they've never found a connection."

"Who did you tell about Mays?" Kate asked, wondering why that information had never been conveyed to Kahler.

"I really don't know. At first..." The deep voice hesitated, and Kate recognized some trace of emotion, but again the pause was brief and whatever she had heard was gone when he continued. "At first there was only an endless confusion of voices. I never learned to separate them. Thank God, that was a skill I wasn't forced to acquire."

Thank God whatever damage there had been to his eyes hadn't been permanent, Kate realized. That had certainly sounded heartfelt and for the first time she thought about what blindness would have meant to the man Barrington had been. But at least he wouldn't have been a prisoner in his own home. Maybe what *had* happened had somehow been worse than the loss of his sight.

"And later on? Did you tell Kahler about Mays?"

"I don't remember mentioning the school bombing to Detective Kahler. I suppose I assumed that whoever I had told at first had investigated Mays and that the possibility of his involvement had come to nothing. There's never been any mention of him in anything that's been written about the mail bombings."

She wondered suddenly if that meant Barrington had read her stuff. He had been familiar with her name, so even with his disdain for the media, he had still followed the investigation.

"There's been nothing in *my* series, because I just heard Mays's name last week," she said.

"Who mentioned him to you?"

"A good reporter always protects her sources, Judge Barrington," she said, smiling. "Or pretty soon she doesn't have any," she explained the pragmatism behind that particular ethic.

"Thorne," he said.

"I beg your pardon."

"I was simply suggesting that you might use my given name."

"Of course," Kate said, her voice almost as breathless as when she'd realized whom she was talking to on the phone. "If that's what you prefer," she added.

"May I call you Kate?"

"Of course."

"Why do I feel that I've just made you extremely uncomfortable?" Barrington asked. The amusement was clearly back, touching the deep baritone with intimacy.

This was the way his voice must have sounded before, Kate

thought, back when those beautiful debutantes had hung on his every word, their eyes drinking in the perfection of feature that had not changed. He was still as handsome, hiding here in the shadowed existence that he had chosen or had been forced to choose. The sexual magnetism was still there. With the dark, honeyed warmth of his tone she had felt its power move through her body, sensual and inviting.

"Thorne," she repeated obediently. She had never even called him that in her imagination.

"I know it sounds like one of those names Hollywood dreamed up—Rip or Rock or Cord. I *do* realize how ridiculous it is, but given the options available to her, I confess that I'm grateful my mother had the good sense to settle on Thorne."

Harlan Thornedyke Barrington, Kate thought—and then she laughed. He was right. By far the lesser of the possible evils. His laughter joined hers, and when she became aware of the sound, she was again unprepared for how intimate it was. He was just a man, she reminded herself. With her fascination, she knew that she truly had made him larger than life.

Just a man. Just like Kahler. Just like any of the other guys she had been involved with through the years. *Been involved with?* she repeated mentally, incredulous at what she had just thought. *Slow down,* she reminded herself. Just because she was here, finally talking to Barrington did not—definitely did not—mean they were involved.

"I thought I'd try talking to Mays," she said, attempting to get back on track, back to the reason she was here. This might be the only chance she would ever have to discuss these things with Barrington. She couldn't afford to blow it.

"My advice is to stay as far away from Mays as you can."

"You think he's still dangerous."

"The school bombing isn't the only crime Mays was involved in. The informant mentioned a lynching, and there were other things. Nothing Mays could be tied to legally, but he was a man filled with hate and more than willing to act on his feelings."

"Surely after all this time—" Kate began.

"A rattler's not any less dangerous because he's old. He's just bigger and meaner. More full of venom."

It was a Southernism. Something her grandmother might have said, and like all truisms, it was probably a very accurate opinion where a snake like Wilford Mays was concerned.

"Stay away from Mays," he warned. "Chances are he has nothing to do with the current bombings. The police would surely have investigated that possibility."

Only, Kate knew, that wasn't the case. No one, despite Thorne Barrington's initial request, had ever checked out Mays. She had even discouraged Kahler when he'd suggested an investigation of the alleged school bomber.

"Why don't you tell me the things Draper's widow told you," Barrington said. "It's possible there may be something there. At least, I think that's more likely to result in something useful than pursuing a seventy-year-old bigot."

Kate glanced down at her notebook and realized that in the dimness of the room she could barely make out her notes, a confusing mixture of real shorthand and her own personal variety. She could hardly ask Barrington to turn on the lights, and he was so accustomed to this omnipresent darkness that he apparently didn't realize there was a problem with what he'd just proposed.

Her eyes still lowered to the barely discernible words she had scrawled across the ruled paper, she realized there was only one thing to do. She would have to recount from memory what Jackie Draper had told her.

Kate took a deep breath, trying to think where to start. As she began to talk, however, she found that the events of Hall Draper's life—so ordinary as to be unremarkable—had made an indelible impression. She wasn't aware of the passage of time, eventually as lost in the narrative as she had been when she had listened to it in that sun-striped room in Tucson.

"And finally, when I asked her if her husband had ever been mixed up in anything…unsavory, she could only think of one thing, almost an afterthought. It was about a girl who had gotten pregnant at fourteen with what *might* have been Hall Draper's child. She had an abortion, either because she was forced to by her family or because that's what she wanted. Not what Draper had wanted maybe, but he had felt he was too young to have much effect on that decision. Mrs. Draper said that's the one thing in his life he regretted. That poor lost baby.''

The words drifted away into the silence. The room was darker now, she realized. The man who had listened without comment to the story of Hall Draper's life was almost completely enveloped in the shadows that had deepened with the approach of twilight. Suddenly she was embarrassed for having taken up his afternoon on what was apparently an exercise in futility.

''Nothing in that story meant anything to you,'' she said. It wasn't even a question. Barrington had asked for no repetitions, had not commented on or questioned any of what she'd related.

''Perhaps not. Not in the way you'd hoped.'' The deep voice was almost disembodied, simply coming out of the darkness. ''But obviously, it meant something to you.''

She hadn't intended to reveal how moved she had been by the images of the Drapers' private lives, by the decency of Hall Draper, the grief of his widow.

''It just seemed to me that whatever mistake he made—at whatever point in his life—the way he had lived the rest of it should have made up for it. It should have been enough.''

''But it wasn't,'' Thorne said softly.

''No,'' she whispered. ''He died, and there doesn't seem to be a reason for his death. Not in anything she told me.''

''Or for any of the others?'' he asked.

She shook her head, and then wondered if he could see her, given the darkness. ''No,'' she whispered.

''Perhaps you won't understand this, but knowing you feel that way helps.''

''Knowing…?''

''That none of *them* deserved what happened.''

''And that means that you didn't deserve it either,'' she said, suddenly understanding.

"I've spent three years wondering what I did. Maybe the answer is, I did nothing."

"But like Hall Draper—like all of us, I suppose—there are things in your life you aren't proud of."

"Like all of us," he acknowledged.

"What do *you* regret, Judge Barrington?"

It was the question any good reporter would have asked, but she was curious on another level. What did a man, highly respected for his integrity, his dedication to duty, a man who had lived the kind of life Thorne Barrington had, have to regret?

"Perhaps I'll tell you that the next time we talk," he said softly. "Now, if you'll excuse me, I'm afraid I have another appointment." It was certainly a lie, graceful and polite, but still a lie.

"Of course," she said, pushing the unused notebook back into her purse. "I appreciate your agreeing to see me. Thank you for your time."

"A commodity of which I seem to have an unlimited supply."

"Does that mean I can come back?" she asked, deliberately injecting the teasing note. "When I have other questions?"

"As long as our conversations remain simply that," he surprised her by agreeing. "I'm not interested in having my name or my comments appear in your paper. I can assure you that...my situation attracted all the attention I ever desire in this lifetime. If you want my input, then like your other sources, I expect our relationship to remain completely confidential."

"Of course," Kate agreed. *Our relationship.* He meant professional, of course, but for some reason the words had echoed more strongly than the rest of the warning. "I never intended to make any part of our conversation public."

"Thank you," Thorne said. "Shall I ring for Elliot or do you think you can find your way out?" There was a pause before he added, his voice touched with humor, "Again."

His timing had been impeccable, and she paid tribute by laughing. "Thank you, but I believe I can manage."

She stood up, gathering up her bag, and began to cross to the sliding doors. Before she reached them, she remembered the retriever. "Where's your dog?" she asked.

"Elliot's fastened him in one of the rooms upstairs. He was afraid he'd frighten you." The amusement was still there, pleasantly intriguing in the deep voice. "For some reason Elliot is under the impression that the retriever's a guard dog."

"Then I'm glad you've got a fence," she said.

She let herself out of the parlor, but she stopped in the wide foyer, looking up the stairs where Elliot and the puppy were waiting for her to leave. Then they would once again become a part of the limited world of the man they obviously adored. The man who had, for some reason, allowed her to enter this very private domain. Who had indicated he would allow it again, providing she, too, guarded the privacy which he seemed to value above anything else—even, it seemed, above human companionship.

HE LISTENED to the closing of the front door and the faint noise made by the crystals of his grandmother's Waterford chandelier. When those sounds had faded, he sat alone in the shadows, the house again completely silent.

It had been far too pleasant to sit and listen to her voice, to listen as she told the story of Hall Draper's life. It had been obvious that she had been deeply moved by her encounter with Draper's widow. The emotion had been there, enriching the quiet narrative. Clearly, she admired the kind of man Draper had been. Perhaps as she might have admired the man Thorne Barrington had once been, the kind of man he knew he was no longer.

She was a reporter working on a story. That was why she had come here. Nothing else. *I'm not news,* he had told her the first night, but even then he had known that he was, and that despite the passage of time, he probably always would be. He understood exactly why Kate August wanted to talk to him. What he didn't understand was why, given the situation, he had agreed.

Chapter Seven

Kate had spent another nearly sleepless night. She had not even entered the bedroom this time, having learned during the dawn hours of the night before the futility of trying to sleep there. She had instead pulled out spare bedding and made a nest on the couch, but sleep again eluded her. It might have had something to do with the fact that she couldn't bear to turn off the lamp and plunge the apartment into darkness. Or it might have been because of the voices that kept invading her mind.

The soft warmth of Barrington's amused baritone. Kahler's, slightly accented, in the darkness of the restaurant parking lot in Tucson, telling her about another bomber. Jackie Draper's whispering tribute to her husband—a good man.

The lack of sleep was beginning to show, she thought, putting on her makeup the next morning. The small bathroom light clearly illuminated the shadows under her eyes, and in them was the same frustration she had heard in Kahler's voice.

This had all gone on too long. Too many people had died, and she knew in her heart that there was a connection between them. Figuring out what that link might be was the key to stopping Jack. Dangerous or not, she knew that she could not give up the story. She didn't bother to deny, to herself at least, that there were a couple of personal aspects to the puzzle that she wasn't ready to step away from. Especially not now.

It had only taken her a couple of hours after she arrived at her desk to locate Wilford Mays. He was still living in the same house where he had been born. He was even listed in the local telephone directory. However reprehensible the rest of the world felt his actions to be, Mays had felt no need to hide from them.

She hadn't called to make an appointment. She had simply left a message for Lew and then driven out to the small rural community. It was only as she drove up the unpaved road the locals had told her led to Mays's house that she allowed herself to admit this might not be a good idea.

The sprawling farmhouse-style board-and-batten sat under the spread of an oak that was at least a couple of hundred years old. The house itself had probably been built in the early years of the century. There was a profusion of multi-colored impatiens and petunias trailing from baskets hanging between the square white columns of a porch that ran the length of the house.

As she walked up the liriope-bordered sidewalk, Kate could see that someone was sitting in the old-fashioned porch swing. The woman, whom Kate guessed to be Mays's wife, had stretched her small, rounded body to its full height in an attempt to identify the driver of the car that had pulled into her yard.

"Hello," Kate called, as she climbed the wooden steps. She knew that despite the xenophobia of city dwellers, she was not likely to be unwelcome here, even if she were uninvited. "Miz Mays?" she questioned, using, without any conscious decision, the old Southern form of address she had been taught as a child.

"I'm Velma Mays," the woman answered, stopping the gentle sway of the swing with one foot. Mrs. Mays stood up, holding the blue-and-white-speckled colander into which she'd been snapping beans. Her print dress had been carefully ironed, the starched cotton appearing as fresh as it must have when she'd put it on this morning. There wasn't a strand of iron-gray hair out of place, the curls so tightly permed that they didn't look capable of escaping from the style they'd been tortured into.

Her face was relatively unlined for her age, smoothly white.

Kate's grandmother had this nearly flawless complexion—fed by the constant humidity and vigilantly protected from the damaging rays of the sun. It was the mark of gentility in their generation, a Southern legacy of climate and convention.

"Ms. Mays, my name is Kathrine August," Kate said, smiling. She didn't offer her hand. It was perhaps acceptable in the city for women to shake hands, but it was not the custom in rural Georgia. "I'm a reporter for an Atlanta newspaper, and I'd like to talk to your husband, if he has time."

The curve of Velma Mays's mouth, a small Cupid's bow, widened. Her blue eyes sparkled behind the wire-frame bifocals. "Time?" she questioned, poking fun at Kate's politeness with her friendly smile. "Wilford Mays's got nothing *but* time, and that man surely likes talking, especially to somebody as pretty as you. Just as pretty as a picture. You from Atlanta originally?"

They were about to play an old Southern game called *Who Are You Kin To*. Kate was as familiar with its rules as her hostess. "Tupelo," she said readily.

"I don't believe I know any Augusts," Velma said, raising her chin to get a better view of Kate through the half-moons at the bottom of her glasses, as if trying to judge her genealogy by an examination of her features. "Who's your mother, dear?"

"She was a Montgomery. Her daddy was Boyd Montgomery, but he was raised on the coast. Near Savannah."

"Montgomery," Velma said, crinkling her forehead in an attempt to place the family. "There's a big family of Montgomerys lives near Dalton. Wilford had some business with a man there named Herbert. Any kin to your granddaddy?"

"I don't think so," Kate said truthfully. She knew it didn't really matter if they made a connection. It was the attempt that was important.

"Well, no matter. I'm sure your family's real proud of you. A reporter, you say. Why, when I was growing up, we'd never have thought about a woman being a reporter."

Kate smiled again, feeling no reply was necessary. Apparently none was expected because Velma continued.

"Why don't you sit down, Miss August, while I take these beans in and then find Wilford for you. He won't have gone far. There isn't far to go out here," she said with a laugh. "And I'll bring you some tea while you're waiting. This weather is just awful. I don't know how you people in the city stand all that concrete. It just seems to magnify the heat."

Kate sat down obediently in one of the white wicker rockers that flanked a matching table. All the furniture was lined up in a row, backs against the front of the house, facing outward for the best view of the passing traffic on the narrow road.

"I'll be right back," Velma promised. She bustled by to disappear through the screen door. Kate had caught the faintest whiff of rose water as she passed, pleasantly reminiscent.

Despite what Barrington had told her about Wilford Mays, despite the trepidation she'd felt in coming out here alone, the visit so far seemed as pleasant as an afternoon spent on her grandmother's wisteria-shaded veranda in Mississippi. After a few minutes, Velma Mays pushed open the screen with her elbow to carry out a glass of tea, the clinking movement of ice inviting. She put it down on the table by Kate and handed her the small paper napkin she carried.

"Now you just sit here and try to keep cool while I locate Wilford," she said. She walked to the side of the porch and, putting her hand on the column, she stepped down the three low steps, and then disappeared around the corner of the house.

Kate picked up the glass and sipped. The tea was sweetened of course, and flavored with something that she couldn't identify. The taste was tantalizingly familiar, but elusive. She took a larger swallow, rolling the coldness over her tongue.

"Grape juice," Wilford Mays said. He was standing on the bare patch that Velma's small feet had made through the years, trampling the grass as she had stepped off those low steps always in the same exact spot, the repetition demanded by the placement of her steadying hand on the porch column.

"Of course," Kate said. "I couldn't quite figure it out."

"Velma's mother always put grape juice in her ice tea."

"It's wonderful," Kate said, preparing to stand.

"Don't bother to get up. Velma said you wanted to talk to me. Something about a paper in Atlanta."

"I'm Kathrine August—" Kate began only to be interrupted.

"You're doing that series on the bomber," he said. "The one they're calling Jack the Tripper."

Kate felt a tug of unease that he had so readily recognized her name. He was watching her reaction, his eyes penetrating in a way his wife's had not been. He was as spare as Velma was rounded, dressed in overalls over a plaid shirt, both as meticulously starched and ironed as his wife's housedress.

"That's right," she said, offering the same smile that had created a matching friendliness in Mrs. Mays. His eyes remained cold, and the thin lips never moved. He ascended the steps and folded his length into the swing his wife had vacated.

"I don't have nothing to do with those," he said. There was no rancor in his denial. Only a statement of fact.

Kate was surprised. She had been prepared for coyness, a denial of his reputation even, but not this open disclaimer of responsibility for the current murders. She needed to be careful of what she said, she reminded herself. Mays was no fool. Barrington had characterized him as both shrewd and cunning.

"That *is* why you're here, ain't it?" he asked.

"Not really," Kate lied. "I wanted to talk to you about Judge Thornedyke Barrington."

"I read your piece. You seem to think mighty highly of that conniving bastard. Talked about him like he's some kind of hero. He's got you just as hoodwinked as the rest of 'em."

"Hoodwinked?" she repeated.

"All that mess you wrote about his fine record, his *integrity*." His inflection of the word was an insult. "That's all it is, Miss August. A bunch of mess. He railroaded me, and if he'd do it to me, then you can be sure he done it to a heap of others. I'm surprised somebody ain't tried to blow up that crooked son of a bitch before now."

"Why would Judge Barrington want to railroad you, Mr. Mays?"

"'Cause he was in cahoots with the cops. In their pockets.

They spit, and he had to jump. He needed to make a name for hisself. His daddy had a career in politics all laid out for his boy, and then ole Jack come along and ruined it.'' He laughed, the sound without humor, bitter and vindictive.

"And you've always blamed Judge Barrington for your conviction," she suggested.

"You trying to get me to say I got a motive for blowing the bastard sky-high? You got a microphone hid somewhere? That's been tried, only I wasn't born yesterday."

"I just thought, since you feel so strongly, that you might like to comment on Judge Barrington's character, to provide a different slant. Something I could include in the series as a contrast to the view of him we offered our readers before."

"You ain't interested in my views. You're just interested in making a case against me for being the one trying to blow him up. Only you ain't quite figured out why all them other people got blowed up, too. Why do you think I'd do those, Miss August? What's your explanation for all those other people dying?"

"All I know is, from what you've told me, that you aren't an admirer of Thorne Barrington."

"I ain't told you nothing," he said. There was no discernible change of expression and his voice had not changed, but suddenly malice toward her was in his eyes. "And I don't *intend* to tell you nothing. You or no other reporter."

"Did the authorities ever come out to talk to you about the bombings, Mr. Mays?"

His lips moved, deepening the creases age had carved into the lean cheeks, but his cold eyes didn't change. "Somebody come all right. Scared Velma to death. She thought they was fixing to put me away again on some other trumped-up charge, 'cause I keep fertilizer in the barn, maybe, and folks been known to make bombs out of that. Took me more'n a week to calm her down."

"And you still deny that you had any part in the school bombing?" she asked. That wasn't what he'd been charged with, but she wanted to see how he responded to the suggestion.

"Somebody told you I did that?" he said, a pretended disgust at the ridiculousness of that accusation in his tone. "Do I look like a man that would want to blow up a school or want to kill some poor little children? Do I strike you as that kind of man?"

His eyes were openly mocking now, the questions sarcastic, and Kate felt a shiver of apprehension. Barrington had been right. A venomous old snake. Still dangerous, still deadly.

"I'll let you in on a secret, Miss August. One you might do well to remember. A bomber's a special kind of man 'cause he ain't real particular about who gets blowed up by what he does. He can't afford to be particular. Anybody could have opened those packages. A secretary. Anybody. Or they could have gone off by accident 'fore they ever reached the person they was intended for. A man who sends bombs just don't care. You understand what I'm telling you? He don't *care* who gets blowed up in the process of getting what he wants. A bomber's got to have that kind of mind. You remember that. He purely don't care."

"Even if it's children who get blown up?" Kate asked, forcing her eyes to hold his.

"You ain't old enough to remember how it used to be down here, are you?"

"No," she agreed softly. There was some shadow of the irrational in his eyes and clearly now there was hatred, gray and cold as winter. "I don't remember. I'm just glad, despite the efforts of people like you, it's not *that* way any longer."

"You get off my property, girl," he said, his voice as low as hers had been. "Don't you ever come near us again. I don't like you, and I sure don't like that piece of trash paper you write for. Now you get out of here before I regret lettin' you."

She stood up, frightened, despite her determination not to be, by the bizarre transformation. Mays was openly menacing now, no longer bothering to hide his hostility.

"You ready for some more tea, dear?" Velma asked, coming out of the screen door with a cut-glass pitcher in her hand. "Oh, surely you're not thinking about leaving," she protested in dismay when she saw Kate was standing. "You just got here. And you haven't even touched your tea."

"Now, Mother," Wilford said, the polite veneer again in place before his wife. "Miss August has a long drive ahead of her, and she knows her business better than you. Besides, she don't *like* your tea." There was a deliberate cruelty about the comment, considering the effort Velma had made to be kind.

"Oh, I'm so sorry, dear. I should have asked. I can fix you another. Fix it any way you like."

"The tea's delicious, Ms. Mays, but your husband's right. I do have a long drive, and I better get started."

"I hope Wilford told you what you wanted to know. Since you came so far to talk," Velma said, smiling at her.

Kate stepped off the porch onto the front steps. She could still feel his eyes focused on her, cold as a snake, although she didn't look at him again. "Mr. Mays has been very helpful. Thank you, ma'am, for your hospitality."

"You come again, dear. We're always glad to have company."

IT WAS AFTER FOUR before she got back to the office. She had spent the drive into Atlanta thinking about what Mays had told her. Every time she remembered the madness in his eyes, she shivered, but she was really no closer to knowing whether or not he had had anything to do with the current bombings.

She still was left with the possibility of three different bombers, and no way to know if there was a connection between them. Obviously, she had been targeted because of the series—obvious unless she was willing to believe that Thorne Barrington had sent the confetti-filled package because she had entered his house uninvited. If he had, then he had also been the person who had broken into her apartment while she was out of town and put the matching confetti in her bed.

But if that were true, why would he agree to meet with her—despite his well-known hatred of the media? And what did Wilford Mays have to do with the Tripper bombings? There was no doubt he hated Barrington enough to do almost anything, but as he had reminded her, there would also have to be a link between him and the other victims. Logic told her there couldn't be three bombers, but she couldn't decide where the incidents overlapped.

She stopped by Lew's office on her way to the newsroom. He was working, on the phone, top shirt button undone and his tie loosened, but he motioned her in. She sat on the other side of the cluttered desk and listened to him handle whatever problem had arisen with his usual efficiency. He hung up, jotted a final note on his desk calendar and then looked up to smile at her.

"Change your mind?" he asked. In contrast to the gray hatred in Wilford Mays's, Lew's brown eyes were full of understanding. He thought she had come to beg off the series.

"No, but I probably should," she admitted. "I just spent the afternoon with Wilford Mays. Remember him?"

"Mays?" Lew repeated, questioning, but his memory was better than hers had been. "The school bomber?"

"*Alleged* bomber," she corrected, smiling.

"You think he has some connection to what's going on now?"

"Not if you consider only method, but the interesting thing is that Barrington was the judge who finally put him away. On some lesser charge, of course, but he burned him with as much time as he could. Barrington's convinced Mays did the school bombing. Mays, as you can imagine, hates Barrington's guts."

"So what does that mean as far as the Tripper bombings are concerned?" Lew asked carefully.

"Damned if I know," Kate said, shrugging, feeling the frustration of not knowing as strongly as she had on the way back into the city. "But it's *got* to mean something. Doesn't it?"

Lew said nothing for a moment, thinking about whether it did or not, she guessed, trying as she had been to fit the pieces of the triangular-shaped puzzle together. Only, Lew was probably not considering the confetti bomber as part of the equation.

"Even if that's a motive for sending a bomb to the judge, why would Mays hit the others?" he finally queried.

"He asked me that—why would he want to kill those other people. I didn't have an answer. I still don't. But that's a hell of a coincidence. Barrington and Mays."

"How many cases was Barrington involved in through the years, on and off the bench? Is it such a stretch to imagine that one of them might involve another bomber? Have you talked to Kahler about this?"

"He's the one who mentioned Mays. Barrington says he told the police about Mays from the first, but somehow the word never got back to Kahler. He just picked up the connection on his own, going back over the cases Barrington had handled one more time."

"But he thinks there's some connection?" Lew asked.

"Kahler's like the rest of us, grasping at any possibility."

"What did you think about Mays?"

"That he's one scary old man. You believe at first he's this harmless old coot, and then all of a sudden, you see something in his eyes. I think he's capable of almost anything. He certainly hates Barrington, but that doesn't mean he had a reason to kill the other people Jack targeted. To be fair, it's been a long time since Mays was even rumored to be involved in anything violent—thirty or thirty-five years."

"Any current association with the hate groups?" Lew asked. He had picked up the pen he'd been jotting notes with and doodled along the edge of his crowded appointment calendar.

"I don't know. You think I should try to find out?"

"Let me ask around, talk to Kahler about running the membership lists, and I'll let you know. Maybe we ought to do exactly what Kahler did."

"Which is?"

"Go back over everything we have one more time. Reread it all. Try to see if anything reaches out and grabs us."

"I don't have to reread it. I know it all by heart. I swear, Lew, there's nothing else there. And I'm still left with the confetti bomber. I don't even know if that's connected to the others."

"A one-time shot. Some kook thought it'd be cute to send the person writing about the bombings a fake bomb. It probably has *no* connection. Kahler said everything was different."

"There was confetti in my bed when I got back from Tucson."

It took a split second for the impact of that to be reflected in his eyes, and another few while he sorted through the implications. "In your *bed?*" he repeated. His voice was still calm and restrained, but his eyebrows had arched, his forehead wrinkling upward into the receding hairline.

"It was worse, somehow, than the other. I felt violated. Invaded. He was in my home."

"That's it, Kate. No more. This has gotten beyond crackpots sending letters. It's too damned dangerous."

"I had a new lock put in. Kahler says my lack of security was just an invitation to trouble."

"At least that should take Barrington out of the picture for you. There's no way he would have anything to do with that."

"Given the fact that he never leaves home," she agreed. "At least not in the daylight. Counts Dracula and Barrington."

Lew laughed. "Don't you think you're letting your imagination run away with you? Are you picturing Barrington as some kind of night crawler? A monster who only comes out after dark? Come on, Kate. Think about the reality of the man we're talking about. Even given your theory about head injury, you know that's a stretch."

"That reminds me. What have you found out about Barrington's injuries? You said you'd check around."

"Yeah, I know. I haven't found out much of anything yet, but I'll try again," he promised, making a note. "I want you to understand that I'm not doing this because I think the judge had anything to do with your harassment. That's way off base, Kate. Way out in left field."

She nodded, relieved that Lew was as adamant in his denial as he had been before. She didn't want to believe Barrington was capable of doing the things that had been done to terrorize

her. It didn't fit with any of her impressions of the judge, either
before or after she had met him. Unlike Wilford Mays, her
sense of Thorne Barrington was free of menace, and she acknowledged to herself that she really wanted it to stay that
way.

THE GATE WAS CLOSED, standing guardian again against the
invasion of the outside world. She turned off the engine and
sat in the darkness, looking at the wrought iron patterns and
thinking about what Mays had told her.

   Had Barrington allowed the state to frame the old man because he needed the goodwill of the political establishment?
A different picture from the one that had formed in her mind
and from the one Barrington had painted when they'd discussed the case. It was obvious that the old man believed he'd
been done wrong. The ring of that conviction had been in
every word. And insanity behind his cold eyes, she reminded
herself.

   Because she didn't want to go home, dreading again having
to walk into a place she knew had been touched by a different
kind of insanity, she opened the car door and then after a
moment stepped outside. The heat was less intense since the
sun had gone down, but the humidity was still as oppressive.
As she stepped up onto the sidewalk in front of the Barrington
house, she lifted her hair up off the back of her neck. She
should have put it up, she thought. Or maybe she should just
get it cut. She was getting too old to wear it this long. Everyone said—

   A hand touched her arm and she gasped, turning around
with both fists raised defensively. At some point before she
completed the blow her terrified brain had ordered, she recognized the man standing behind her. Her right hand almost
connected with the side of his jaw anyway, her flash of recognition not quick enough to override the motion she had begun. Thankfully his reflexes were faster than hers. Thorne Barrington caught her arm, holding it high between them, holding
tightly enough to prevent another blow.

   "God, I'm sorry," she whispered. "I thought—"

Her gaze had fallen to where his right hand was wrapped around her wrist. At least what was left of his hand, she realized. The thumb and the first two fingers seemed to be intact, heavily scarred as was the back of the hand, but at least they were still there—unlike the other two that should have been and were not. Her shocked eyes moved to his face to watch all the muscles tighten, his mouth firming to a slit and his eyes narrowing. His hand unclenched suddenly, freeing her wrist.

"Sorry," he said.

She knew what he was apologizing for. For touching her with that mutilated hand. He had told her he no longer shook hands and this was, of course, the reason. She could imagine the polite, veiled reactions that damage might provoke, especially if one was aware of the way in which he had been injured.

The dark eyes were still stubbornly holding hers, but there was something different in their midnight depths. Not a coldness like Mays's, but still, something.

"What are you doing out here?" he asked, without making any reference to his damaged hand. "Were you coming to see me?"

"I came..." she began and then wondered what in the world she could tell him. "Because I couldn't stand to go home," she finished, a truth she had certainly not intended to share.

"What's wrong?"

"The bastard put his damn confetti in my bed. It was there when I got home from Tucson. I just couldn't face walking in there again tonight. I know how stupid that is, but I couldn't make myself go home. I was just driving around, putting off the inevitable, and somehow...I ended up here."

He was still looking at her with that focused intensity. "You don't have to go home. Not until you're ready. Come inside," he said. "We can talk. Have you eaten? Elliot's probably got something stashed away."

It was an invitation she had no right to expect, and for some reason, her throat tightened with its unexpected kindness. *Come inside*, her subconscious echoed, recognizing how unusual this situation was. Thorne Barrington was standing beside her on the sidewalk outside his house.

"What are *you* doing out here?" she blurted out her unthinking question.

"Out with the *normal* people?" he mocked her surprise, the amusement she had heard before suddenly back in his voice.

"Considering the folks I've been around lately, I'm not so sure about the normal part," she said smiling. "You seem far more normal to me than the people I've been dealing with."

"At least I promise not to put confetti in your bed," Thorne said, and suddenly she remembered Kahler's comment about foreplay. She took a breath, fighting the images the word had produced in her head and knew that despite everything, her obsession with him was still there.

Her eyes fell, determined not to let him see the effect he had on her. When she raised them again, he was smiling at her. Just the smallest lift of that very sensuous mouth. She felt her own lips move, answering. "I'll count on that," she said.

He turned back to the darkness behind him and whistled, the sound low and pleasant. It was apparently as compelling to the dog that bounded out of the shadows along the fence he had been investigating. Kate bent to welcome the cold-nosed greeting, and then watched the retriever return to dance around his master as if they had been separated for days instead of the few minutes Barrington's attention had been directed to her.

"This is why I'm outside," Barrington explained, allowing the dog's unrestrained welcome without the least trace of annoyance. He caressed the silken ears with his damaged hand, and when Kate realized she was watching that movement, she deliberately pulled her eyes away. "Elliot's gone to visit his sister. She had a stroke a few days ago."

"So you had to walk the dog."

There was a small silence before he said, his hand still touching the puppy's head, "Despite the fact that you believe I'm in hiding."

"I had no right to say that to you, Judge Barrington. I wish—"

"Thorne," he corrected. "I thought we'd settled that."

She didn't repeat the name this time, still hesitant to believe that he wanted to be on a first-name basis with her.

"Why is that so difficult for you?" he asked.

"Since I started working on this story, in my head you've always been Judge Barrington. Someone who was not quite...real, I guess."

"Not real?" Again his tone was openly amused.

"Someone I had read about. I wanted to interview you before I did the profile, but you had an unlisted number, and you didn't answer my written request. You just seemed...unapproachable. Unknowable. Always at a distance."

"Do I still seem unapproachable?" he asked.

"No," she said.

"Would you *like* to come inside, Kate?" he asked again. Patiently. "At least it would offer a respite from having to face your apartment."

"I'd like that," she said, managing a smile, although incredibly her mouth had gone dry, her stomach nervously fluttering. She didn't know why he affected her this way. She could only hope her fascination wasn't obvious.

"So would I," he said. The line of his mouth was controlled, no answering smile, but again there was something in the dark eyes that she had not seen there before.

If this had been any man other than Thorne Barrington, she would have had no doubt about what was in his eyes, but he was so far removed from the world she inhabited that she wasn't quite ready to assign to him its normal masculine attributes.

He was being kind because she had told him she was afraid. That's all it was. She shouldn't imagine there was anything else involved in his invitation, she reminded herself. Despite that very sound advice, her heartbeat had accelerated slightly because what she thought she had seen in the depths of Barrington's eyes had been a very different invitation, one not motivated by kindness or decency. Very compelling to someone who had spent a major part of the last four months day-

dreaming about him, she admitted, and when he turned to un
lock the gate, like the puppy, she followed him inside withou
question.

Chapter Eight

"Would you like something to drink?" he asked. The retriever had bounded ahead, disappearing into the darkness behind the staircase, but they had stopped in the shadowed foyer.

"I thought you mentioned something about food," she reminded him, smiling.

"You haven't eaten?"

"That was something else I didn't want to do alone in my apartment. I thought about grabbing a bite somewhere, but…"

She paused, because she didn't really know how to explain why she hadn't. She had tried to phone Kahler at work, only to be told he was out. She hadn't left a message, because she didn't know where she was going to be. Not at her apartment. Maybe at some restaurant. Indecisive, she had simply told the policeman who had taken her call that she'd try again later.

She hesitated over confessing to Barrington that while she had daydreamed about him the last four months, Detective Kahler had been her only dinner partner. It sounded as if her relationship with Kahler was more personal than it really was.

"I know," Thorne said. "I always hated eating out alone." His left palm rested lightly against the small of her back, directing her toward the dark into which the dog had disappeared. "There's something about the way people look at you, as if they're wondering why you don't have a friend to join you."

"Or if you're a woman, they decide there's something wrong with you because you couldn't get a date."

She must have hesitated as the passage behind the stairs narrowed to a small hallway, so black she couldn't see three feet in front of her face. The pressure of the guiding hand increased minutely and then disappeared.

"Sorry," he said. "I forget how dark this must seem."

The explanation faded as Thorne stepped around her to lead the way. The white knit shirt he was wearing made following him easy, even through the shadowed hallway. The kitchen was better, illuminated by the filtered glow of the streetlights outside.

"I can make you a sandwich. And there's peach cobbler left from dinner."

"I'll settle for the cobbler. If it's not too much trouble," she added.

"You're sure?"

"Just the pie. I have a sweet tooth."

"Confessions of the damned. Me, too. That's why Elliot plans dessert before anything else."

As he talked, he opened the refrigerator and took out a casserole. Kate wondered why the action seemed vaguely wrong, and then she realized there had been no automatic flash of light when he opened the refrigerator. He closed the door and set the dish on the counter.

"You want it heated?" he asked.

"Not really. When I was a kid I used to eat the leftover cobbler cold. I'd stand in front of the refrigerator, grab a couple of spoonfuls straight out of the bowl, and gobble them down. My mother would have died if she'd caught me."

He laughed. Like Kahler's, his laugh was deep and pleasant, nice to listen to. She watched as he dipped two generous portions into bowls and then opened a drawer to supply them with spoons. The damage to his right hand didn't seem to have caused any loss of dexterity. He had learned to compensate for the missing fingers, and here in his familiar darkness, it seemed he had also forgotten to be self-conscious about them.

He carried the bowls to the small round table set in a windowed bay. He pulled one of the chairs out for her and then seated her. He sat down across from her, unconsciously licking the thick juices of the cobbler off his thumb. The dark eyes looked up to discover she was watching him.

He grinned. Not distant. Not unapproachable.

"My mother would have killed me, too," he said.

She laughed, and then embarrassed to have been caught staring at him, she concentrated on the cobbler and not on Thorne Barrington. The pie was cold and delicious, the peaches sweet and the thickened juices congealed under the sugar-glazed crust.

"This is wonderful," she said after a few mouthfuls. "My compliments to the chef."

"I'll tell Elliot you enjoyed it."

"You don't have a cook?"

"Elliot's the only staff I have. We have a cleaning service that comes in once a week, but Elliot cooks. He's wasted on just me, I'm afraid. His talents were appreciated in my mother's day when there was a lot of entertaining."

"Then he hasn't always been your butler?" she asked, taking another bite of Elliot's cobbler.

"He started in service here when my great-grandfather was alive and worked his way up. Or, as he explains it, he simply outlived everyone else. Becoming my butler was the only way he'd consider letting me pay him half of what he's worth to me. Elliot's standards of being in service are rigidly pre-war."

There was something archaic about his speech patterns, she thought. She had noticed it before. Maybe it was simply the rarefied social atmosphere he had grown up in. Maybe they all talked this way. It wasn't that she didn't like the way he talked. It was just a little more formal than she was used to, a little out of her league, as she and Kahler had decided. She hadn't even been sure which war Thorne meant. Someone accustomed to those who were "in service" would probably have known what the phrase implied, but her family had never had a butler or a cook, other of course, than her mother.

"The first time I saw Elliot," she said, "I thought he looked like something out of those thirties comedies, Carole Lombard's butler maybe."

There was a small silence, strained, and belatedly she re-

alized she had reminded him of the day she had met Elliot
The day she'd come to accuse Thorne Barrington of sending
her the confetti package. The day she'd decided to let a little
light into his darkness. "That day," she said, remembering
"Did throwing up the shades cause—"

She cut off the question. The migraines were something he
didn't talk about. He had never publicly discussed his injuries
He was a very private man, and just because he had relaxed
that vigilance with her tonight didn't give her the right to
probe.

Embarrassed, she looked down into the cobbler. She pushed
her spoon through a piece of the crust, breaking it into two
pieces, the thick, pink-tinged juice seeping up between them.

"Obviously..." he began, and she looked up when he hesitated. "Obviously, you now know some things about me that
you didn't know when you came here that day. I find myself
curious as to how you know them."

A good reporter protects her sources, she had told him before, but that excuse wouldn't suffice any longer. He had invited her into his home out of kindness, because she had admitted that going into her apartment gave her the willies. He
deserved an explanation rather than a brush-off.

"Detective Kahler told me some of them," she said.

"Kahler?" He sounded surprised by the revelation, and
given the detective's normal reticence, she understood why.

"And my editor knows some people who...know you."
That certainly was vague enough.

"Lew Garrison?" he questioned.

She nodded, pushing her spoon into the cobbler again.

"I see," he said.

When she glanced up, his face had tightened, the line of his
mouth again straight and uncompromising. Probably the way
he'd looked at the about-to-be-condemned standing before his
bench.

"It's not really the way it sounds," she offered. "I just
thought I needed to understand what had happened to you."

"I'm always surprised when people I know are willing to

talk about me. It's disappointing that friends would share that kind of personal information."

"At first, I believed you'd sent me the package, and I thought that…it was weird that you live the way you do. Lew and Kahler both defended you, gave me some background, some reasons for…"

"The fact that I *hide* in the darkness," he finished for her. His eyes were steady on her face.

"Yes," she said. It was only what she had already said to him. Why bother to deny it? There was another silence. She realized that he had stopped eating a long time ago, his cobbler almost untouched.

"As a matter of fact, a friend of mine called today," he said. "He wanted to warn me that someone had been asking questions about the bombing, specifically about my injuries. He seemed to think it involved an upcoming news story. He suggested I might want to take some kind of legal action to stop it. To stop the invasion of privacy. I'm not a public figure, Kate. I haven't surrendered my right to privacy."

That must have been Lew, she thought, following through on the request she'd made. An entirely personal request for information, now that she was sure Thorne Barrington hadn't been involved with the package she'd received.

"*That's* why you invited me to come in tonight," she said, realizing the truth. "To issue a warning. *Not* because I told you I was afraid to go home." She had wanted him to be some kind of knight in shining armor, so she had made him into one. She had made a fool of herself. Surely she was smarter than this, she thought in disgust.

"Did you have anything to do with that inquiry?" he asked.

She considered lying to him. Denying that she had been the one who had set it in motion. If she didn't deny it, she knew she'd never see him again. But, she reminded herself, what did it matter? Tonight hadn't been what she had thought. Just because she was obsessed with him didn't mean…

"Kate?" he said.

"Yes, I did."

He said nothing in response, although she met his eyes, had

made hers make contact until his fell. He was still holding the
spoon with his right hand. He put it back into the bowl and
pushed it away from him. She could see the depth of the breath
he took before he spoke.

"I see," he said. "I suppose I shouldn't be surprised. You
did try to warn me."

She shook her head, wondering what he meant. She couldn't
remembering trying to do anything of the kind.

"If you'll forgive me, Ms. August, I think that it might be
wise if we call it a night," he said. Despite what he believed,
he wouldn't be rude to her. It wasn't in his nature or in his
training.

"It's not what you think," she said and watched the subtle
realignment of his mouth. Cynicism this time and not humor.

"I believe that's what you told me the first time," he said.

She remembered then the conversation he was referring to.
The parking lot outside the police station. Her confession.

"I could have lied to you. Both times."

"Why didn't you?"

"Because you'd have found out sooner or later."

"And that mattered to you?"

"Yes."

"Because you thought I'd eventually give in and give you
a story? Something about my life after Jack? About the bombing itself? How I felt?"

Now she should lie, she thought, hide her real motivation
behind what he believed, the easy out his contempt of her
profession provided. "No," she said instead.

He didn't probe, but she knew he was still looking at her.
She could feel his gaze. She couldn't confess the real reason
she had always told him the truth, the real hope behind the
things she'd done. Not if he hadn't figured it out on his own,
if he didn't feel whatever this was between them.

Between them, hell, she ridiculed. What was between *them*
was all in her head. Since she'd collected his pictures. Since
she'd done the profile. It had all been just in her head.

She pushed her chair away from the table suddenly and
stood up. She had been guilty of doing all the things he hated.

She had pried into his private life, had even asked Lew to question his friends. It didn't make any difference that she was really trying to help Kahler catch a madman. If she couldn't convince herself that was the reason for her interest in Thorne Barrington, how could she think she might convince him?

"Thanks for the cobbler," she said. "And for the company," she added, almost bitter that this had all turned out to be something very different from what she had been imagining when he'd invited her in.

She crossed the room and entered the small, dark hallway. Barrington moved fast for a big man. And silently. He caught her before she had emerged into the part of the foyer under the grand staircase. This time he didn't release the grip he had taken on her arm, not even after he had pulled her around to face him and her eyes had fastened again on the damaged hand holding her wrist with such strength.

"Was that *all* it was?" he demanded. "Just for some damn story? Is that what all this is about?"

She struggled, but he refused to let her go.

"Answer me, damn it," he ordered. Although his features were hidden by the shadowed darkness, the black eyes glittered, hard and demanding.

"No," she whispered.

He was close enough that she could smell him. Closer than in the big car the first night. The scent of his body more intimate here in the shadows. Still pleasant. Warm. Male.

"Then what?" he said. "If not for a story, then why the hell do you keep coming here?"

"Please let me go," she said. "You're hurting my arm."

It was a lie, but the hot moisture had begun to burn behind her eyes. She didn't want him to see her cry, and she couldn't tell him the truth. *I'm here because I've fantasized about being with you like this, held close against your body in the darkness.* That was the truth, but not one she could confess. Too humiliating. Too bizarre.

He released her. She had known he would. He was too much a prisoner of his upbringing to do anything else. She didn't move, held motionless by her obsession as she had been from the first. She could see nothing of his expression. There was no clue in his darkness to tell her what she should do.

Leave, her brain ordered suddenly. *Get out.* The instinct to flee was primitive, but very strong.

Obeying it blindly, she began to turn. His left hand, the one that had survived the attempt on his life virtually unscathed, was suddenly pressed, palm flattened, against the wall beside her, his outstretched arm a barrier to prevent her escape.

She hesitated, unsure again. His hand left the wall and moved to the back of her neck, slipping under the fall of her hair. She didn't react, couldn't have moved away from him had her life depended on it. His fingers slowly threaded upward through the long strands and then spread out against her scalp, cupping the back of her head. The lobe of her ear rested in the V formed between the spreading fingers and the caress of his thumb, which had begun to move back and forth over her cheekbone.

Her eyes closed, her breath sighing out in a small unintended whisper of sound. At her response, his hand shifted, drifting forward so that his fingers trailed over her jawline and the sensitive skin beneath it. His thumb teased along her lips, which opened, without her volition, to allow her tongue to touch him. He used his thumb to force her mouth open more widely, pulling downward against her bottom lip, the moisture on his skin cool against her own as his thumb skimmed down her chin to lift her face for his kiss.

His mouth tasted of peaches. Sweet. So sweet. Just as she had imagined. Through the long months. Imagining this so long. His tongue found hers, demanding response. Touch and retreat. Savoring the warmth of his mouth, finally where it belonged. Over hers.

He was exactly the right height, tall enough that she found her body straining upward, made small and somehow more fragile, more feminine by his size. She liked how that made her feel, but she had always known it would feel this way. This rightness.

The kiss wasn't long. He broke the connection, leaning back slightly as if to read her expression, and she wondered suddenly if his vision were more acute than hers in the darkness. Because this was the way he lived. Surrounded by darkness.

"Not just for a story," he said softly. His voice was deep and intimate, not colored with amusement and not cynical. An acknowledgment of all that had been in her response.

"I told you the truth," she said. "It wasn't for the series. That wasn't why I was asking questions."

He stepped back, half a step farther away, but she felt exposed by the distance between them, by what she had confessed. There was always vulnerability in admitting how you felt. It was inherent in caring for someone and probably necessary, but so risky. The possibility always existed that the other person wasn't interested or wasn't affected in the same way.

"Now what?" she whispered. Get it over with. Find out if she had been as foolish as she felt right now.

The pause was too long. He didn't touch her, and he didn't answer her question. She felt the elation of the kiss begin to fade, and humiliation grow to replace it, rising hotly into her chest and then upward to fill her throat.

She had thrown herself at him. Her mother used to warn her about doing that when she was a teenager, madly in love with her latest crush. *Just don't throw yourself at him, honey.* The words taunted from her memory.

"I don't know," he said, but finally his left hand came up to find her upper arm, thumb smoothing over her bare skin, exposed by the sleeveless silk blouse she was wearing. "I don't know," he said again.

She thought she heard pain in the whisper. "Okay," she said. "It's okay. You don't have to know. As long as you understand that…it isn't the series. I'm not working on a story about you."

"It's been a long time," he said.

The silence that had preceded his comment was not as strained as before because he was still touching her, but then he didn't go on, didn't finish whatever thought he had had. *Since he'd kissed someone?* she wondered. *Felt this way? Made love?*

"Since?" she prodded softly.

He laughed, a breath of sound.

"Since I kissed a woman. Or wanted to."

"Then I guess I should be flattered."

"Probably not," he said. He had moved closer to her again. She could feel the breath of that comment against her forehead.

"Why not?"

His lips touched where his breath had, almost as lightly.

"This used to all come so easily," he said instead of answering.

"Gettin' women?" she teased, her own laughter soft, buried against the warmth of his throat.

"Knowing what to do. What to say."

"You don't know?"

"My life…" he began. When he stopped, she waited through the pause. "Everything's a lot more complicated than it used to be," he finished finally.

"It doesn't have to be. Complicated."

"Given my…situation, it probably does," he said.

"It wasn't tonight. We sat at the table together. We ate. We talked. It seemed pretty simple to me. Uncomplicated."

"Normal," he said, his tone mocking.

"You're not some kind of…" The phrases Lew had used were suddenly in her head. *Night crawler. Monster.* And then her own. *Vampire.*

"Recluse?" he offered, and her brain relaxed, relieved he hadn't known what she had been thinking. "Yes, I am, Kate. That's exactly what I am."

"By choice," she argued.

"Not really."

"It doesn't matter," she said.

For the first time she took the initiative, moving against him, putting her hands on the wide shoulders. Raising her face for his kiss. Inviting it now.

There was time to wonder what she would do if he didn't respond before his mouth closed over hers. Deeper now, more intense. They both knew now that this was what the other wanted, too, and there was freedom in knowing that. No one was going to have to pull away in embarrassment.

His arms closed around her, and he held her, pressing his body into hers. She realized, a little surprised by the discovery, that he was already strongly aroused. Her back was against the wall of the hallway, his hands possessive over her bottom, pulling her upward into the hard evidence of how much he desired her. It was all happening a little faster than she had expected. She had known how she felt, but he had given her no clue before tonight that he found her attractive. Obviously, he did. At least—sexually attractive.

For some reason she was disconcerted by that idea. Maybe it made no sense, but faced with the unexpected reality that this man was flesh and blood, and not the fantasy she had created, she was suddenly unsure. Her hands flattened against his chest, exerting their own pressure. He released her immediately, again stepping backward into the shadows.

"Maybe you better go," he suggested.

"While the going's good?" she asked, still breathless.

There was again the whisper of his laughter. "It might be easier."

"Easier?"

He took a deep breath, the broad shoulders in the white shirt lifting, visible in the darkness. "Cold showers. Think about something else. All that good advice."

"Do those work?"

"Not with you," he said softly, and her throat closed, hard and tight. "Sometimes I'll wake up in the middle of the night wanting you. Thinking about you being there with me. Where the darkness doesn't matter. Where it's an ally, a friend."

He had left her with nothing to say. She had thought she was the one taking the risk in confessing how she felt, but what she had done had been not nearly so brave as that.

"Thank you for telling me that," she said.

"I thought it was already rather obvious," he said, and again self-amusement underlay the words. "Pretty damn difficult to hide. Women have all the advantage when it comes to that."

"I guess we do," she agreed.

"When can I see you again?" he asked.

She almost said: Anytime. It was what she wanted to say, but somehow she was still a little guarded. His was a confession to be examined. When she was alone. Just to see if it was as promising as it had sounded when he'd made it.

"You could call me," she said instead.

"I will," he promised.

His left hand was touching her hair. She knew suddenly that if she didn't get out of here pretty soon, she was going to end up...just where he'd said he wanted her. In his bed.

"I really need to go," she said, forcing her voice to remain steady. His fingers were touching her earlobe now.

"I know," he said.

"Thank you for inviting me in."

He put his mouth over hers, enclosing the last word, caressing it with his tongue. More demanding this time. Wanting her. She knew now that he wanted her. She pushed away again, knowing how close she was to giving in to him, giving in to her own obsession. She walked toward the rise of the steps, black against the light filtering around them from the beveled glass door. When she opened it, the crystal tears moved, a small cascade of notes falling into the silence. Then she closed the door behind her, stepping out into the heat of the summer night.

HE STOOD in the shadowed darkness of the hallway, listening. There was no place in his life for the emotions that had flared between them tonight. He had told Kate August the truth—about that, at least. It had been a long time, and it all seemed too complicated now. Too hard to explain. Or too hard to justify.

He knew she was destroying the world he had created—the safe world into which he had retreated. She had accused him of hiding in the darkness and had forced him to contemplate exactly what he was hiding from.

He closed his eyes, but he could still smell her perfume, the scent caught in the shadows that surrounded him and had sur-

NO COST! NO OBLIGATION TO BUY! NO PURCHASE NECESSARY!

PLAY "LUCKY 7" AND GET FIVE FREE GIFTS

HOW TO PLAY:

1. With a coin, carefully scratch off the silver box at the right. Then check the claim chart to see what we have for you—FREE BOOKS and a gift—ALL YOURS! ALL FREE!

2. Send back this card and you'll receive brand-new Harlequin Intrigue® novels. These books have a cover price of $3.75 each, but they are yours to keep absolutely free.

3. There's no catch. You're under no obligation to buy anything. We charge nothing—ZERO—for your first shipment. And you don't have to make any minimum number of purchases—not even one!

4. The fact is thousands of readers enjoy receiving books by mail from the Harlequin Reader Service®. They like the convenience of home delivery...they like getting the best new novels BEFORE they're available in stores...and they love our discount prices!

5. We hope that after receiving your free books you'll want to remain a subscriber. But the choice is yours—to continue or cancel, anytime at all! So why not take us up on our invitation, with no risk of any kind. You'll be glad you did!

THIS SURPRISE MYSTERY GIFT CAN BE YOURS _FREE_ AS ADDED THANKS FOR GIVING OUR READER SERVICE A TRY!

PLAY "LUCKY 7"

**Just scratch off the silver box with a coin.
Then check below to see the gifts you get.**

YES! I have scratched off the silver box. Please send me all the gifts for which I qualify. I understand I am under no obligation to purchase any books, as explained on the back and on the opposite page.

181 CIH CCNM
(U-H-I-11/97)

NAME

ADDRESS   APT.

CITY   STATE   ZIP

 **WORTH FOUR FREE BOOKS AND A SURPRISE MYSTERY GIFT!**

 WORTH THREE FREE BOOKS

 WORTH TWO FREE BOOKS

 WORTH ONE FREE BOOK

Offer limited to one per household and not valid to current Harlequin Intrigue® subscribers. All orders subject to approval.

© 1990 HARLEQUIN ENTERPRISES LIMITED   **PRINTED IN U.S.A.**

DETACH AND MAIL CARD TODAY

THE HARLEQUIN READER SERVICE®: HERE'S HOW IT WORKS

Accepting free books places you under no obligation to buy anything. You may keep the books and gift and return the shipping statement marked "cancel". If you do not cancel, about a month later we'll send you 4 additional novels, and bill you just $3.12 each plus 25¢ delivery per book and applicable sales tax, if any.* That's the complete price–and compared to cover prices of $3.75 each–quite a bargain! You may cancel at any time, but if you choose to continue, every month we'll send you 4 more books, which you may either purchase at the discount price…or return to us and cancel your subscription.

*Terms and prices subject to change without notice. Sales tax applicable in N.Y.

rounded him so long. He was no longer sure which was more powerful—the darkness that protected him or what he felt for the woman who had touched him, who had wanted to touch him, despite what he was.

He put both hands flat on the wall before him. The left was as finely made, as strong and powerful as it had ever been. The other was as scarred and damaged as he knew himself to be. His lips twisted with the irony that he had believed—even briefly—that a woman like Kate August might really want to enter his darkness.

Vampire, he thought again, and the mutilated hand curled into a misshapen fist.

KATE DIDN'T go straight home. Not because she was afraid. She just wanted to savor what had happened, to think about what it might mean. Her professional concerns had taken a back seat to events that might have begun as a result of her work but were, as she had suggested to Kahler, very personal.

It was almost eleven when she pulled into the parking lot of her apartment house. Although it was well lighted, the lot was deserted at this hour on a weeknight. She sat in the car a moment, looking around the expanse of concrete and the low plantings around the building. For some reason she hesitated to get out of the car and walk the short distance to the entry door. This was a good neighborhood, which was why she had chosen it, but since the invasion of her home, nothing had felt the same.

Angry with herself for letting the confetti bastard make her lose her courage, she opened the door and stepped out, pressing the automatic lock. She started across the browning strip of heat-dried grass that separated the lot from the entryway.

With every step she took, the feeling she'd had in the car grew. The silence surrounding her felt wrong. Eerie. Like someone was watching her. Eyes following her passage. Only a few more feet. A few—

"Hey!"

Her blood froze. Congealed and stopped, clogging her veins

with ice. She whirled around and found Kahler walking toward her. Her relieved gasp was audible.

"What the *hell*, Kahler! You scared me to death. What the hell do you think you're doing?" She was overreacting, but given that he was very well aware of what had happened in her apartment two nights ago, it seemed that he'd have more sense than to sneak up behind her. At least he hadn't touched her. Not like Barrington had earlier. She *would* have had a heart attack.

"Waiting for you. I was worried that you hadn't come home," he said.

His eyes were studying her face. She knew she looked like hell. It had been a long day, and she'd had almost no sleep for the last two nights. "Well, thanks, I guess, but you just came closer to doing me in than anything else that's happened lately."

"Working late?" he asked.

She hesitated. She supposed she could classify the visit to Barrington as work. It wasn't, of course, but he was a legitimate part of the bombing story. "Yeah," she said. "And I'm really tired. Since the home visit of our prankster, I haven't been sleeping too well. I've just been putting off coming back. Dreading finding something worse in my bed."

"You got the lock," he reminded her.

"I know. Maybe he can pick locks. Who knows?"

"Want me to walk in with you? Check the place out?"

It was a nice offer. He was a nice man, and she truly appreciated his concern. Concerned enough to sit in a dark parking lot waiting to make sure she got home all right.

"How long have you been here?" she asked.

"Sergeant Arnold said you'd called. You didn't leave a message, so I thought maybe it was…personal." The hesitation had been revealing. Kahler had given her enough clues in the last couple of weeks to know that he wanted their relationship to be personal. Only, after what had happened tonight—

"Give me your key," he said, holding out his hand. "I'll

take a look around, and then you'll feel better. Sleep deprivation plays hell with your nerves."

"To say nothing of your looks," she suggested, smiling.

"There's nothing wrong with the way you look, August. Even sleep-deprived."

She wasn't sure how to respond to that. His eyes were still on her face. She put her key into the outstretched palm and said simply, "Thanks, Kahler. There's nothing wrong with the way you look, either." She wasn't sure if that was supposed to be comfort for the fact that she knew he felt differently about her than she did about him. It was a pretty lame remark even if concern had been her motivation.

He put his left arm around her and turned her in the direction she'd been headed when he had stopped her. His hand squeezed her shoulder slightly, and he said, "Come on. You'll feel better inside."

Probably not, she thought, remembering the last two nights, but she obeyed. She really didn't have a choice, unless she wanted to ask him if she could go home with him. Or unless she wanted to go back to Thorne Barrington's dark mansion, to curl up in his arms, safe and sound from night terrors, maybe, but very vulnerable to a lot of other kinds of danger.

KAHLER EXAMINED the apartment with a casual efficiency. She checked her answering machine while he walked back to the bedroom. There were two messages. She glanced toward the hall leading to the back and decided to play them while Kahler was doing his thing.

After the familiar machine noises came the recording of the slightly accented voice of the man in her bedroom. *"Kahler. They said you called. Give me a ring as soon as you get home."* Short and to the point, she thought, smiling.

The second message was from Lew. It was longer and far more intriguing. *"I did what we talked about, Kate. And I found something that might be... I don't know. Maybe important. Maybe nothing. Just call me. I'll be at the office for a while. I need to run this by you."*

The second call had come in at 7:40 p.m. Sometime while

she'd been driving through the twilight streets of a subdivision trying to decide whether to go home or to eat out alone. More than an hour before she had ended up at Barrington's mansion.

"That sounded important," Kahler said from the doorway.

She nodded. Lew rarely called her at home. It was part of his unspoken code of management. "I better call him."

"It's pretty late," he said.

"I'll call his office. If he's not there, I won't bother him at home. Whatever he wants can surely wait until morning."

She had already picked up the phone and begun punching in Lew's private number at the paper. She let it ring maybe fifteen times, but no one picked up. She put the phone back in its cradle and looked up to find Kahler watching her.

"He must have gone home," she offered.

"I guess I'll do the same," he said, moving toward the door.

"Thanks for coming in with me. And for waiting for me."

"You weren't at the paper?" he asked.

She had told him she was working late, but if she thought Lew had been at the office when he tried to get in touch with her, then it was obvious she hadn't been.

"I had an interview," she said.

"They must work the night shift," Kahler suggested. He had stopped at the door, hazel eyes assessing.

She shook her head, knowing he was too smart for her to lie to. Especially a lie as stupid as that one.

"Whoever you were interviewing," he explained, pretending to believe she was puzzled by the comment.

"I went to see Barrington," she said.

"Pretty late for a social call. Or maybe the…interview lasted a while."

"I drove out to see Mays today. I wanted to touch base with the judge about what he told me."

"What did Mays say?"

"Pretty much what you'd expect. That he has nothing to do with Jack. That the state and Barrington framed him on the firearms charge. That Barrington's an SOB who put him away in order to advance his political career."

"Sounds like he gave you an earful."

"Of hate. He's still spewing it out. Barrington's a favorite target."

"You think he's Jack?" Kahler asked.

"What does it matter what I think? Do *you* think he's Jack?"

"Give me a gut reaction," he suggested.

She took a breath, trying to decide what she thought, remembering the cold gray eyes. But it didn't feel right. Gut reaction. "No," she said. "I don't know why, but I don't."

Kahler nodded.

"Are you still going to talk to him?" she asked.

"Eventually. I *do* have a couple of other cases I'm working on. I haven't had time to get around to Mays yet, but I will. It's too big a coincidence to ignore."

"Is he right about Barrington? About going along with a frame? You read the transcript."

"I didn't have time. But what if Barrington *did* do what Mays said? What's so wrong about putting a killer away, however you can, for as long as you can?"

"The same thing that's wrong with cops planting evidence. With federal labs skewing test results to favor the prosecution. You know what's wrong with it."

"The idea of the judge screwing the old man—metaphorically, of course—" Kahler said, an edge of sarcasm in his voice, "doesn't sit too well, does it?"

"It just doesn't fit with what I believed about him."

"Maybe you better reexamine some of your beliefs," he suggested. "And in the meantime, come put the chain on the door. Things will look better in the morning. They always do."

He closed the door behind him. Kate waited a moment, listening to his footsteps fade. She crossed the small living room to slip the chain into place. When she turned around, the apartment looked cold and empty. It was home, but it sure didn't feel very welcoming.

She didn't want to go into the bedroom the prankster had invaded, but the idea of spending another night trying to sleep on her couch wasn't appealing. She hated it, but there wasn't any need to try to deny how she felt, at least not to herself.

Her eyes found the phone and her mind replayed the message Lew had left. She glanced again at her watch. Maybe she should try Lew at home. He'd certainly understand her need to know just what he thought he'd found out about the case that had baffled everybody for the last three years. Lew would certainly understand—even if she woke him up to ask.

She looked up Lew's home phone number in her address book and again listened to the phone, counting the rings before the answering machine picked up. She put the receiver back in its cradle without leaving a message. If Lew wasn't at home, that meant he must still be at the paper, maybe just not in his office. Looking at microfilm, maybe. Reading the articles the local papers had done on the Barrington bombing. Trying to decide if the "might be nothing" thing he'd discovered might be something instead. And if he were still at the paper…

Without giving herself time to decide it was a bad idea, Kate picked up her purse, scrambling through the junk to find the car keys she had dropped inside. It might be a wasted trip, but at least it would burn a few more minutes of the night— a few minutes' reprieve from trying to sleep in the contaminated apartment.

Chapter Nine

Lew wasn't at the paper. They told her that he'd left around eight, which didn't make a lot of sense, given the contents of the message on her machine. Lew had definitely indicated he would be working for a while, and then he'd left the office less than half an hour later.

She even went upstairs to see if he might have put a note on her desk to explain where he was going. He must have known that the enigmatic message on her machine would set her wondering. There was, however, nothing on the surface of her desk except the same mess that had been there when she'd left the office this afternoon. And the door to Lew's office was locked.

It took her about ten seconds after she got back into her car to make the choice between going back to her apartment or heading to Lew's house.

As she drove, she fought the useless speculations about what Lew might have discovered. She tried to remember his exact wording and wished she'd saved the message so that if this journey turned out to be a wild-goose chase, she could at least play back the tape when she got home. *I did what I promised… Or I did what we talked about…* She wasn't positive how Lew's opening sentence had been phrased.

But she did know that he had told her he'd check out Mays's possible association with any of the current hate groups and that he would contact people who knew Barrington and make some inquiries about his injuries. Based on what

Thorne had told her, she knew that Lew had done exactly what he'd promised as far as pursuing information about the judge's injuries was concerned, so if he'd found out something that might be important...

Her mind retreated from that conclusion. She didn't want to believe that Lew had learned anything that might have made him change his mind about Barrington's involvement in the confetti package or in invading her apartment to leave that distinctive message between the sheets of the bed she slept in every night.

Into her head drifted Thorne's confession. *Sometimes I'll wake up in the middle of the night wanting you. Thinking about you being there with me.* Was it possible that because he was sexually attracted to her he had...

Again, she forced the rejection of the thought that seemed disloyal, somehow, after what had happened between them tonight. *Between them,* she thought, remembering her earlier fears. Despite her worries over how whatever Lew wanted to tell her might reflect on the man she had admitted she was obsessed with, she liked the sound of that. The reality of it. *Between them.*

There were lights on inside Lew's house. He must have had some errands to run between leaving the paper and coming home. Maybe he had talked to someone else between the time he'd put the message on her machine and the time he'd left the office. That would help explain why he wasn't there when he'd clearly indicated he planned to be around a while.

She opened the car door and stepped out onto the brick driveway. She had been here before. Lew had hosted a few employee Christmas parties before his wife's death from ovarian cancer almost four years ago. To everyone's surprise, Lew had chosen to keep this house in the suburbs rather than moving into a town house or an apartment, smaller and more convenient for a man living alone. It must get lonely at times, she thought, rattling around in this big empty place alone. Lew didn't talk about his private life, and she didn't ask. She considered him a friend, but they didn't have that kind of relationship.

She rang the bell and heard the distant melodious chime. The street behind her was as quiet and peaceful as you'd expect from a neighborhood with houses in this price range. Very far removed from the crime and violence that plagued the hearts of major cities. Out here in this pricey neighborhood the inhabitants could imagine themselves safe from that particular taint of society's ills.

There was no response to the bell. She hesitated, wondering if she could be mistaken about the meaning of the lights. Maybe Lew simply left a few burning downstairs as a safety precaution. She was going to feel like an idiot if he showed up in his pajamas and robe, awakened by her repeated demands at his door. Even as the image formed, she pressed the ivory-colored button again and listened to the interior chime once more.

Her hand dropped to touch the elaborate brass handle of the door and without her conscious direction, her thumb pressed the release. The latch moved downward and the door opened. A sense of unease twisted in her stomach. Not the slight worry about embarrassing herself she had felt before, standing outside ringing her boss's doorbell at eleven-thirty on a weeknight. This was much stronger, much more compelling. Doors were supposed to be locked at night. That was the twentieth-century reality, even in the old, exclusive neighborhood where this house stood.

The foyer the opened door revealed was dark, but there was light filtering in from somewhere beyond the hall. The white-and-pink marble squares of the foyer floor reflected the shadowed illumination from the house's interior, softly gleaming in the dimness, inviting in their timeless beauty. She opened the door a little wider, leaning into the entrance hall without actually stepping inside.

"Lew," she called, pitching her voice into the waiting stillness. There was no answer, so she called again, more loudly this time, her voice echoing slightly, bouncing off the cold expanse of the marble. Unanswered. The feeling that something was wrong was growing, fear, as it had in the parking lot tonight, mushrooming with sick certainty inside her body.

What was she so afraid of? she wondered. Why the hell was she making such a big deal of this?

Because she was spooked, and she had been for a couple of days. Because of the confetti and maybe because she had talked to Mays today, had seen the cold hatred in his eyes. The craziness. All of this was crazy. She ought to get out of here. Lew would be at the office in the morning. She could talk to him then, and he'd never have to know she'd come to his house tonight. This was as stupid as walking into Barrington's mansion that night because the gate had been open. *I don't know why he didn't shoot you,* Kahler had said. That was the normal twentieth century response to someone entering your house at night. What she was doing was dangerous. Stupid and dangerous.

Except, her rational mind reminded, there *had* been something wrong at Barrington's. Her instincts then had been right on the money, and something wasn't right tonight. Despite the urge to cut and run, she knew that something was very wrong here.

Steeling herself, she stepped inside the foyer, but she left the door open behind her. She tried to remember the layout of the house from the parties she had attended here. That had been several years ago, and the house then had echoed with noise and color, filled with Christmas smells. Candles and holly and perfume. Spiced cider. While she stood uncertainly in the darkened foyer, the pleasant memories swirled inside her head.

"Lew?" she called again, questioning the silent darkness. There was still no answer, so she walked across the marble squares, her footsteps echoing as hollowly as her voice had. She remembered the layout as she walked, the pieces of memory floating into her head. Spacious living room to her right. Dark. The dining room where Lew's wife had arranged the buffets during those Christmas parties was on her left. She kept walking, past the stairs that rose beyond the double doorway to the living room. They were nothing like the curving staircase at Thorne's house. Only the darkness at the top was the same.

The room at the end of the entrance hall was lighter. The den or great room or whatever people were calling it now. But the light she had seen from the first was coming from the kitchen. She headed across the den to the left, remembering white, glass-fronted cabinets, and a lot of hanging brass. It had been a nice blend, new and old elements, clean and open.

It, too, was deserted, looking ordinary and functional in the cold fluorescent light of the above-the-sink fixture. Nothing scary here. The wide windows that surrounded the breakfast table were uncurtained to let in the morning sun. The neatly landscaped backyard and the subdued underwater lights of the pool they looked out on were beautiful in the moonlight.

She turned around, looking back across the kitchen, back the way she had come. Nothing was wrong, her brain reassured. *Gut reaction?* Kahler had asked. And her gut reaction right now was that something here was very definitely wrong.

Lew's office, she remembered. He had been very proud of his new computer system the night of the last party. A relatively recent convert to the wonders of technology, at least home technology, he had dragged anyone willing to be dragged back to the office to examine the equipment, delighted to show it off.

The study was on the other side of the den. She walked back to the doorway of the kitchen and looked across the shadowed den. The door to Lew's office, almost directly across from where she was standing, was closed. There was a thread of light under the bottom, just visible between the mahogany and the thick pale peach of the den carpet. As she started across the room, the phrase from childhood games of hide-and-seek intruded. Getting warmer. Much nearer to whatever was going on, she thought, when she was standing before the door. "Lew?" she called. There was no answer. She waited a moment before she repeated the word. She raised her hand and tapped against the solid wood as she spoke. "Lew?"

Then, as it had at the entry door, her hand made its own decision, reaching downward to touch the knob, which turned easily under her fingers. She pushed the door open, her eyes seeking the big antique desk that dominated the opposite end

of the room. The light she had seen under the door had come
from its green-shaded lamp.

The reason Lew hadn't responded to her repeated calls was
apparent. Behind the spread of equipment, she could make out
his body slumped forward, his head pillowed on his right arm
that was resting on the top of the computer system's printer.

Working too late, she thought, smiling in sudden compassion. And no one to miss him upstairs. She debated leaving
him, but given his cramped position among the electronic pe-
ripherals on the crowded surface of the desk, she knew he'd
pay the price tomorrow. A sore neck. A short temper. Some
price.

"Lew," she said again, relief making her voice stronger.
She took a farther step into the room and then stopped. All
the images from the devastation in Austin burst into her head.
This was a different devastation, but even in the play of light
and shadow, there was no doubt, now that she was this close.
Lew Garrison wasn't asleep. There could be no doubt about
that either, given the fact that the back of his head...

Retching, she turned away, stumbled across the small office
and out into the den. She had enough presence of mind to
realize she had to get out of the study. Not just because of the
horror it contained, the splatter of blood on the wall behind
the desk, the smell hot and strong and distinctive as no other
smell, but because whatever she touched would be contaminated.

Crime scene. The familiar words were in her head, their
importance fighting her natural inclinations to go to Lew, to
make sure of what she already knew. And fighting also that
other inclination. The one that screamed at her to run, as far
and as fast as she could manage. To get the hell out of this
house.

She stopped in the middle of the expanse of expensive
peach carpeting and made herself take a couple of calming
breaths. Her head swam sickeningly when she closed her eyes,
so she opened them and held them open by sheer will to look
for a phone.

She knew she couldn't go back into Lew's office, even if

that was the most likely place to find a telephone. She couldn't go upstairs, into the unknown darkness where, perhaps, whoever had killed Lew was hiding. How could she be sure the killer had left? she thought, the panic building again.

She fought it down, knowing that what she *had* to do was call the cops. No one had known she was coming here. It had been impulse. Lew's murderer wasn't waiting for her. He was long gone. Her rational mind knew that. She was reacting like a child and not like an adult. Not thinking, just feeling. But when she began to move again, it was toward the light, toward the pleasant openness of the white kitchen.

Thank God there was a phone on the wall. She dialed 911, trying to remember Lew's exact street address before the operator picked up. She had looked it up in her address book before she'd gotten on the interstate, so the numbers were still in her head, despite the fact that she'd left her purse in the car.

She had to repeat her story a couple of times, and then she did exactly what she had been told to do. Despite all her instincts screaming at her to get out of the house, she stood in the kitchen, waiting for the patrol car they had promised was on the way. But she never took her eyes off the doorway.

IT WAS PROBABLY half an hour after the first police car had arrived that Kahler got there. She had told the cops she believed Lew's death had something to do with Jack and had urged them to call Detective Kahler. The men she had talked to were so calm, accustomed to dealing with violence and its aftermath. Once she would have claimed that after her years on the paper, she was pretty acclimated to man's inhumanity to man, but Austin had taught her better. And tonight.

They had sent her out onto the patio that surrounded the pool. One of the cops had stayed with her, taking notes on what she told him and then probably staying just to keep her company. Eventually, with her repeated assertions that she was fine—just as false as those she'd made the day in the office when the fake bomb had gone off in her lap—he'd gone back inside.

Through the glass of the patio doors, she had watched Kahler arrive and disappear with the forensics people into the study. She was still watching when he came out and posed his questions to the cop who'd taken her story. The cop pointed to the backyard, and Kahler looked up, his eyes meeting hers through the glass.

She watched him cross the den and open the patio door beside the fireplace and walk over to stand in front of her. He didn't say anything for a moment, and then, as she had once before, she moved into his arms, which opened automatically to enclose her.

Kahler held her tight, safe and protected. "What the hell made you decide to come over here tonight, August?" he asked.

She could feel the words rumble through his chest, his breath stirring against her hair. She knew she should step away, formulate some kind of answer, quit hiding, but it was physically impossible to move. All her reserves of strength had been sapped by the realization that Lew was dead, so she answered with her cheek still resting against the starched blue oxford cloth that covered Kahler's shoulder.

"The message he left on my machine. I couldn't get it out of my head—the thought that finally Lew might have found something. I knew I wasn't going to be able to sleep, so I went back to the paper. Lew had left about eight, but that didn't make any sense to me. So, I decided to come over here on the chance he might still be awake." She shivered, remembering her initial reaction to the body.

"Why did you come in?" Kahler asked, his lips against her hair. His hand was making comforting circles over the tightness in her shoulders. Relaxing a little of the tension and the fear.

"There was a light. I thought..." she paused, trying to re-create exactly what she had thought. "I rang the bell and no one answered, and then I opened the door. It wasn't locked, Kahler, and I knew it should have been. I looked around, and when I remembered Lew's study, I went back there."

"It's all right," he said, apparently feeling the shuddering force of the breath she took. "Everything's okay. I'm here. Nothing's going to happen to you, Kate. I won't let anything happen to you."

An official promise maybe, but his tone had not been very official, she thought. Definitely not. She was infinitely grateful for his personal attention, grateful for his kindness, and especially grateful for that assurance.

"Did you touch anything?" he asked.

"The phone in the kitchen. The front door. The door to the study. I can't remember touching anything else."

"Good girl," he said, his voice warm, complimenting.

"I went about halfway into the study. I thought he was just asleep. Then I went in far enough to see..."

"It's all right," Kahler said again. His voice was still calm, soothing her obvious distress.

"Whatever he found out," she said, leaning back from his embrace far enough to see his face, "it was enough to get him killed, Kahler. Something pretty damned important."

He nodded, agreeing with her, still comforting.

"Was there anything on the desk that would give you a clue to whatever...?" she began and saw the quick, denying movement of his head.

"We don't know yet. We have to wait for the lab boys to finish, let the coroner remove the body, before we can look for anything like that."

"Oh, dear God," she said softly, finally feeling the tears begin to slip out past her control. She raised her head, looking upward into the night sky, biting her lips to keep from letting it all pour out. *The body.* Maybe to Kahler, long inured to this, Lew was just "the body," but to her he had been a friend. Someone who had died perhaps because he had asked the questions she had wanted him to ask. *Her* questions had gotten him killed.

Kahler pulled her against him, his hand on the back of her head, pushing her face into his shoulder. He was only a little taller than she, and she buried her head and let the tears come. The words he whispered while she cried weren't official either, but right now she needed what he was giving her, needed to feel the strength of his arms holding her. Very human comfort.

Eventually she cried it all out, her mind drained by the shock of what had happened. The ugly sobs lessened, and she had presence of mind enough to think what a female thing crying like this had been. Someone who broke down into hysterical tears wasn't exactly the image she had always had of herself, certainly not the one she wanted to portray to the world. She pushed away from him to wipe her nose, and then using the back on her hand, she tried to rub away the evidence of her tears.

Kahler pulled out a handkerchief and began to clean the mascara off her cheeks. He worked gently, with steady concentration, and she found herself really looking at his face for the first time. Thinking about him as a man, and not a cop.

Not the flashy good looks Thorne Barrington had, maybe, but a nice face. Strong. She especially liked the lines around his eyes. He looked up from the mess she'd made of her makeup to find her eyes on him, and he smiled at her.

"Thanks," she said, embarrassed to have cried and to have been caught studying his face, maybe her own revealing what she'd been thinking.

"My pleasure," he said, and the corners of his mouth lifted again, the small creases around his eyes moving. "Let's get out of here," he suggested.

She was a little surprised that he wanted to leave, would be willing to walk away from the scene. Somehow she had thought Kahler was as obsessed with this case as she. "Now?" she asked.

"I need to get you home," he said.

The small sound of protest she made in response to that idea was automatic. Her apartment was the last place she wanted to be. Trying to deal with Lew's death, with her guilt over her role in it, and remembering that damn confetti in her bed. She knew that she'd be wondering all night how it all was related.

"My place?" Kahler suggested.

Ordinarily, she'd never have agreed. It was a bad idea, considering what she believed about Kahler's feelings, but right now it felt like an answer to prayer, so she nodded.

"Please," she said.

"Let me tell them inside. I'll be right back. We won't go through the house. I'll take you around. Wait right here."

She was more than willing to follow his instructions. More than willing to let Kahler make the decisions. More than willing to let him take care of her. And she realized that it felt pretty good to *have* someone take care of her for a change.

KAHLER FIXED HER the bourbon and Coke she had asked for, a taste left over from college, and seated her on his oversized sofa while he disappeared into the back of the apartment to make a couple of phone calls. She imagined they were related to Lew's death and that he knew she didn't need to hear them right now.

She sat on the couch, shoes off, feet up, sipping the sweet, smoky darkness of his good bourbon, and let her eyes wander around the room. It was masculine, dark colors, massive, comfortable furniture. There were some nice prints on the walls, well-framed and well-placed, and a lot of books. There was only one photograph, a small, maybe five-by-seven-inch print in a wooden frame. Because she was curious, she got up to look at it, fighting the lethargy of the bourbon and the emotional trauma.

It was a photograph of a pre-adolescent Kahler, the strong features distinctive, even given the difference of more than a couple of decades, and a pretty little girl, maybe three years old. She had the same hair as Kahler. Same shape eyes, but darker than his, more chocolate than hazel. He had told her he grew up with his mother and sister. Obviously, this was the sister. She hadn't realized the difference in their ages. She was still holding the framed photograph in her hand when Kahler came back into the room. She turned to smile at him, and his eyes flicked to the picture she held and then back to hers.

"Is this your sister?" she asked.

He nodded.

"I didn't realize there was so much difference in your ages."

"Nine years," he said. He walked to the counter where the bottle of bourbon stood and poured two fingers into the bottom of a kitchen glass. He leaned against the counter, watching her as she set the photograph back in the spot it had occupied on the small desk. He was rolling the bourbon around on his tongue, obviously more a connoisseur of good whiskey than she. He had probably thought the concoction she was drinking a sacrilege.

She went back to the couch and put her feet back up. *Making myself right at home,* she thought, taking a sip of her drink.

"You want to talk about this or wait a while?" Kahler asked.

"About Lew?"

"You can come down to the office if you'd rather. I just thought it might be easier for you if…"

"If I just told you."

"Whatever you want to do, Kate. There's no hurry. You can just sit here and get soused, if you feel like it."

"That won't make it go away."

"You're right about that," he acknowledged.

He took the last of his bourbon into his mouth and set his glass down on the counter. He walked across to take the chair opposite the couch she'd adopted. Despite their closeness earlier tonight, she appreciated the distance. Appreciated his recognition that this wasn't the time or the place for moving in on her. She didn't need that kind of pressure right now.

"Let's get it over with," she said finally. "I'd rather talk to you than someone else."

"Then start with the message on the machine. Garrison said, 'I did what we talked about.' What did he mean?"

"I couldn't even remember what he'd said. I tried to think, but I couldn't remember, and I'd already erased the message."

"What had you talked about?"

About Thorne Barrington, she thought. *About Lew asking questions about his injuries, talking to his friends.* That was something she knew Lew had done, but telling Kahler that was going to be hard. It made it sound as if Thorne must be involved in Lew's death, and she didn't believe that. Besides, Barrington hadn't been the only thing they'd discussed.

"I'd just gotten back from Mays's house. I went to tell Lew where I'd been because he'd been out of the office when I left. I wanted to run what Mays had said by him, to get his reaction."

She hesitated, trying to remember exactly what had been said. It was the kind of conversation she and Lew had had a hundred times. She couldn't have known, of course, how important what had been said might prove to be. Or that it would be the last conversation she'd ever have with him. She cleared that thought from her mind and concentrated on remembering.

"We talked about Mays. I told him what Mays thought of Barrington."

"Did you tell him you didn't feel Mays was Jack?"

She shook her head. She hadn't made that decision until Kahler's question had forced her to, after she'd talked to Lew.

"He asked me if Mays had any association with any of the hate groups," she said, remembering. "I didn't know, so Lew said he'd ask around, talk to you about that. Did he call you?"

Kahler shook his head.

"He probably didn't have time to get around to it," she suggested. She racked her brain trying to think what else had been said. Now was the time to tell Kahler that Lew *had* had time to do the other thing she knew they'd talked about. He *had* made inquiries about Barrington's injuries. It felt so wrong to tell the police that, but just because she knew Thorne had nothing to do with Lew's death didn't mean she could withhold evidence.

"Lew told me he'd check on the possibility…" she paused, realizing how awful her idea would sound in this context. It hadn't sounded so brutal when she'd believed Thorne might have had something to do with the confetti bomb, but now, with Lew's murder, it sounded…incriminating. "About the possibility that Barrington had some brain damage. From the bomb. If it could make him do things that were…out of character."

"Brain damage?" Kahler repeated, his tone disbelieving.

"Sometimes after a head injury, people do things they would normally never think about doing," she argued. It sounded a lot dumber now than it had the first time she'd proposed it.

"Like blowing people up?" Kahler asked sarcastically.

"No, of course not. I didn't think even then that Barrington was blowing people up. I *never* thought Barrington was Jack, Kahler, but I *did* think for a while he'd sent me the confetti. You knew that. It was just weird enough..." Again she paused, feeling disloyal.

"What did Garrison think about your idea?"

"That it was way off base. Like you, he never thought Barrington was involved with any of this. Other than being the first victim. We talked about that, too. Maybe not the last time I talked to Lew, but sometime. That Barrington was one name we knew was still on Jack's list."

"You think he's going to try for Barrington again?"

"Before he's through," she said, nodding. "We just don't have any idea when that will be."

Kahler didn't comment. There was really nothing to say, but she suddenly realized the possibility Jack wasn't through was a lot scarier than it had been when she and Lew had talked about it. Before she had gotten to know Thorne. Before they had...

She turned her thoughts away from the shadowed hallway in Barrington's mansion. What had occurred there seemed to have taken place a long time ago instead of only a few hours. Too much had happened in between. With Lew's death, the reality of Thorne Barrington's danger had been graphically reinforced.

"Who was Lew supposed to ask about the injury?" Kahler interrupted that sudden realization.

She looked up, wondering how long she'd been thinking about Barrington instead of what she was supposed to be doing. "I don't know. He just said they had some mutual acquaintances. He didn't mention names."

"So we'll probably never know if he got around to asking."

Now, her brain ordered. *Tell him now.*

"He asked *somebody,*" she said, feeling sick.

"How do you know?"

"Judge Barrington told me. At his house tonight."

"How could he know?"

"The friend called him. Told him someone was asking questions for a news story. He thought Barrington might want to fight the invasion of privacy with some sort of legal action."

"And Barrington was willing to talk to you after that?"

Kahler had been the one who had told her how much the judge hated the press. No wonder he was skeptical.

"I think he wanted to pick my brain. Maybe warn me to back off any story about him."

"He thought you were the one making inquiries?"

"I think he knew it was Lew, but he also knew this had always been my story. That whatever Lew was asking was for me."

"Was he angry?"

Before or after he kissed me? Before he confessed that he wanted me in his bed? Or maybe, she thought, maybe he had been just setting her up—a willing and ready source of information. Maybe he believed that coming on to her was the way to get her to drop the story. Suddenly, nothing that had happened tonight seemed to mean what she had thought it meant.

"Kate?" Kahler prodded.

"About like you'd expect. He doesn't like publicity."

She looked down at the drink she still held. The ice had melted. She took a sip, trying to banish the doubts from her mind. *Not what she had thought it was* wouldn't leave her head, circling along with all the other memories of this night.

"Did Barrington kick you out?" Kahler asked.

"No," she denied. *He kissed me. He told me he wanted me in his bed, had thought about having me there. About making love to me.* "No, nothing like that," she said aloud.

"What time did you talk to him?"

"I got there...maybe 8:45. Maybe closer to nine. I don't know exactly."

"Barrington was home when you arrived?"

"Yes," she agreed, and then she realized why he'd asked, the significance of that question. "You don't think—" she began and hesitated while she thought about what that meant. "Kahler, you can't believe Barrington had anything to do with Lew? Because of what *I* said?"

"This is my job, August. Asking questions. It's your job to answer them. Your duty as a good citizen." There was an edge of cynicism in his voice that hadn't been there before.

"What time did Lew die?" she asked.

"We won't know until we get the coroner's report."

"When will that be?"

"A few days."

"Barrington had nothing to do with this," she said, trying to let him hear her certainty.

"Given the fact that he never leaves the house, that should be easy enough to prove," Kahler agreed.

But he had, Kate realized. He had been outside the house when she arrived tonight. Because Elliot had been away. Thorne's explanation had been logical, of course, but—

"Is Barrington a suspect?" she asked.

He didn't answer her immediately, but it didn't matter because she already knew.

"Because of what I told you," she said, despairing. "God, you're so wrong. Don't make a fool of yourself, Kahler. Because you're wrong, and as you reminded me, Barrington's got all the marbles, all the high-powered attorneys."

His eyes studied her face for a moment.

"Just like he always has," Kahler said simply.

Chapter Ten

She spent the night on Kahler's big couch. She even managed to sleep a few hours. After bringing sheets and a light blanket and showing her the bathroom, Kahler had disappeared into his bedroom, and he hadn't come out again. Kate appreciated the privacy as much as she did the comfort of knowing he was there, that she wasn't alone.

When dawn arrived, throwing its weak light into the room, she was ready, welcoming permission not to have to lie there any longer, letting the events of the previous night tumble through her head. She walked barefoot across the beige carpet to push the linen-weave draperies back from the center of the window.

She looked down again at the photograph of Kahler and his sister. She wondered what kind of brother he'd been. Protective, maybe. He had treated her that way last night, like a brother. There had been no embarrassment and no discomfort about spending the night here. Just a safe place to stay.

She picked up the picture, turning it into the fragile morning light, examining both subjects. Kahler, before the reality of what he did for a living made all those intriguing lines she'd noticed last night. Young. Innocent. Like the little girl with her dark, trusting eyes. She had probably worshipped the boy he had been, looking up to him from the far distance of nine years.

Kate smiled, carrying the frame back to the coffee table and again taking her place on the big couch. She pulled the blanket up over her feet and legs, the air-conditioning a little too efficient, especially this time of day.

"Good morning," Kahler said from the doorway that led to the hall. He was already dressed for work, another starched blue oxford cloth shirt, gun and shoulder holster in place. He walked into the kitchen to begin making coffee. "You get any sleep?"

"More than I expected," Kate said. "Thanks for letting me stay. I really don't think I could have gone home last night."

"That couch is available anytime. Just say the word."

"Don't offer unless you mean it. After all that's happened, I might take you up on it too often."

"I don't think you're in any danger, Kate. If I did—"

"How can you say that?" she interrupted. "Lew's dead because of something he found out about Jack. And everyone knows this is my story. What makes you think whoever killed Lew won't think I also know whatever he had found?"

"Because no one was watching your apartment last night. No one was following you. It was Garrison the killer was interested in, because he let the wrong person know that he'd discovered something dangerous."

"I'm the one who went to see Mays."

"I don't think Mays has anything to do with it."

"He's crazy, Kahler. Crazy enough to do anything. You didn't see his eyes."

"If Mays was going to take out after someone, who would it be? Think, Kate. Who does Mays blame for his troubles?"

"Barrington. The authorities."

"*Not* Lew Garrison."

"Maybe Lew found out that Mays *is* involved in one of the hate groups. Maybe he asked that question to someone besides you, asked the wrong person, just like you said. Lew had sources all over this city. This is his city, and after all these years, he knows the people who know where all the bodies are buried."

"I'll check it out," Kahler said, but there was no conviction in the promise, obviously made only to pacify her.

"You think it was some *other* question he asked that precipitated what happened to him last night.'' She knew what he thought. He had already made that clear.

"I'll check that out, too."

"You're the one who told me what an upstanding citizen Barrington was. You and Lew. Why are you now—"

"Because Lew's dead. Apparently he wasn't as good a judge of character as he thought. He confided in somebody or tried to investigate something he should have left to the police. Playing cop will get you in trouble every time. That's something you better remember, August. You let me ask the hard questions."

She nodded. There wasn't much else to say. Something Lew had said or done had gotten him killed, and she didn't want to be next. Kahler was only trying to protect her. Her eyes moved back to the little girl in the photograph. Big brother.

"Did she ever get mad at you for trying to boss her around?'' she asked, indicating with her hand the picture she'd moved.

"Probably,'' he said, hazel eyes studying the photograph as if he hadn't looked at it in a long time.

"Your folks still alive, Kahler?"

He shook his head. "Yours?"

"Yeah, both of them. Same little town. Nothing ever changes with them. And I hope it won't,'' she added.

"Then you're lucky."

"I know. So what was growing up like for the two of you?"

"Ordinary. Small town."

"Me, too."

"I don't remember my father. He wasn't around long enough to make an impression. My stepfather just disappeared one day. Mom kept telling us he was coming home soon. Jenny may have believed her, but I knew better. It was no great loss. He hadn't been much while he was around."

Kahler was leaning against the bar as he had last night, sipping orange juice this time. Relaxed. Discussing what was just another part of the reality of his life, something he had apparently accepted a long time ago.

"Your mom raised you alone, you and your sister?"

"With the help of a succession of...boyfriends." There was an underlying harshness in his pronunciation of the word. It would have been hard for an adolescent boy to accept another man in his mother's life, no matter what the circumstances were. "We were always pretty much on our own. I guess my mother did the best she could, given...the circumstances."

His voice faded, and she watched him lift the glass to swallow the remainder of the liquid it held.

"What does your sister do? She's not a cop?"

"No, not a cop," he said. Kate waited through the pause. His eyes, almost as dark now as the little girl's, were again on the photograph. "Jenny died. Almost eight years ago."

"God, Kahler, I'm sorry. I never dreamed... She must have been very young."

There was no response.

"What happened?" she asked softly.

He glanced up, not at her, but at the light coming from the opening she'd created when she'd pushed the curtain aside.

"An accident. A drunk driver," he said dispassionately, but the emotion was there. Hidden, as always, with Kahler.

"I'm sorry. That must have been really rough."

"It happened a long time ago. You learn to deal."

She nodded.

"You want to take me to work, or you want me to call somebody?" he asked, the memories deliberately cleared from his voice. He had driven her car last night, allowing her time to sit in the darkness and deal with what had happened at Lew's. *You learn to deal*, Kahler had said. And she would.

"No, I'll drive you. I need to get back to my place and change clothes."

"You going in to the paper?"

"Yeah," she said, and she was surprised by how reluctant she was to do that. "It's what they pay me this enormous salary to do. I want to look around in Lew's office. It was locked last night. I thought he might have left whatever he was working on in there. There could be something that might give me a clue as to what direction he was pursuing."

"I'm not sure that's a good idea," Kahler said. "Why don't

you let someone from the department take a look? The less involved you are with whatever Lew Garrison found the better.''

"How can the police know what was new, what Lew discovered only yesterday? I know everything that's in those files, Kahler. If Lew jotted down notes or made a stray comment in the margin, it might tell me what he was thinking. No one else knows what was already there. No one else can recognize what's been added.''

"Given the time frame, Garrison probably didn't have time to make notes. I wouldn't get my hopes up. I've got a feeling he found what he found and then, probably without thinking too much about what he was doing, he mentioned it to the wrong person. Maybe he was trying to feel them out and it backfired.''

"Lew wasn't stupid.''

"I don't mean to suggest that. But he's dead, and my guess is that whatever he was talking about on your answering machine is the cause.''

She nodded again. It was the obvious conclusion.

"If you find something in the files, Kate, don't act on it. That's not your job. Come to me. I'll pursue whatever it is, and unlike Garrison, I'll bring along some backup. I don't want you ending up like your boss.''

"Okay, big brother,'' she agreed, smiling at him. "I can assure you I don't want to end up...'' She paused, the image of the room last night suddenly too vivid in her memory. "I promise, Kahler, not to make a move without you.''

SHE HAD DROPPED Kahler off and driven home in the early-morning traffic, changing lanes and making her exit automatically, her mind still involved with everything that had happened in the last twenty-four hours. It was almost too much to assimilate. Her brain worried at each separate event like a terrier working over a well-chewed slipper, trying to fit them together until, at the end of each train of thought, logic asserted itself to reiterate that they didn't fit. Nothing tied together. At least, not in any way she wanted it to.

Her apartment looked ordinary in the light of day. She wondered why it didn't look this way—safe and nonthreaten-
ing—when darkness fell. She threw her suit coat over the back
of the sofa and began unbuttoning the silk blouse.

She wanted to get out of her clothes, send them out to the
cleaners as soon as possible. She wanted to take a hot shower
and wash her hair. As if by doing those things she could
cleanse the horror of what she had found at Lew's house from
her mind.

She punched the play button on the answering machine by
habit, not even looking at the display. She knew that she'd
almost certainly erased both Kahler's and Lew's messages,
automatically destroyed them, since there had been no phone
numbers left with either. That was the usual deciding factor.

She was right. The voice that filled the room was not the
accented one of the man whose couch she'd slept on last night.
Its timbre was as deep, but it was homegrown, the cadence so
familiar it didn't even qualify in her mind as having an accent.

"I just wanted to say good-night," the recording of Thorne
Barrington's voice said. "Call me when you get in." And then
he gave his number, which she knew was unlisted.

Her hand hesitated over the erase button, and instead, she
hit rewind and listened again. The same tone as in the darkened hallway. Soft and intimate. Deliberately, this time she
punched the erase button and listened to the machine destroy
the message.

SHE WAS MORE than an hour late. It didn't matter, of course,
because when she got to the paper the police were already at
work. Clusters of people stood around in stricken silence. Obviously news of Lew's death had filtered out.

She put her purse down on her desk and stood a moment
watching the shapes move behind the frosted glass walls of
Lew's office. Through the opened door, she caught glimpses
of Kahler's familiar figure, muscularly compact back and
shoulders filling the starched blue shirt or his dark head bent
over Lew's desk. She even overheard the occasional comment,
his voice directing the operation with unthinking authority.

She wasn't surprised that Kahler had come to oversee this search himself. He believed that whatever Lew had found had gotten him killed. As Kate did. She only had to be patient and eventually Kahler would tell her if he discovered anything.

"You okay?" one of the feature editors asked. She was standing almost at Kate's elbow, her eyes filled with concern.

Kate hadn't even been aware when the woman had approached her desk. "I guess," she said, questioning in her own mind if she'd ever be okay again.

"Someone said that...you found him."

Kate nodded. The tightness was back in her throat, and she began to wonder if coming in today had been a good idea. Being here. Exposed. Surrounded by the curious, their eyes all searching for some response, some reaction, a display of emotion.

Why don't you tell our viewers, Ms. August, how it felt to find your editor with the back of his head blown away, his brains splattered against the wall behind him?

"Excuse me," Kate said, managing what was almost a smile. She moved past the sympathetic face of her co-worker to stand outside the opened door of Lew's office. She found that she had put her hands again on their opposite shoulders, smoothing her clammy palms down the short, silk-knit sleeves of the summer sweater set she'd pulled blindly from her closet this morning.

Maybe if she appeared to be watching the police do their job, no one would ask questions or demand that she recount what had happened last night. *The public's right to know,* she thought bitterly. Only not now. Not yet. Please, just not today.

"Did you find anything?" she asked when Kahler came out, pitching her voice low enough that the onlookers couldn't overhear. The hazel eyes assessed her face, so she smiled at him. He shook his head, a single tight movement and then he moved past her, carrying the trailing team of men with him.

The contents of the familiar office were clearly visible from where she stood, the papers on Lew's desk straight and more orderly than she'd ever seen them—Kahler's imposed order, not Lew's comforting disorder.

She wondered again who Lew had talked to yesterday. A friend of Barrington's—that was all she knew for certain. Suddenly the remembrance of Lew jotting something on his desk calendar as they talked was in her head. The image of his pen moving quickly across the already crowded whiteness. She hadn't told Kahler that. Maybe…

She glanced toward the newsroom doorway, but there was no sign of the cops. With their departure, most of the staff had made some pretense of getting back to business as usual. Someone would step in to organize, to direct the operation of the paper as Lew had for so many years. Maybe soon. They might even take over the office, clear out Lew's things. There would be no reason not to. The police were apparently through here.

She stepped inside Lew's office and pulled the door closed behind her. She waited a moment, feeling guilty, expecting to be challenged. She had no right to be here. Except this had always been her story, and Lew Garrison had been her friend.

When nothing happened, no protest concerning the invasion, she walked across the room to Lew's desk. There were too many memories here, and she felt her eyes burn, suddenly and unexpectedly. She fought the emotion by pushing Kahler's neatly stacked pile of documents off the calendar desk pad. She ran her finger down the right-hand side of the page, the place where Lew had been jotting notes as they'd talked. There were names and numbers written there, appointments, reminders as innocuous as "laundry 2:00." Nothing about Barrington. Nothing that seemed to relate to their conversation yesterday.

"Damn," she said under her breath. Just to be sure, she ran her finger across this week's block of days. Maybe Lew had written whatever he'd written on the appropriate day. Yesterday had been Wednesday the tenth. Only it wasn't. It was the thirteenth. Wednesday, the thirteenth. It took a moment for the significance to hit her. She looked up and found that the calendar page she was examining so closely wasn't for July, but for March. Last March. Which meant someone had removed—she stopped and counted backward—four months' worth of pages. She took all the pages out of the pad and rifled quickly through them, just to make sure that the missing months hadn't been shifted to the back during the police search. They weren't there.

Kahler must have taken them. But he'd said they'd found nothing, so why take the calendar pages. Unless it hadn't been Kahler. Unless someone else had taken them. Someone who had reason to fear whatever Lew had jotted on their margins. She took a deep breath, trying to think. Either Kahler had lied to her, or he hadn't noticed the pages were missing.

Kahler would have noticed, she thought. He was bright and he was thorough, which meant he'd taken them. There had to be a reason for that. Something he didn't want her to see because he was afraid if she did, she'd pursue it, despite his warning.

Because it related to Barrington? Because she'd all but admitted to him how she felt about the judge, not exactly unbiased? *Call me,* Thorne had said on the tape. And before that, *When can I see you again?*

To find out what she knew? To find out if Lew had told her whatever had gotten him killed? Kahler said no one had been waiting for her at her apartment last night and no one had followed her. Was it possible that the person involved hadn't had to follow her because...because she had already gone to his house? Because he already knew that she wasn't aware of whatever Lew Garrison had discovered?

But Thorne hadn't even asked her any questions. They hadn't talked about anything dealing with the case—other than Lew's phone call. Was Barrington astute enough to know from the little she'd said that she hadn't been aware that Lew had made that call? That she certainly didn't know to whom it had been made?

She tried to reconstruct their conversation, the exact words, but it was no use. The words she remembered, the phrases that echoed in her head, burned into her memory, all concerned something else. Something very different.

Sometimes I'll wake up in the middle of the night wanting you. Thinking about you being there with me.

She had done her duty. She had told Kahler about Lew's phone call to Barrington's friend. That didn't mean she had to believe Barrington had something to do with Lew's death. The man who had held her, who had kissed her last night, who had confessed how he felt, had *not* just returned from killing Lew Garrison. She had always trusted her instincts, and there had been nothing there last night except what he had openly confessed to—incredibly, the same obsession she'd felt for weeks.

Someone tapped on the frosted glass upper half of the door, and Kate watched it swing open before she could formulate a reply. The editor who had spoken to her before stuck her head into the opening.

"Kate?" she said. "I thought you must be in here. I looked everywhere else."

"What is it?" Kate asked.

"Judge Barrington's on the phone. Line one. I thought you'd want to take it. Since it's Barrington," she added.

"Thanks," Kate said. She had felt a brief flutter of unease at the comment, and then she realized all the woman could know about Barrington was that he'd been Jack's first victim. She would assume the call had something to do with the story. No one could suspect that her connection to him was far more personal. She waited until the editor closed the door behind her, and then she took a deep breath, and she picked up the phone.

"Kate August," she said.

"Kate?"

With the sound of her name, all the doubts she had had about Thorne Barrington's possible involvement in what had happened to Lew last night—doubts she hadn't even acknowledged—seemed to slip out of her head.

"Are you all right?" he asked.

"You've heard?"

"On the news. They said you found the body. Are you okay?"

For some reason his concern caused the moisture to sting behind her lids again, but she fought it.

"Not really. It was... To be honest, it was just as awful as Austin." She realized that he might not know what she meant, so she added, explaining to a man who certainly needed no explanation of the horror Jack wrought, "I went to Austin. I thought I wanted to see... I had thought, if I was going to be working on the story, I needed to understand—"

He interrupted. "Kate," he said softly. Only her name, his voice, again rich with concern, caressing her agitation. And then, "Don't. Don't think about it."

She took another breath, trying to obey. She knew that wasn't what she needed to talk to him about. Not today, anyway. Maybe sometime they might talk about that, but today...

"I told Kahler about Lew's call," she said.

There was a small silence. Maybe he was trying to put that together with what she had said before, but he was as smart as she had always been told he was.

"His call to my friend?"

"Lew left a message on my machine last night. Something about doing what we'd talked about. Asking around about you was one of the things we'd discussed. Kahler heard the message. Lew's call to your friend must have been one of the last things he did." An explanation for why she'd told Kahler.

"Of course," he said simply.

"The police will probably want to talk to you, Thorne. I'm sorry, but I didn't know how to—"

"There's nothing to apologize for. A man's dead. As far as the police are concerned anything he did might be important." There was a silence, and then he added what she hadn't asked for. "His name is Greg Sandifer. We've been friends since elementary school. He's a doctor. Not mine, but...the fact that he is a doctor is probably one of the reasons Garrison called him."

She didn't say anything. She knew why he was telling her this. Not to pass on to Kahler, but for her own information. To satisfy her own need to know what his friend had told Lew. To put to rest the doubts that he must have realized had crept, certainly unwanted, into her head since she'd found Lew's body. For her information—personal and not professional.

"You didn't have to tell me that," she said.

"Call him," he said. "Tell him I said to talk to you. Ask him anything you want about his conversation with Garrison." He began to reel off a number, and her hand automatically found a pen, adding the seven digits to the crowded calendar page on Lew's desk. "That's his private number. The fact that you have that number should be introduction enough."

"I don't—" she began, not really certain what she needed to tell him.

"Call him," he ordered, interrupting, and then the connection was broken.

She stood a moment with the phone in her hand, the dial tone annoying. Finally she put the receiver back on the cradle and looked down on the number Barrington had given her. He was right. She did need to know exactly what had been said to Lew Garrison. She needed to know for her own information. *Personal.*

DESPITE THE FACT that Thorne had given her Dr. Sandifer's private number, she still had some problems getting through. He refused to speak to her at first. She had thought it only fair to give her name and the paper's name, and he had refused to take the call. She had then used Barrington's name and the reminder that she had been given Sandifer's private number. The masculine voice that finally replaced the smooth politeness of his secretary's was brusque.

"I told Lew Garrison everything I have to say to you people. If Thorne *did* give you this number—"

"Lew's dead," Kate said, breaking into his indignation.

"Dead?" Sandifer repeated, as if it were a word he'd never heard before.

"He was murdered last night. Apparently your conversation was one of the last he had. The police will almost certainly want to talk to you to confirm exactly what was said. Because Lew was working on my story, asking questions I'd suggested, I'd like to know what you told him. Judge Barrington gave me your name and number and said to tell you to talk to me."

"Why? Why would Thorne want me to talk to you?" he

asked. The voice that had been full of anger and then shock was ripe now with suspicion. It was certainly a legitimate question. Kate wasn't sure she had a legitimate answer.

"For personal reasons," she admitted finally.

Sandifer said nothing for a moment. He was so quiet she could hear background noises from his end of the line, voices, faint and indistinct.

"Are you trying to tell me..." he began, and then he stopped. Apparently the thought of Thorne Barrington being involved with a reporter was simply beyond his comprehension. "You and Thorne are..." Again, he paused, and despite the situation, at the obvious disbelief in his tone Kate's mouth moved, almost a smile.

"Involved," she affirmed. The word had been in her mind and it had simply come out. Why not? It was true, given last night.

"Peg said you're a reporter."

"That's right," Kate said.

"Look, in spite of what you claim, I can't tell you anything about Thorne. I don't talk to the press about my friends."

"You talked to Lew," she reminded him.

"That's exactly what I told Garrison."

"That you wouldn't talk about Barrington?"

"That's right."

"Nothing else?"

Sandifer didn't say anything for a moment, and then he sighed, deeply enough to be audible.

"He came up with some crap about Thorne's migraines being emotional."

"Psychogenic," she said.

"As a matter of fact, that's the exact word he used."

"We had a mutual source," Kate acknowledged.

"But the way Lew said it, he made it sound as if it equated with crazy. That's not what the term means, Ms. August."

"Are they?" she asked.

"I wasn't Thorne's doctor."

"But?" Kate asked softly, because the qualifier had been in his tone.

"In my opinion, they're not."

"In your opinion? Or based on something you know? Something you've heard."

Again there was silence. "I don't discuss my friends with reporters," he said finally.

"But that *is* what you told Lew yesterday. Nothing else?"

"Our conversation was very brief. I was ticked off that Lew would even ask, that he thought I'd supply any information about a friend's medical condition. Even if I *had* any information. I've known Lew a long time, and frankly I was surprised he'd call me and ask that. I thought it was out of character. I remember telling him to leave Barrington alone. I called him a couple of less than complimentary epithets, and I hung up. Then I called Thorne and told him what had happened. I was angry at Lew, but I didn't kill him if that's what y'all are thinking. If you and the cops are trying to make some kind of case out of me calling Lew a couple of names—"

"No one thinks anything like that," she reassured him, smiling slightly. "You're not under suspicion, Dr. Sandifer. That's not why I'm calling you. It's not why the police will call. They'll just want to know if you told Lew anything..." She hesitated, searching for the right word. "Incriminating."

"Incriminating? About me?"

"No," Kate said.

"About Thorne?"

"Yes."

"They think *Thorne* had something to do with Garrison's death?" The question was derisive. Apparently, Greg Sandifer was just what he'd claimed to be, a friend of Barrington's.

"I think it's more a matter of checking out all the possibilities. They know Garrison called you concerning Judge Barrington's injuries, and they know someone killed him shortly after your conversation. They'll just be trying to determine if the two are in any way related."

"I can tell you that they're not. Not in *any* way," Dr. Sandifer said. "If that's all, Ms. August?"

"You can call Judge Barrington. He really did give me your number."

"You can be assured that I will," he said succinctly, and then the connection was broken.

Kate put Lew's phone back in the cradle and stood a moment looking down at it. She hadn't handled that conversation very professionally, but at least she knew that the friend of Barrington's Lew had called hadn't told him anything that might have gotten him killed. Apparently Dr. Sandifer had given her editor no real information at all about Barrington's injuries. She took a deep breath and realized only then how tense she had been. Now she could relax, knowing that the doubts that had begun to circle in her head like vultures were groundless.

She would have to call Kahler and give him Dr. Sandifer's name. Barrington would, of course, but she needed to confess to the detective that she had made her own call. Kahler would probably chew her out, but the relief she felt as a result of Sandifer's comments would make his lecture a lot more bearable.

She took another careful survey of the materials on Lew's desk, but Kahler had apparently told the truth about that. With the exception of the missing pages from the calendar, nothing else here seemed to relate to Jack. The material she had collected through the months she'd been involved in the story was in the file drawer of her desk—with the exception of the pictures of Barrington that had been taken from her apartment. That was something else she needed to confess to Kahler. Since he now knew something of what she felt about Thorne, that confession would finally be possible. She could pretend that she had just discovered the photographs were missing.

She walked out of Lew's office and closed the door behind her. She was a little surprised that Kahler hadn't ordered the office locked, but maybe their search had been thorough enough that he was convinced there was nothing else to be learned from Lew's papers. Or maybe Kahler, bless his heart, had left it open so that she would have the opportunity to do exactly what she had just done—to take her own look around.

She sat down in her chair and opened the bottom left-hand drawer of her desk. It was immediately apparent that something was wrong. Half the file folders were lying face down in the front of the drawer, the rest propped drunkenly against them.

She hesitated a moment, trying to decide what was going on. Finally, she picked up the fallen folders and pushed them to the back of the drawer, all upright again. She began to thumb through the tabs on top, but she knew what was missing. The thick collection of her materials relating to the Tripper bombings was gone, just like the newspaper pictures she'd taken home. She wouldn't be able to do what she'd told Kahler she'd do, read through all the material to see if there was anything—

Suddenly she remembered. That was the other thing she and Lew had talked about. She had told Lew that Kahler had found the Mays connection by reading back through the dockets of Barrington's cases, and then Lew had said something about maybe that's what they ought to do. *Read back through everything to see if there was anything they'd overlooked.*

She had been so smug that day, bragging about knowing every detail included in the material. But maybe she'd been wrong. Maybe Lew had done exactly what he'd suggested they should do—read back through all the files. Maybe he'd taken them into his office, sat down at his desk, the material she'd collected spread out before him, and gone over it all with a fine-toothed comb.

She pushed her chair back and walked to Lew's office. Instead of putting the files back in her drawer where he'd gotten them, maybe he'd simply stuck them in his own file cabinet, in a hurry because he'd found whatever he'd found. But first, she prayed, he'd marked whatever it was, underlined it, made a notation. *Something* that would let her follow the path—

She stopped, suddenly remembering where that path had led, the darkened study in the silent house, Lew's lifeless body slumped over his desk and behind him— She jerked her mind away from the image, and she knew she had to remember what Kahler had told her. *Don't play cop.*

She moved to the tall, five-drawer cabinet and pulled out the first drawer. She had no idea about Lew's filing system and the drawers were unlabeled, so she began to methodically go through the folders. Lew's careful lettering on the tabs, the printing small and very precise, was so familiar that she had to blink to clear her vision.

She worked her way through the files, even the two drawers that held material clearly not related to any ongoing stories. Her folders on the bombings were not here. And, she had realized sometime during her search, neither was the material the stringers were sending in from the cities where the murders had taken place. Lew had been collecting those for her for the segment dealing with the official hunt for the bomber. Everything they had collected about Jack had disappeared.

She closed the bottom drawer and stood up, aware of how long she'd been searching by the cramping ache in her legs. Either Lew had taken everything with him when he'd left the office last night or someone else had at some point cleaned out the files. If Lew had taken the material, it was probably at his home. Maybe lying on that blood-soaked desk. But of course, whoever had killed Lew would not have left those folders there if he had been aware of them, and he must have been if they had indeed contained whatever information Lew had indicated he'd discovered.

She knew that she couldn't put off calling Kahler much longer. There were too many things she needed to tell him, things that might help him find Lew's killer. Or help him find Jack. One and the same? That seemed obvious unless you considered the roles of the confetti prankster and Mays. None of them fitted together, but that wasn't, thank goodness, her job. She was going to take Kahler's advice very seriously. She didn't intend to play cop. She didn't intend to end up—

She forced her mind away again from what had happened to Lew and left his office, pulling the door closed behind her.

Chapter Eleven

It was after lunch before Kahler returned her call. She had spent the morning rereading the articles she had done on the bombings. Those were, of course, still available. It was all the material that had provided the sources for these very condensed versions that was missing.

"August? I had a message to call you," Kahler said when she picked up the phone. "Something wrong?"

"I'm just the bearer of bad news now?" she asked, smiling at the concern in his voice.

"I didn't mean that. I know how hard last night was. Finding Garrison. I was worried about you."

"I know," she said. She did know how he felt about her. He hadn't made much of a secret of his feelings lately, and she appreciated his automatic concern. "I'm grateful, but I didn't call just to listen to your voice, Kahler, as pleasant as it is."

Somehow that came out wrong. Personal. She didn't know why it was so hard to find the bantering tone their conversations had always had. Maybe because too much had happened, because the violence they were dealing with was now very up close and personal. No longer murder at long distance.

"You found something," Kahler said. His voice was controlled, the tone tight and almost flat.

She hated to have to disappoint him, so she gave him the little bit of information she did have. "The friend of Barrington's was Dr. Greg Sandifer. He didn't tell Lew anything, refused even to talk about the judge's injuries. He called Lew a couple of names and hung up. Then he called to warn Barrington that the paper was asking questions.'' There was a small silence, and Kate pictured Kahler jotting down the information. ''I have his private number if you want it,'' she added.

''You called him,'' Kahler said. It was not a question.

''Barrington told me to.''

Silence again, and then he asked, ''What did you tell Barrington, Kate?''

''Tell him?'' she asked, puzzled by his tone. ''*He* called me. He'd heard about Lew. When I mentioned that I'd told you about Lew's call to his friend, he gave me Sandifer's number. I didn't 'tell' him anything, Kahler. What's that supposed to mean?''

''He asked you to pass Sandifer's number on to the police?''

There was an edge to the question. Sarcasm? Anger? She wasn't sure what she was hearing, but it was clear Kahler didn't like the idea that she'd talked to Sandifer. Or maybe...the idea that she had talked to Barrington? Personal? she wondered. If so, maybe it was time that she made it clear exactly how personal her relationship with Thorne Barrington had become.

''I don't think that's why he gave me the number,'' she said. ''I think he knew that...I had some questions of my own about what Sandifer had told Lew. Some personal questions that I needed to have answered. I'm just passing on the information to you because I thought you'd want to talk to Sandifer yourself. In your case, talk to him professionally, of course.''

None of that had come out as she'd intended. It had sounded abrupt, as if she thought it was none of Kahler's business why Barrington had given her the number. That hadn't been what she'd intended to convey, but she could tell by the coldness in the detective's tone that that was indeed how she had come across.

''Then thank you for the information. Anything else?''

''Don't,'' she protested softly.

He made no response for a long heartbeat, but he didn't pretend not to understand. "How did you expect me to react?" he asked. The coldness was gone, but his voice was not the same, not what it had always been before.

"I don't know," she said. "I don't know what to say, Kahler. I'm sorry," she added.

"Yeah," he responded. Flat, dispassionate. "Me, too."

"I can't help what I feel. You should understand that," she added, and then knew that was the wrong thing to say. She wasn't sure there *was* a right thing in this situation.

"Would it make any difference if I told you that I don't think being involved with Barrington is a good idea?" he asked.

"I don't think it would. Not now."

"For professional reasons, Kate. Not personal."

"Because?" she asked.

"Gut reaction," he said.

"That's not an explanation."

"It's all I've got."

"Well, thanks for the advice, but I don't think that's enough. Not anymore."

"You sleeping with him?" The tone of his question was bitter, and given what she knew about his feelings, she supposed it should not have been unexpected, but it was. Totally out of character. Totally hurtful.

"What the hell, Kahler? What gives you the right—"

"Eight people are dead. Is that enough *right?*"

It stopped her outrage as he had certainly known it would.

"What's that supposed to mean? That Barrington's involved in those deaths? Is that what you're trying to suggest?"

"I'm trying to remind you that eight people are already dead. I don't want you to be another victim."

"Of *Barrington?*" she mocked, angry now. No matter how he felt, it didn't give him the right to make unfounded accusations. "You might want to remember that Judge Barrington was one of Jack's victims. Or are you suggesting that he sent *himself* a bomb? Tried to blow himself up? Is that your proessional opinion, Detective Kahler? Because if so, I have to tell you—''

"Maybe he had an accident. Did you ever think about that?''

"Never once," she said in disbelief. "But then I'm not blind with jealousy. You have some proof that's what happened? Because if not, I'd like to remind you of *who* you're accusing. Now, if you have some legitimate reason for telling me not to see Thorne Barrington, then spit it out. Otherwise I just might think your motives in issuing that warning are not as pure as you'd like me to believe.''

"You think whatever the hell you want to, August. I'm just offering advice. Stay away from Barrington. You don't know what you're dealing with.''

"But as always, I'm sure you're dying to tell me.''

"My best advice," he repeated and hung up.

Kate sat stunned for a moment, still holding the phone, angry enough to slam it down, but since Kahler had beat her to the punch, she resisted the urge.

She hadn't told Kahler about the missing files or about the calendar pages, she realized suddenly. That had really been the reason she'd called, and instead she'd been given a lecture—not exactly the one she'd anticipated. *Stay away from Barrington,* he'd said, but he hadn't be able to come up with any reasons. Personal. Almost certainly personal.

She lowered her head, resting her forehead against her joined fingers, elbows propped tiredly on her desk. Now there was no one to talk to. Not Lew. And not Kahler. No one to offer comfort and support. Except…there was, of course.

Sometimes I'll wake up in the middle of the night wanting you. Thinking about you being there with me. Where the darkness doesn't matter. Without giving herself time to decide it might be a bad idea, she picked up her purse. Suddenly she knew exactly where she wanted to be.

WHEN ELLIOT CAME to the gate, he didn't wait for her to ask to see the judge. He unfastened the inside lock and pulled the heavy wrought iron inward. "Miss August," he said politely. "Is Mr. Thorne expecting you?"

"He should be," she said, smiling at the old man.

"If you'll come this way. You don't have to be frightened," he added, and Kate spent a second attempting to figure that out.

"Frightened?" she asked.

"Of the dog," he explained. "I always fasten him upstairs when I hear the bell."

"Thank you, Elliot, but I'm not afraid of the dog. What's his name, by the way?"

They were almost to the front steps, Kate again matching her longer stride to the slow one of the old man.

"Prince Charles Edward Stuart," he said. "They're Scots, you know."

For a moment Kate couldn't think who "they" might be.

"Retrievers," Elliot explained. "They originated in Scotland."

"I didn't know that," she said.

The old man opened the front door, and its movement sent the crystal tears into their small ballet. "Mr. Thorne persists in calling him Charlie," Elliot said, disapproval in his voice.

"And you prefer?" Kate asked.

"Something with a bit more dignity."

"Prince," she guessed.

"Oh, dear me, no." He looked horrified at the thought, and Kate found herself smiling again. "Stuart," he announced solemnly. "I think it's very fitting for such a fine animal. Royal, you know," he added as if that settled the entire issue.

Kate smiled at his obvious love for the dog. He was such a nice old man. She suddenly remembered what Thorne had told her. "By the way, Elliot, I was so sorry to hear about your sister. I hope she's improving."

"Oh, she's doing very well, thank you. Much better than expected. She may even be released from the hospital today."

"That's wonderful," Kate said. There was a small silence, the exchange too personal perhaps for Elliot's idea of his role.

"Mr. Thorne is in the parlor. Shall I announce you?"

"I believe—if he won't mind—I'd rather just go in."

"I can assure you he won't mind," Elliot said simply.

Kate smiled at him again and pushed open the sliding door. Thorne was standing, both hands resting on the mantel of the white marble fireplace, looking down into the empty grate. He turned his head at the small noise made by the door. In the ever-present dimness, Kate couldn't read what was in the dark eyes, but they watched her as she crossed the room. When she was almost to the fireplace, he straightened, removing his hands from the mantel and turning to face her.

"I didn't really need to talk to your friend," she said.

"I called Kahler and told him what I had told you," Thorne said. "I gave him Greg's name and number."

"Apparently, Dr. Sandifer didn't give Lew any information. That should certainly prove…"

She hesitated, reluctant to put exactly what it should prove into words.

"That I had nothing to do with Garrison's death?"

"I never thought you did," Kate said.

The midnight eyes held hers, assessing, and finally he nodded. "And Kahler?" he asked. "What does he believe?"

"I don't presume to speak for Kahler."

"Don't you, Kate? Somehow I've gotten the impression that you two are…close."

"Close?" she repeated carefully, wondering what he'd been told and who had told him.

"Close enough that some time last night he was in your apartment, listening as you replayed your messages."

She had told him that, she realized, not thinking about what interpretation he might put on Kahler's presence.

"I tried to call you last night, Kate. Several times. I even left a message. Did you get in too late to return my call?"

Kate didn't say anything. She couldn't think of anything to tell him but the truth, and she knew how that would sound.

"You didn't spend the night at home," he said, statement and not question.

"No," she agreed.

He turned his head, looking down again into the shadowed recess of the fireplace.

"I told you my apartment gives me the creeps. Because of the confetti, the idea that someone had been inside, in my bedroom. Then last night... After finding Lew, I knew I couldn't go back there."

He turned his head toward her again, his gaze tracing over the line of her mouth and then almost reluctantly lifting to meet her eyes. "You could have come here," he said.

She knew that was true. She had known it last night, but for some reason, she had chosen not to. "I didn't think coming here was a good idea. After we..." She paused, trying to decide what to call what had been between them.

"After I kissed you," he said into her hesitation. "Told you that I've thought about you for days. Did that make you afraid to come back here?"

"Not afraid. Not because of that. It just seemed it would be...rushing things."

His eyes held hers a long moment. "I see," he said finally.

"I came today," she reminded him.

He touched her then. He put the tips of his fingers on her cheek, and she turned her head to press her lips into his palm, because she had realized that she wanted his touch, wanted it very badly. His right hand came up to smooth around her shoulder, urging her body closer to the solid strength of his. She raised her face, watching, almost mesmerized, as his head lowered, his mouth moving inexorably toward hers, which opened in response. Anticipating.

The impact of his kiss was as powerful as it had been last night. His tongue moving against hers with familiarity now. With sure expertise. And with emotion. It didn't last long, and then he raised his head to look down into her eyes, his own still dark, almost fathomless. The beautiful line of his mouth curved. The perfect features were enhanced by his smile, and her own lips moved in answer.

You don't know what you're dealing with echoed suddenly in her head, and to banish Kahler's voice, she stretched on tiptoe, her body straining to Thorne's. His arms enclosed her, his size again making her feel fragile, in need of protection. That wasn't a feeling she would ever have imagined could be as pleasurable as she was finding it to be. Fragile and feminine weren't adjectives that she had sought as descriptors of herself, but that was how Thorne made her feel, and she was a little surprised to find how much she enjoyed that feeling.

She was also surprised that their embrace was having the same immediate effect on him that their kiss last night had had. His body was already hardened with desire, and he wasn't embarrassed to let her become aware of that. For some reason, today she wasn't uncomfortable with the realization of how he felt. She raised her hand to touch the back of his head, her fingers splaying through the thick, black hair. It curled around them, seeming to welcome their caress. It had been so long, he'd told her last night. *So long.*

He drew her closer, pressing his body into hers. She could feel his breathing change, the small, telltale increase in his heart rate. His hands cupped under her hips, pulling her into his arousal, holding her to him. His mouth turned, deepening the kiss. Wanting her. Making it obvious that he wanted her.

Her breathing shortened, tremulous, anxious, feeling the force of desire move through her own body. Surging upward. Hot and powerful and almost new, like nothing she had felt before. Stronger. Deeper.

Perhaps he became aware of her response, her loss of control imminent. For some reason he eased his big body away from her, the distance between them slight, but suddenly far too wide, the space unwanted and invasive. Involuntarily she moved toward him, seeking again the pleasant heat of his body. His hands found her shoulders, and he held her. His denial was gentle, but there was no doubt that he was holding her away from him.

She opened her eyes to find him watching her. Whatever emotion had been briefly revealed in his face shifted before she could name it, altered subtly as she watched, realigning itself into something more familiar, safer.

"It's all right," she comforted. Maybe he thought he was rushing her. Because of what she'd said about last night.

Maybe he didn't realize how she felt about him. Maybe he still thought that Kahler—

"Don't tempt me, Kate," he said. He didn't smile, but she had already been aware of his desire. There was no doubt that she was doing exactly that.

"Why?" she asked, smiling at him.

"Because becoming…involved with me probably isn't a good idea," he said.

"*Becoming* involved?" she repeated, letting him hear the emphasis.

"Becoming intimate," he said simply.

Old-fashioned, she thought. The wording was uniquely Barrington. *Becoming intimate.* She couldn't think of a nicer way to express it, even if the phrase was archaic. Intimate. An intimate relationship.

"I think I like the sound of that," she offered.

He made another small movement. Away from her again. His hands exerted a quick pressure, a small squeeze, against her shoulders, and then he released her.

"What's wrong?" she asked.

"I had a lot of time to think last night. While I was waiting for you to return my call."

"Look," she said, knowing this was too important for misunderstanding. Such a stupid misunderstanding. "It was nothing. I was in shock from finding Lew. Kahler offered me his couch for the night, and I accepted. It didn't mean anything."

"It's not that," he said quickly. And then nothing else.

She shook her head, feeling some of last night's anxiety resurface. If not the fact that she'd spent the night at Kahler's apartment, then what? What was wrong? "Then what is it?" she asked.

"I realized you'd been right about a lot of things."

"What kinds of things? I don't understand."

"The things you told me. About myself."

"Thorne," she said, her tone full of regret. She shook her head slowly, knowing how far she had come toward understanding. "When I said those things—" she began.

"You were far more objective than you are now," he suggested. For the first time since he'd touched her, he smiled at her. "Far more apt to tell me the truth."

"I thought you'd sent me a bomb. How objective is that?" she argued. "I wanted to hurt you. I had no idea of the reasons…"

When she hesitated, he turned back to face the marble fireplace. Unthinkingly he put his hands again over the edge of the mantel. The marred right one was nearer, and she found her eyes drawn again to the scars, the mutilation. Marked forever by what had happened.

Suddenly she remembered, against her will, what Kahler had suggested. *Jealous*, she thought, *and striking out blindly. We all do it.* Kahler wasn't exempt from human emotion. He'd apologize the next time she saw him, and until then she certainly didn't have to give any credence to his jealous speculations.

"I didn't understand all that had happened to you," she said.

He turned his head to look at her again, dark eyes examining her features, slowly, as if imprinting them on his memory.

"I realized last night that I *have* been hiding," he said.

She felt her throat tighten, and she swallowed, fighting the emotion. Something constricted in her chest, hating his humiliation, hating that he felt compelled to make that confession to her. She wasn't surprised, given what she knew about the caliber of the man standing before her. She had never heard anything derogatory said about Thorne Barrington by anyone in Atlanta. Only recognition of his abilities. His integrity. This was a manifestation of that same integrity. He was being brutally honest with her. Honest about himself.

"I think you had cause," she said quietly.

"To be a coward?" he asked. There was derision in his voice. Mockery. All self-directed.

"You're not a coward."

He turned back to the fireplace. There was a long silence, and she didn't break it. She had said the truth. What she felt. Even if he had hidden, that didn't make him a coward.

"You have an image of yourself. Everyone does," he went

on. "A perception. And for most of us, that perception *is* who we are. What we *think* we are." His voice stopped, but she knew from the tenseness of the muscles in those broad shoulders that this wasn't all. Not complete. "I think that's what I hate most about what happened. He destroyed my perception of who I am."

"You're not a coward," she said again. "Sane people don't put themselves into situations where they can be hurt or injured. If light causes pain, you avoid it. The burned child avoids the flame. That's called self-preservation. It's called sanity."

He turned to look at her again. Once more assessing.

"You have headaches," she said. "No one would choose to do anything that might trigger a migraine. Especially a severe one."

"Are you quoting Kahler?" he asked.

"He told me about the migraines," she admitted.

"Because they couldn't pinpoint the physical cause of my headaches, couldn't stop them, they suggested I see a psychiatrist." There was no inflection she could read in the statement. No longer hiding.

"Did you?"

He laughed, the sound short and bitter.

"I *knew* the headaches were the result of the injuries. They just couldn't find out what was wrong, so therefore I must be at fault. I was furious that they suggested it."

"So you never went."

"Maybe I was just afraid of what he might discover."

"I'm not sure I blame you. I never had much desire to have all my neuroses exposed to the light of day."

The silence stretched, expanded, became uncomfortable long before he broke it, his tone less emotional than it had been before. "I have migraines," he said, speaking as if she didn't know, finally explaining. "Triggered by light, especially a bright or unexpected light. A camera flash, even something as small as a refrigerator bulb in a darkened room."

"The photographer," she realized suddenly. "After the bombing. Is that...?"

"That was the first. Luckily, I was still in the hospital. I didn't even understand what was happening. I thought something had exploded in my head, some damage from the bomb they hadn't found."

"But that wasn't the only one?" she asked.

"No, but you're right. The burned child learns very quickly to avoid the flame."

"And there's nothing they can do for them?"

"Injections. Something to knock me out. I'm still aware of the pain on some level. I lose a couple of days of my life. And even afterwards...there are residual effects. So I...avoid the cause. I live in the darkness."

"There's nothing wrong with that. I told you. Self-preservation. Sanity."

He said nothing, still leaning forward against his hands which gripped the mantel.

"I thought," she said finally, "when I left work today, when I decided to come here... I thought about what you said. About being here where the darkness doesn't matter. It doesn't matter, Thorne. I want to be here."

He turned to look at her. She remembered that he had made his confession last night. Braver then than she had been. It was only fair that she tell him now how she felt, how she had felt for so long. "I've wanted to be here far longer than you can possibly imagine."

"Will you come back tonight?" he asked, still watching her face. "Stay here with me? If the darkness really doesn't matter," he added.

Seeing what was in his eyes, she smiled at him, and then she nodded.

SHE WENT BACK to her apartment. She still wanted the long soaking bath she had needed this morning when she had made do with a quick shower and shampoo. Before she went back to Thorne's tonight, she intended to soak out some of the tension of the past few days. Not her grief over Lew and probably not her fear. That had become an almost constant anxiety. But maybe she could do something about her nervousness over her stalker, the confetti bandit. The tensions of her argument with Kahler. His accusations. She'd climb into the tub and try to banish all of those from her mind. Then she'd dress and go back to Thorne's.

She wasn't sure if he had simply been offering a refuge or if he intended something different. A seduction, maybe, she found herself thinking as she undressed in her small bathroom. She thought she'd probably like whatever old-fashioned ideas about seduction Thorne Barrington had. Maybe even like pretending that he needed to seduce her, that she wasn't coming to him already seduced—by his voice, his pictures, by his reputation even. By every experience she had had with the man himself. At last, reality and not fantasy.

She had just been stepping out of the tub, unconscious of how long she had spent there, thinking about tonight, again anticipating, when she heard the doorbell. She picked up her watch that she'd placed on the tile counter and found that it was after seven.

Kahler, she thought. *Coming to apologize. To back off the stupid things he'd said out of jealousy.*

She pulled on her white terry robe and leaned over, letting her long hair fall forward. She wrapped a towel, turban-like, around her wet head. She thought briefly that Kahler had never seen her like this. No makeup. Wet hair wrapped in a towel. Then she acknowledged that she really didn't care. Somewhere inside she was disappointed in Kahler, that he'd let his personal feelings enter into his investigation of a murder case.

"Who is it?" she asked automatically as she approached the door. She looked through the peephole and saw her neighbor from across the hall.

"It's me. Carol Simmons."

Kate released the chain and opened the door slightly.

"Sorry," her neighbor said. "I got you out of the shower."

"It's okay."

"I just wanted to give you this," Carol said, holding a blue-and-white Ty-Vek envelope toward the opening in the door. "It wouldn't fit into the mail slot, and when I came out to get my mail, I told the postman I'd take it and give it to you when you got home. Only, with the noise the kids were making, I guess I missed hearing you come in.''

Kate opened the door wide enough to accept the bulky envelope, glancing automatically at the address block. Her name and address and the sender... The sender had been Lew Garrison.

The envelope wasn't the folder thing the post office had—not the letter-size cardboard mailer. This one was big. Big enough to hold... Files, she realized suddenly. Big enough to hold all the Tripper files. She forced her eyes up from Lew's careful lettering, just as neat and precise as it had been on the tabs she'd examined today, to meet her neighbor's.

"The postman gave it to you?" she asked carefully.

"Uh-huh," Carol said, a brief puzzlement in her green eyes.

"The regular postman?"

Carol shrugged. "Yeah. I mean I don't know if he delivers our mail every day, but I've seen him before."

"The real postman?" Kate said.

Carol laughed. "The honest-to-God, real-life postman," she said, still smiling. "What's wrong with you?"

"Paranoia, I guess," Kate said, knowing she was making a fool of herself. "I've been working on the bomber thing. Jack the Tripper."

"Oh, God, Kate, and you're afraid this might be..." Instinctively, Carol stepped back a couple of feet and with that automatic reaction, Kate realized how silly she was being.

"That was just paranoia. It's from my boss. I recognize his handwriting. My...hesitation was just a momentary insanity," she explained.

"You better call the cops," Carol said. "Don't you open that thing without having the cops check it out. That guy blows people up."

"I know," Kate said, "but I promise this isn't from Jack. It's from Lew Garrison. He's my editor."

She held out the envelope to allow Carol to see the return address, but as the package approached her, Kate's neighbor moved another step back, toward the safety of her own door.

"But I thought..." Carol began and then hesitated. "I thought he was dead."

"He is. He must have sent this..." *Before he was killed.* A message or a warning. From beyond the grave. Kate shivered and then realized how melodramatic those words were. Lew Garrison would certainly have red-lined that phrase had she been dumb enough to use it in a story. Despite the fact that he was gone, she smiled. *Lew's not stupid,* she had assured Kahler, and apparently she'd been right. If this was what she thought it might be...

"Thanks, Carol," she said, in a hurry now to get back inside and open the envelope.

"You call the police, Kate. You hear me? You call the cops. Don't you open that thing. Anybody could have sent that. Just because it's got somebody's name on the front—"

"Thanks," Kate said, closing the door on the last part of that warning. She turned and walked across the room and laid the package on the coffee table, on top of the magazines Kahler had been reading that day as he'd waited for her to come home.

She briefly considered doing exactly what Carol had suggested: picking up the phone and putting in a call for Kahler. Only... Too much had happened between them. Too many things had been said. She felt as if she'd forfeited her right to ask for Kahler's help.

Besides, she thought, sitting down on the couch in front of the blue and white envelope, this was Lew's handwriting. She'd certainly seen enough of that today that there was no doubt. She didn't want to wait for the cops. She wanted to know what was in the package Lew had mailed, apparently shortly before he'd been killed. Truly a message from beyond the grave, and at that thought she shivered again, even as she reached for the opening of the envelope.

Chapter Twelve

Despite Kate's surety that Lew's hand had addressed the package, she examined by touch what it held as fully as she could through the thin, tough skin of the envelope. She could feel the thicker manila of the folders and even the sheaf of papers each held. She briefly considered whether there could be explosives concealed in the center of one of the files, but in handling the package when she'd taken it from Carol, it had been obvious that it contained only flexible materials.

She looked again at the address. Everything was correct. It wasn't marked Private or Personal. If it had been, that would have been a clue that it might contain a bomb, intended exclusively for the hands of one person. There was nothing suspicious—no lumps or bulges, no wires, no stains on the outside—none of the signs you were supposed to look for in a mail bomb. And without a doubt, the handwriting was Lew's, by far the strongest argument for its safety.

She didn't realize she'd been holding her breath until she had carefully peeled the last section of the adhesive flap away from the envelope. She knew better than to try to pull the contents out, so she got up and walked around to the end of the coffee table.

She stood as far away from the opening of the envelope as she could and stretched out her right hand to lift one corner of the bottom. The image of Thorne Barrington's right hand was suddenly in her head, and she hesitated again. *Coward,* she mocked herself, trying to gather her faltering courage, *you know this is from Lew. Just do it!*

She turned her face away, closing her eyes, and dumped whatever the package contained onto the table. The mass of material slid out without resistance. When she opened her eyes, only a stack of manila folders lay on the surface of her coffee table, looking totally innocent. She took a deep breath, feeling foolish and relieved and very lucky all at the same time.

What the hell did you think you were doing, August? Kahler would say. *You got a death wish?* She didn't, of course, especially after seeing the room in Austin, after finding Lew.

She remembered to take another breath, finally feeling her heart rate begin to steady. This had probably been the dumbest thing she'd ever done, but she had *known* the package was from Lew. Thankfully, she'd been right. *Stupid risk,* her subconscious screamed, *no matter who you thought it was from.*

She laid the empty envelope on the table beside the folders and realized only then that she had handled it without gloves, maybe destroying whatever evidence it contained. But, of course, so had Carol and the postman and the dozens of people who had processed the package on its way to her. Her fingerprints were already all over the files—as were Lew's. Especially if he had really done what he'd said they should do, if he had really again examined everything they contained.

If he had, it was obvious he'd found something—something that had gotten him killed—but not before he'd sent the files on to her. Maybe on his way to meet his killer? She didn't know, and it didn't make much sense to speculate on what had happened that night. What was important was that Lew had sent these to her, and whatever he'd found that had gotten him killed, almost certainly lay within these files.

Unconsciously, she pulled the damp towel off her head, letting her the hair fall around her face and shoulders. Impatiently she pushed it back, finger-combing the damp strands out of her eyes and away from her face with both hands.

There was enough material here that it would take her hours to go through it all. Unless, she thought suddenly, Lew had stuck a note in one of the folders, or marked something in one of the files, something that would direct her search.

She sat down on the couch and opened the first folder in the stack. A file for a victim profile. She quickly fanned through the pages, but there seemed to be nothing there. No note, nothing that didn't belong. She opened the second folder in the stack, doing the same thing. She continued the process through all of them, carefully restacking the folders she'd searched upside down in the order they'd been in when they'd arrived.

There appeared to be nothing in any of the folders except what she had put into them originally. In her cursory search, she hadn't seen any notations, no circles or stars. Only her files and the ones Lew had begun collecting from the stringers in the scattered cities where the bombings had taken place. She supposed she had looked at those at some time in the past, maybe when they'd come in, but she couldn't really remember too much about them because she hadn't written that article yet.

Interviews with the hunters, Lew had called these files. Profiles of the men who were desperately looking for Jack because he'd killed someone in their jurisdiction, someone who was supposed to be under their protection. Murder had been done on their watch, and they were still looking for the murderer. She laid the final folder on top and then lifted the entire stack, turning it over so that the files were again in the order in which they'd arrived.

Whatever message Lew had intended to send her, he hadn't made it easy. Maybe he hadn't had time. Maybe— She'd probably never know, she realized. It was useless to speculate. Only Lew and the killer knew what the situation had been last night.

She picked up the stack of folders and carried them to her kitchen table. Because the terry robe was damp and becoming uncomfortable in the air-conditioning, she took a moment to go back into her bedroom to slip out of it and into a pair of shorts and a T-shirt before she sat down in one of the kitchen chairs. She ran her fingers again through her drying hair, securing the curling tendrils behind her ears, and then, opening the first folder, she began to read.

She jumped when the phone rang, sharp and unexpected in the hours-long silence. She lifted her head from where it rested, propped on her hand, and the ache in her stiffened neck was a reminder of how long she'd sat in this same position, carefully reading through her own material. She thought about letting the machine pick up, and then she realized the caller might be Kahler. She felt a moment of guilt because she knew she should have called him hours ago, when the package had first arrived. She stood up and moved across the room on legs that were also stiff, catching the phone on its fourth ring.

"Hello," she said, anticipating the accented voice of the detective. After all, she'd been expecting him to call all afternoon to apologize for the things he'd said.

"Kate?" Barrington said.

It took a second to make the shift in her thinking. With the arrival of the package, she had forgotten the arrangement she and Thorne had made this afternoon. She glanced at the kitchen clock and realized with shock that it was almost eleven.

"Are you all right?" he asked.

"I forgot about you," she said truthfully, an answer to the question he hadn't asked, and it was not until the lack of response stretched that she realized how that would sound.

"I see," he said finally, his tone carefully neutral.

"No," she said. "No, you don't. Something's happened."

"What's wrong?" he asked.

She was grateful for the immediate concern, as welcome as Kahler's had always been.

"Kate?"

"I got a package from Lew."

"Don't touch it," he ordered harshly.

He was certainly qualified to give that advice. Thorne would think she was as stupid for opening the envelope as Kahler would.

"I've already opened it. It wasn't a bomb."

"Thank God." Barrington's deep voice breathed the words. "What the hell, Kate—"

"It's the files. *That* was the other thing Lew said he would do that afternoon. The last time I talked to him. I didn't remember until today. He said we needed to read back through the files because that's how Kahler had found Mays."

"Did he read them?"

"I couldn't be sure. I looked for them today at the paper, but everything was gone. Then tonight, when I got home, my neighbor brought over this package. It was the missing files. Lew had sent them to me."

"And you've read them?"

"Not all of them."

"Have you called Kahler?"

"Not yet. I thought you might be..." She paused, remembering what he believed about her relationship with the detective. "When the phone rang, I thought it might be Kahler. I was going to tell him."

"Come over here, Kate. Right now. Get the hell out of that apartment. I don't want you there alone."

"I know I told you I get the willies here, but I don't—"

"Something in those files may have gotten Lew Garrison killed, Kate. Don't be a fool."

"I know, but when Kahler finds out I've got these, he'll pick them up and give them to someone else to read. He wants me to back off, to play it safe. But no one else will be able to recognize what's important. I *know* there's something here. Why else would Lew have sent the files if he didn't think they'd tell me something? I'll be all right. No one knows I have them. I just need to finish reading them. I have to. This is my job."

"The public's right to know," he said bitterly.

"The public's right not to be dead."

Again there was long silence across the line, and then she heard the depth of the breath he took before he spoke. "I can't stand the thought that you might be in danger."

She waited, knowing what was going through his mind, the horror of the memories he lived with. *Make the offer,* she urged him silently. *Come over here and stay with me while I do my job, a job we both know I have to finish.* There was only silence until she broke it.

"I could bring them with me," she offered. "You could look at them. Maybe someone who hasn't seen everything a dozen times might spot whatever it was Lew found. Maybe I'm too close to all this. And I haven't changed my mind. I really don't want to sleep here tonight. The invitation still open?"

"Of course," he said. She could hear relief in his voice. "Bring everything with you. We'll look at them together."

"Could you..." she hesitated, hating to let him know that his reminder of the dangers posed by whatever was in these files had struck home. Too many people dead, she had acknowledged, and she really didn't want to be next. "Would you meet me at the gate?"

"How long will it take you to get here?" Thorne asked, as if he didn't even think it was a strange request.

"Ten minutes," she guessed. Traffic certainly wouldn't be a problem at this time of night.

"I'll be at the gate," he promised.

HE WASN'T. The gate was unlocked, standing slightly open when she arrived. She pulled her Mazda along the curb and sat a moment in the car, trying to decide what to do. Was it possible that something had happened to him in the short space of time since she'd listened to the comforting assurance of his promise?

That sudden fear propelled her into action. She opened the door and ran around the front of the Mazda and across the sidewalk that bordered the fence. She touched the gate, pushing the narrow opening wide enough to allow her to slip through and onto the grounds. "Thorne?" she called.

There was no answer from the surrounding darkness. She hesitated briefly before she pulled the gate shut behind her, feeling infinitely better when the iron lock slipped into its niche with a metallic clang. She was safely inside the urban fortress the Barringtons had built against the encroaching violence of the twentieth century. The only question was: Where was Thorne? She ran up the steps to the porch, but she hadn't had time to cross its narrow expanse to the glass-paneled front door, when she heard her name from the shadows behind her.

"Kate."

She looked back and saw Thorne standing outside his own security fence, a restraining hand on the collar of the retriever. The puppy stood beside him, panting, his tongue lolling out of his friendly dog-grin, looking up trustingly at his owner, whose tall frame was bent sideways in order to maintain his hold.

Running back down the steps, Kate hurried down the sidewalk and then spent a seemingly endless minute struggling with the gate's release. "I thought something had happened to you," she said breathlessly when it finally yielded.

Thorne laughed, the sound deep and warm, totally relaxed. The prosaic explanation for his absence was also comforting.

"I made the mistake of letting Charlie come out of the house with me. When I unlocked the gate, he thought we were going for a run. He pushed through before I could grab him. I couldn't let him roam around loose. He hasn't figured out that cars are dangerous. I thought we could get back before you arrived. I left the gate unlocked," he explained, "in case we didn't."

By that time he was inside, pulling the gate inward again, and she listened once more to the satisfyingly secure clang of its mechanism engage. The dog's greeting was cold-nosed and enthusiastic, and she found herself smiling, forgetting briefly what had sent her hurrying through the darkness to this man.

"I'm glad you're here," Thorne said. He drew her against his side, his body big and solid and protective. He touched his lips to the top of her hair. "You smell good," he said.

She remembered that she had washed her hair, allowing it to dry naturally, a process that she knew would have resulted in a mass of uncontrollable curls. "That's good," she said, "'cause I probably look like hell."

He laughed.

"Do you think we could go inside?" she suggested. "Despite your fence, I still feel a little exposed out here."

"Of course," he said. He put his arm around her shoulder, pulling her to him again, and they walked together to the porch where the dog was patiently waiting, his gaze fixed on the closed door, anticipating being allowed back into the familiar domain as much as she was now. The house seemed welcoming, in spite of its ever-present darkness.

Thorne slipped his long fingers into the front pocket of his jeans, his hand flattened to fit into the skin-tight material, and fished out the key.

"Where's Elliot?" she asked. Maybe the old man was already asleep, and Thorne didn't want to disturb him.

"I suggested he spend the night at his sister's. She was released from the hospital today. I thought you might be more comfortable if...we were alone," he offered.

He was right, she realized. For some reason, she *would* have been embarrassed for Elliot to know she had come here to spend the night with Thorne, and she was grateful again for his consideration of feelings she hadn't even anticipated that she might have. But he had. Kindness or old-fashioned good manners? Either way, it was especially welcoming.

Thorne fitted the key he'd retrieved into the lock and then turned the handle. When the door swung inward, the soft cascade of glass notes shimmered into the silent hallway as the draft of night air touched the crystals of the chandelier.

The retriever padded like a golden shadow across the foyer, his nails ticking softly on the parquet, disappearing again into the darkness behind the staircase. Heading to the kitchen and his dishes, Kate thought, in need of a long drink of water after his unexpected midnight run.

Like the Southern gentleman he had been raised to be, Thorne allowed her to precede him into the dim foyer, and then he pulled the door closed behind them. "Have I told you how glad I am that you're here?" he asked.

"Despite the fact that I'm about four hours late?"

"Apparently you had a good reason. Where are the files you wanted me to look at?"

"Damn. I left them in the car. When you weren't at the gate..." She hesitated, again hating to admit how paranoid all this was making her. Thorne's warning that even possessing the files was dangerous had somehow made the threat seem more real. What she was doing was not an exercise in intellect, but a search for a killer.

"Did you think *I'd* forgotten *you?*" he asked. There was a trace of self-directed amusement in the question, and she knew he was remembering the confession she'd made over the phone.

"I thought something had happened to you," she admitted.

"To me? Why would you think that?"

If he hadn't realized, as she had told Lew, that his was one name they knew was still on Jack's list, she wouldn't be the one to suggest it to him. Thorne Barrington had had enough to deal with during the last three years. Her idea that Jack would try again wasn't something that would help in this situation.

"Just an indication of how shook up I am, I guess. You'd said you'd be there and when you weren't..." She shrugged, letting him put his own interpretation on that fear. Fear for him. A very real fear, she believed, whether he had confronted it yet or not.

"I'll go back out and get them," he offered.

Suddenly, she didn't want him out there, out in the darkness. "We could leave it until tomorrow," she surprised herself by suggesting. "There's not much left to read. I had read all the victim profiles."

"Everything?" he prodded softly. "Every word?"

"Except yours," she admitted. She had laid the thick folder to the side when she'd come to it. She already knew everything it contained. There were no secrets there. It had seemed far more important to examine the others. "I'd already read it a dozen times before, and I *knew* you weren't involved."

"I appreciate the vote of confidence," he said. There was a hint of amusement in his tone, and she knew he had recognized the significance of that confession. She had read his file a dozen times before because of her fascination with him.

"I had read a couple of the files on the investigators, and then you called. I swear I didn't see anything I hadn't read a hundred times before. I can't imagine what Lew found."

"It's always possible that it wasn't something in those files. It's possible that Garrison uncovered something else."

That was a possibility, of course. Lew had promised yesterday to pursue other things. Mays's connections with the current hate groups. Thorne's injuries. She had been the one who had asked for that, a long time ago, before she had come to know the man standing beside her. But of course, those scenarios wouldn't explain why Lew had mailed her the files.

"We could start fresh in the morning," Thorne's voice broke into her thoughts. "Maybe when you're less tired..." He let the suggestion trail.

"I just want it over. I just want to find whoever killed Lew. Whoever—" Whoever had sent the bombs. Like the one that had arrived here three years ago and had forever changed Thorne Barrington's life. "Just over," she finished.

"I know, but I think you've probably dealt with enough during the last couple of days. You don't have to figure it all out tonight."

"You have another suggestion?" she asked, smiling at him.

"Let it go," he said. "Don't think about it. About what's happened. About the files. Don't think about anything. Not tonight. Just let me hold you while you sleep."

Don't tempt me, he'd said, and now he was tempting her. A very tempting offer. To forget about it all. Finally to feel safe again.

"I'd like that," she said simply, the absolute truth. "I'd really like that."

THEY CLIMBED the dark stairs together, Thorne's arm still comfortingly around her shoulder. The bedroom he led her to was huge, with furniture massive enough to fill its soaring dimensions. The draperies had been pushed back from the expanse of windows, so that the moonlight filtered into the room through the leaves of the trees that lined the street outside.

Even in the moon-touched dimness it was obvious that the room's decor was masculine.

"This is your room?" she asked.

"The phone's here. I thought—"

"That wasn't a complaint. Only a question."

She took a breath, acknowledging the inherent awkwardness in their situation. Like the first kiss, neither of them could be sure what the other was feeling.

"It's all right," Thorne said. "I meant what I said. You need to sleep tonight—far more than you need anything else."

"What about the other?" she asked, smiling at him. She was relieved that he seemed able to read her so well.

The dark head tilted, questioning, and a faint crease formed between the winged brows. "The other?" he repeated.

"To hold me while I sleep. Is that offer still good?"

"I can't think of anything that would give me more pleasure than to hold you," he said softly.

She couldn't resist, despite the quiet romanticism of that. "Not...anything?" she teased, lips tilting.

"I'm trying to be a gentleman, Kate, but I have to warn you that you're pushing your luck."

She laughed. Despite everything that had happened in the last few days, despite the horror and fear, something relaxed inside.

"Come to bed," he invited.

He held out his hand, like a courtier from another age, and she laid hers in it. He led her to the wide bed and sat down on the edge, still holding her fingers. He looked up from them, his gaze moving over her features, and then he smiled.

"I like your hair like that, soft and loose, as fine as a child's."

In spite of what he had promised, the deep voice was seductive. Suddenly, she knew that she wanted his fingers entangled in her hair, touching it. Touching her. Finally, touching her.

Drawn by that image, she moved closer to him. He opened his legs, creating a space between them for her to stand in, welcoming her body between the strength of his thighs. Freeing her fingers from his, she laid her palms on the wide expanse of his shoulders. His hands found her waist, and with their movement against her body, she could feel the play of muscle under her palms.

She looked down into his face, the features masculine and strong, yet perfectly aligned, perfectly formed. She had thought about Thorne Barrington for months, but being with him was different from anything she had imagined. Because *he* was different from the man he should have been. Despite the fact that he must have grown up accustomed to the adoration of the opposite sex, there was none of the sexual arrogance often found in men who were this attractive.

His hands had slipped under her T-shirt, their slight roughness pleasant against her skin. The big fingers skimmed slowly upward, over the small, regular protrusions of her ribs. He wasn't smiling now, and again she could see the starkness of desire etched in the spare planes of his face.

He wanted her, and she was fascinated that he did. Fascinated by the idea that someone like Thorne Barrington could be attracted to her. Fascinated by him. By his touch. There was no resistance in her mind to what he was doing. She wanted him to touch her, had wanted it for a long time, far longer than she had ever admitted, even to herself.

Finally his hands found the full, unrestrained softness of her breasts, cupping under their weight, holding her, still gentle, carefully controlled. She heard the depth of the breath he took. Trying to maintain that control. "Kate," he whispered.

"I know," she said. This was not what he had intended—not what he'd promised—but it was what they both wanted.

His thumbs swept across the sensitive swell of her breasts, across nipples hardened with her own desire, taut with the promise of his caress. And then back. No demand. Only need. A need she shared.

She moved closer, putting one knee on the bed beside his narrow hips—leaning against him, letting him support her—and then the other knee on the other side, so that she was kneeling above him now.

His hands shifted under her shirt. Behind her now. Holding

her. Pulling her to him, to be locked against the wall of his chest. She eased down into his lap, put her head against his shoulder, and was held in his arms like a child. His size seemed to give her permission to feel fragile, permission to be vulnerable, and she no longer needed to fear that vulnerability. He was certainly strong enough to protect her.

His hands slid over her spine, moving under the thin shirt, soothing out tension and fear. "It's all right," he promised. "Everything will be all right."

She eased her body away from his, only far enough to look into his eyes. This was inevitable. Their relationship had been building to this for days, weeks. Months, she acknowledged. Long months when she had only looked at his pictures, had dreamed about him.

"Make love to me," she whispered. She hadn't intended to ask him that. She had hoped that he, too, would be aware of the inevitability of this, but she was afraid that he might have meant to do exactly what he had promised. She knew now that to be held was not what she wanted from him tonight. Not *all* she wanted.

His hands had stilled. He held her, unmoving, apparently trying to read what was revealed in her features.

"Please," she added.

"Are you sure, Kate?"

"I don't think I've ever been as sure of anything in my life," she admitted. "I want you to make love to me."

Something shifted in the taut lines of his face. It was not a smile, but a softening, a relaxation of tension, perhaps. Relief that the restraint he had promised was not what she needed from her? Relief that she, too, needed something else? Something very different from the control he had been seeking.

"I want to see you," he said. Already his hands were tangled in the loose fall of her shirt, helping her ease it off over her head. The curling tendrils of her hair were caught up briefly in the fabric, and when the shirt was off, they fell back against her neck and shoulders in a mass of shampoo-fragranced confusion. Unthinkingly, she raised her hands, run-

ning her fingers through the disordered strands, pushing them
up and away from her face.

"Don't move," he ordered softly.

Surprised by the tone of the command, which she had instinctively obeyed, her eyes sought his. He wasn't looking at
her face. His gaze was instead on her breasts, thrown into
prominence by her raised arms, their small peaks thrusting
upward as if seeking...

She knew exactly what they were seeking as she watched
his lips lower to touch against one and then the other. She
held her breath, feeling his against her skin, warm and damp
and feathering over the too-sensitive flesh she had exposed for
his touch. Because she had wanted him to touch her there.
Had wanted him for such a long time.

His mouth fastened over one nipple. His tongue mimicked
the motion his thumbs had begun, slowly across and then back.
She could feel her skin tightening in response and wondered
what that movement felt like against his tongue, wondered if
he could know what he was doing to her.

Her breath caught, a small half sob of sound, like a child
fighting the onslaught of tears, struggling now for her own
control. Her hands deserted the wild profusion of her curls.
She lowered her head over his dark one, which was still bent
to allow his mouth its torturing contact with her body. She put
her lips against his hair and then turned her face so that its
silken caress was under her cheek. Her breath shivered out in
small, audible gasps. His mouth was suckling, pulling and releasing in a pulsing rhythm, slow and strong. Too strong. Too
demanding. The pulse was echoing somewhere in her body.
Low in her belly. Demanding. Aching. The sweet, age-old
ache of desire.

"Please," she whispered again, her mouth moving against
the coal-black softness of his hair.

His lips hesitated, the rhythm he had created broken. In the
silence between them, she was aware again of the slightly
sobbing quality of the breath she drew into lungs hungry for
air. Had she forgotten to breathe as he touched her? Or did

her body need more air, like a furnace that demanded oxygen for the fire he had ignited?

When he didn't move, his stillness too prolonged, she put her hand over the back of his downturned head, cupping the smooth roundness of his skull and then moving down the strong column of his neck.

Suddenly, he fell back against the mattress, carrying her with him, her body lying on top of his. With the change in position she was very aware of how much he wanted her. The evidence of his desire was blatant through the thin material of his worn jeans, straining upward into the soft cotton knit of her shorts. So little between them. But she wanted nothing between. Nothing between the hair-roughened skin of his chest and her bare breasts. Nothing between the small convexity of her belly and the ridged muscles of his. Nothing between...

His mouth found hers. It was open, waiting for him. His tongue invaded. Seeking. Demanding. His hands were against her back. Despite the damage Jack had inflicted, they drifted again with sensuous grace over the slender, contoured planes of her body. Touching her shoulder blades, covered by skin that shivered into his caress. Along the ridge of her spine. Big hands slipping into the waistband of her shorts to curl over her bare bottom.

She could feel his breathing beginning to deepen, his hips straining upward into hers as his hands pushed her body downward. Their mouths released, and his slid, opened, across her cheek, a pulling sensation, dragging against her flushed skin. His lips touched the dampness of the curling tendrils that gathered at her temple and then moved to her ear. She turned her head, accommodating, seeking whatever intimacy his touch suggested he wanted. The warmth of his breath first, softly stirring against the outer fold of the sensitive channel. His tongue moving inside. Caressing. Tantalizing. Hot and wet.

He breathed her name again, so close, speaking it into the small, ivory cavern of her ear. She allowed her knees to slide away from him, lowering herself, millimeter by millimeter, her desire fusing now with his. She could feel the heat of his body through the barrier of their clothing. No barriers, she thought again. No barriers of any kind. Not tonight.

She was more aware of his breath, slipping out in small aching gasps almost over her ear. The other sound was subliminal. She would have ignored it, not unheard but unacknowledged, had she not felt the sudden stillness of his body beneath the bonelessness their lovemaking had reduced hers to.

She felt the change and wondered, and then into her head came the belated recognition of the sound she, too, had recognized. The same sound that had echoed into the darkness of the mansion each time she had come here—the small, crystal teardrops of the glass chandelier touching together in the draft created by the opening front door.

Chapter Thirteen

"What the hell?" Thorne said. His voice was almost sound-less, a breath, but with the shocked whisper there could be no doubt that he had heard and recognized the same noise that had finally penetrated her desire-drugged brain.

She sat up, pushing away from him. Suddenly she was aware that she was half-naked and cold. Cold with her sepa-ration from the solid warmth of his body. Cold with fear.

Thorne still lay motionless on the bed, the pale fabric of the coverlet he was lying against a frame for his darkness. Dark hair and shirt, black eyes holding hers. She knew that he was listening. Both of them listening, without breathing. Listening in the eerie silence of the old house whose night sounds he would be infinitely familiar with.

There was nothing else. No other ghost of noise drifted, almost but not quite soundlessly, upward to the second floor.

"Elliot?" she whispered.

Against the ivory of the counterpane the dark head moved once, a negation, but that movement seemed to free Thorne from whatever spell had held them motionless. His body began to lift, and she scrambled off the bed to stand beside it on legs that trembled. Thorne touched a button on the speaker phone, and she finally remembered to take a breath. The cops had arrived quickly enough the night he called them to pick her up. The first night she had come here. So long ago.

Then, suddenly, Thorne's long fingers were turning the phone. "Son of a bitch," he said, the words again only a breath, the comment made to himself and not to her. At what was in his voice, her stomach roiled, moving upward toward her throat from the cold, hard knot of fear that had begun to grow within it.

He picked up the receiver then and put it to his ear, but given the silence that surrounded them, she already knew. There was no dial tone. There was no longer any connection between the mansion and the outside world.

"The line's been cut," he confirmed, and the coldness in her stomach shifted and reformed, enlarged and blossomed, threatening to engulf her.

He pushed her shirt into her hands, which were trembling so much it was hard to put it on. Before she had the crumpled material completely in place over her body, Thorne had grasped her arm, drawing her away from the bed and toward the shadows of the hallway. She resisted, knowing that the danger they faced was below. Surely they were safer here in the upstairs darkness.

"We can't go down there," she protested, still whispering. "There's someone inside. We have to get out."

Thorne pulled her out into the hall, not toward the curving central stairs they had climbed together, but deeper into the dark bowels of the vast house. They hurried, moving almost noiselessly over the carpeted hall, passing closed doors. The farther they got from the streetlights, the darker the interior of the mansion became. She ran into him when he began to slow.

"Stairs," Thorne warned, the command almost silent. He released her arm, placing her hand on the smooth wood of the stair railing. She heard him move in front of her, and she knew she had no choice but to follow him.

The kitchen was lighter, more open, as it had been the night they had sat at the table and talked. Thorne didn't give her time to enjoy the openness, a welcome contrast to the claustrophobic narrowness of the walls on either side of the steep stairs they had just descended. He pulled her across the room. Awakened from some puppy dream, startled and confused, Charlie barked once, the sound echoing, too revealing. The shock of the unexpected noise paralyzed her, like a thief discovered in the act. By that time Thorne had the door open. He turned back to grab her hand, drawing her out into the now-safer blackness of the urban night.

He led the way unerringly through the small grounds that surrounded the mansion. Behind them, she could hear the echoing frenzy of Charlie's barking increase. Then the sounds faded as they rounded the front corner of the house. The gate was open again and beyond it stood her car.

"I have a phone," she gasped, the words ragged from lack of breath. It was only after she had spoken that she realized how ridiculous that comment was. They didn't need a phone. In her earlier panic that something might have happened to Thorne, she had not only left the folders in the car but also her keys. All they had to do was to reach the Mazda, get in and drive away.

She led the way to the sidewalk, but it was Thorne who moved automatically to the driver's side. She stood by the passenger door, breath sobbing, from physical effort now and not desire, waiting for him to release the lock that would let her in. Looking down into the car, she realized with shock that the folders she had piled on the passenger seat were no longer there. But when Thorne's fist pounded once on the roof of the car, his expletive soft but expressive, she became aware that they had a more immediate problem than the disappearance of those files.

"Locked," he said.

Suddenly the lights came on in the mansion behind her. She glanced back at the house through the bars of the surrounding fence. The chandelier in the foyer, which she had never seen lighted before, was blazing out into the dark stillness.

"Come on. Across the street," Thorne ordered.

She turned back in time to see him sprint toward the darkened hulk of the mansion that was being renovated. She followed, rounding the front of the Mazda as the porch light came on behind her.

Thorne seemed to melt into the shadows of the ruined house that loomed out of the darkness before her. She had always thought his vision must be more acute than normal because of

the way he lived, and now she realized that their very live
might depend on his ability to negotiate in the blackened in
terior of the silent, ghostly ruin.

He was waiting for her beside the opening where the fron
door had once been. His damaged hand closed around he
wrist, and despite the fact that she had known instinctivel
that he wouldn't leave her behind, she jumped with the shoc
of that unexpected contact.

"Upstairs," he breathed, his mouth pressed against her ear

From the street came the sound of footsteps, unmistakabl
in the surrounding night. Thorne drew her into the foyer. Sh
wondered briefly about the safety of climbing the stairs tha
loomed before them, about the safety of walking on the uppe
floors, but she had seen the workmen there. And would sh
and Thorne be safer to stay below? To wait for whoever wa
following them, for whoever was working, fairly successfull
now, to keep the sound of his pursuit hidden?

Her tennis shoes made no noise on the wooden risers, an
surprisingly, for such a big man, Thorne moved almost a
silently, guiding her again with unhesitating certitude into th
darkness at the top. She could barely see, following hir
blindly, forced to trust his superior night vision.

She thought once that she heard someone moving behin
them, but the fire-damaged beams of the structure might hav
produced that sensation. Just as they might be revealing thei
progress, she acknowledged ruefully. Thorne guided he
around workmen's paraphernalia, leading her ever toward th
back of the house.

They climbed another set of dark, narrow stairs, up to th
third floor now. The hallway they ran down was becomin
brighter, and when she looked up, she realized why. The doo
it led toward had, like most of the outer doors, been removed
and the passage ended in a view of the night sky beyond th
sagging banister of what must have been the back stairs of th
mansion.

As she watched, a figure moved up those stairs into the dim
illumination provided by the backdrop of moon-touche

ky—a man, silhouetted suddenly within the framework of the missing door.

A flash of light exploded out of that darkness. She flinched before its brightness even as she realized the powerful beam wasn't directed at her. Its intensity had pinned the man moving ahead of her down the hall. Thorne's hand raised in automatic response, trying to protect himself from the glare.

"Kate?"

She identified the speaker immediately, although she could see nothing beyond the glare of the flashlight. *Kahler,* she realized. *My God, it was Kahler.* And the police? Even as she thought it, she realized there had been no sirens, no arriving patrol cars. Only Kahler.

"Are you all right?" Kahler asked, shifting the light slightly to include her figure within its illumination. "He hasn't hurt you, has he?"

"I'm all right," she said automatically. Why would he think Thorne would hurt her?

"You don't have to be afraid, Kate. Everything's under control," Kahler went on, his voice reassuring.

"What the hell's going on?" Barrington's voice, as coldly furious as the night she had first walked into his house. "What were you doing in my house?"

I picked up a few tricks of the trade, Kahler had said the day she had found him inside her apartment, and she realized Thorne was right. It had to have been Kahler who had entered while they were upstairs. There was no one else. At Barrington's question, the flashlight had been refocused, its powerful light again directed at Thorne's face.

"It's over," Kahler said, his voice as cold as Barrington's. "Finally, you're going to pay for what you did."

"I don't know what you're talking about," Thorne said. He had lowered his head, his hand still shielding his eyes. "Get that damned light out of my face," he ordered.

"You couldn't leave Kate alone. Maybe because of your hatred of the media, but whatever you intended tonight is not going to happen. You're not going to hurt her."

"I don't know what you're talking about. Kate came here

because—'' Thorne's voice stopped suddenly, whatever he intended to say deliberately cut off, and she wondered why Because he had realized that Kahler was jealous? That telling him why she had come tonight would only make him more angry?

"Because you tricked her into trusting you," Kahler said "Because she believed what everyone else believed about you Because she doesn't know what you really are."

"And you do?" Barrington asked. His tone had changed anger overlain by a rigid control and by an emotion she couldn't read.

"I know *exactly* what you are. A murderer. A fine, highly respected, sanctimonious murderer."

"Kahler," Kate said, a protest. She could sense the unraveling fury in his voice, and thankfully, with her interruption the beam of light came back to her.

"What are you doing here, Kate?" he asked. "Didn't you get my message?"

"What message?" she asked.

"About the lab results. The results on the physical evidence from Garrison's office and from the sheets I took off your bed The hair and fiber samples."

He said it as if it should mean something to her, but it didn't. In all that had happened, she had even forgotten about the sheets he had taken from her apartment that night. The realization that he seemed to be implicating Thorne Barrington in that break-in and in Lew's murder began to filter into her head.

"What's that supposed to mean?" she asked.

"They're consistent. I told you. On the message. I couldn't figure out why you'd come here tonight…" He paused, and then the voice she had always thought so pleasant continued "They match the DNA."

"What DNA? What the hell are you talking about?"

"Barrington's. From the bombing. They match Barrington' DNA."

"That's a lie," Thorne said softly, almost as if he were

speaking only to her. "There was no DNA profile done. There was no reason for that to be done."

"Are you saying that Thorne put the confetti in my bed?" she asked. Her lips felt numb, unwilling to form the question.

"*And* killed Garrison," Kahler agreed. "There's enough physical evidence to tie him to both. I told you all this. You didn't get my message?"

"No," she said. The cold knot was back. Was it possible that what Kahler was saying was true? She had gone straight into the bathroom when she'd gotten home today, too eager to get out of her clothes, too eager to return to Thorne, and then Lew's package arrived. She had never bothered to check her messages.

"If you really believe what you're saying," Barrington said, his voice still controlled, still enforcing a calmness she knew he couldn't feel, "then I would like to call my attorney."

"You can call from the precinct," Kahler said dismissingly. "Kate, come down the hall toward me. Don't try to touch her, Barrington. I'm not likely to miss at this range."

"He said there was no DNA profile done," Kate said. "There was no reason for one."

"We were suspicious from the start," Kahler said. "Despite the old man's explanation about destroying the wrappings from the package, none of the rest of it made any sense. It always seemed strange that the judge would be opening his mail in the basement, but given Barrington's reputation—"

"That's a lie, Kate," Barrington said, speaking over the detective's explanation, his voice still low, directed only to her. "That's not how it happened. You know that."

But she didn't. She couldn't remember anything in the files about the location of the explosion, perhaps because of the press blackout Barrington himself had imposed or because the police had tried to protect his privacy.

Again Kahler's voice came from the darkness behind the light, almost an echo of her thoughts. "We were suspicious, just not enough. We were too willing to believe what he said because of who and what he was supposed to be."

She wished she could see Kahler's face. He had told her

none of this before, despite the times they'd talked about the case, about Barrington. Something here didn't ring true.

"Are you telling me that the police have suspected all along that the first bomb *didn't* originate outside Barrington's house?"

Kahler *had* suggested that, but only recently. *Maybe he had an accident. Did you ever think about that?* And she hadn't. She had been so certain that Kahler's warning had been born of his jealousy. Certain because she had already been caught up in her own fantasy about Barrington? A fantasy that had become so real that it had interfered with her judgment?

Standing in the darkness of the narrow hallway, she was no longer sure of anything. Her instincts about Thorne Barrington had been completely free of threat. She had trusted him, and now…now she didn't know who to trust.

"You're alone?" she asked. That wasn't right. No cop went into an unknown situation without backup. Kahler was too good a cop not to follow the rules.

"My backup hasn't arrived," he said.

"Then you *have* called someone? They're on the way?"

"Of course."

But with the word "call" she remembered that the phone lines from the house had been cut. The police didn't cut lines. Kahler shouldn't have done that, even if he were acting alone, even if he'd been worried about her safety. And why would he take the folders from her car? Unless…

Oh, dear God, she thought, the realization producing a roller coaster of sensation in her stomach. Because there was, of course, a folder in that stack about Byron Kahler, one of the hunters, his name neatly labeled in Lew's script. A folder she had never read, had never seen before. But maybe Lew had. *Oh, dear God,* she thought, *Lew had.*

Kahler had come to take care of the unfinished business he had begun three years ago, and the knowledge that she was in Thorne Barrington's house had not been a deterrent to his plans.

"I got a package tonight, Kahler," she said softly. "It came through the mail."

"Kate."

That was Thorne, trying to warn her. He had already figured it out. That's why he had stopped before, why he hadn't told Kahler the reason she had come to his house. Now he was trying to warn her not to mention the folders, but he didn't know what she knew. Kahler had already discovered she had the files. He had taken them out of her car, and he must be aware of whatever damaging information was in the one with his name on it.

Obviously Lew had given himself away. Somehow he'd revealed whatever he'd found, perhaps unthinkingly, maybe in a phone conversation to the detective, jotting those habitual notes of his on the desk calendar as they talked. Then, belatedly realizing that what he had said might be dangerous, Lew had thrown the files into one of the big Priority Mail envelopes, conveniently on hand in the newsroom, and addressed it to her—the only person he could be certain would understand the significance of what he'd found.

Had he then rushed to the seeming safety of his suburban home, trying to decide if he should act on whatever he'd found? *Maybe important. Maybe nothing,* his voice echoed in her memory.

Oh, God, Lew, I wish you'd been right. I wish it had been nothing. She knew that she was not mistaken. It all fit. Even the profile the FBI had done so long ago matched what she knew about Byron Kahler. A loner. Product of a dysfunctional family. Very smart, meticulous about details. It all fit. As a bonus, he had an insider's knowledge of how the game was played.

And if Kahler *were* Jack, he wouldn't let her go. He couldn't afford to. He knew she had seen the files. He had removed them from her car. What he couldn't know was that she hadn't finished reading them. And he would never believe that, she realized. It had been so against her character not to read them all. She hadn't, but only because of Barrington's invitation, only because of what she had heard in his voice.

"A package?" Kahler said finally. Although the thoughts had been tumbling through her mind at lightning speed, she

knew the pause before his response had been fractionally too
long.

"Don't," Barrington said again. He didn't know that the
files had been taken out of her car. He was still trying to
protect her, as he had been when he'd requested to be allowed
to call his lawyer. He didn't realize, as she now did, that Kahler *had* to kill them both. Thorne still thought she could be
saved, but she knew better. Kahler wouldn't leave a witness
to whatever was going to happen tonight. No witnesses at all.

*A bomber don't care who gets blowed up in the process of
getting what he wants. He purely don't care.* Wilford Mays's
voice was in her head, cold and full of hate.

Kahler had given her Mays's name, she remembered suddenly. When she had mentioned she might go to Hall Draper's
hometown, he had thrown out the information about Mays's
long-ago contact with Barrington to stop her. When she had
indicated that she might try to find the girl Jackie Draper had
told her about, Kahler had sent her off in another direction,
pursuing a thirty-year-old case against another bomber. A
wild-goose chase—to direct her away from whatever connection Draper had with Kahler. Through the girl? she wondered.
Through the girl Hall Draper had gotten pregnant so many
years ago? The image of a dark-haired child in an old black-
and-white photograph flashed into her mind.

With that realization, she must have made some sound,
some movement, because Barrington said again, questioning,
"Kate?"

He couldn't see her, of course. He stood with his head lowered, both hands raised now against the intensity of the light
Kahler kept focused on his face. She knew that what Kahler
was doing was deliberate. The migraine had probably already
begun. Thorne was trying to protect her, even as he was fighting the maelstrom of pain pounding sickeningly in his skull,
and suddenly she *knew* who to trust. No longer any doubt in
her mind.

"What kind of package?" Kahler asked.

"The files," she said. "All the Tripper files. Lew mailed

them to me before he died.'' She took a step closer to them both.

"You've been through them?" It was said without inflection, but despite his effort, the tone was subtly wrong, more obviously wrong perhaps because she *couldn't* see his face. There was only the voice she had admired speaking from the darkness.

"I didn't have time," she said. She needed to be closer. Whatever happened, she could do them no good so far away from the gun. She had to keep up the pretense. Keep him talking until she could get closer. "I brought the folders with me. That's why I came here tonight. I thought Barrington might be able to see something I hadn't seen. I'd been through them a hundred times. I thought he might see something, and instead…''

"It's all right," Kahler said. "It's over, Kate. You're safe. Move past him.''

Was he only trying to get her to move so they would be closer together, a more certain target in the darkness, or was it possible that he had believed what she'd said?

"They're in the car," she added. "I'll get them before we leave. We'll take them with us to the station." She took another step, near enough now that she could have reached out and touched Thorne.

"I don't think there's anything there," Kahler said. "If there were, someone would have found it by now." It was the same lie he had told her from the beginning.

"You're probably right. You don't think that's why he killed Lew? Because of something Lew found in the files?" she asked. She took another step, turning her body so that she could slip between the wall and the shoulder of the man who stood unmoving beside her, hands still shielding his eyes.

"He killed Lew because Garrison discovered what he really is. Maybe one of Barrington's friends revealed something about his medical condition. Maybe the brain damage you suspected. *Something* unhinged him and turned him into what he is.''

"A murderer," she said. Another step. Past Thorne now.

Nearer to Kahler. "Why would he kill all those people?" she asked. "Why would anybody kill all those people?"

"I've told you from the first I don't have any idea why he's done the things he's done. That's for someone else to figure out. All I know is I've got evidence tying Barrington to two crime scenes, one of them a homicide."

"You're going to take him in."

"As soon as help arrives. Then I'll take you home and all of this will be over."

"I guess you must be right," she said softly. She was almost to Kahler, able to see him clearly now that she was past the intensity of the beam. He looked just the same. The flashlight and the gun were remarkably steady, professionally held. *And why not?* she thought bitterly. He was a professional, with years of training at his command. A real insider. That was why he had been able to get away with it so long.

"I can't help but believe he must have had a reason. *Something* set him off," she went on, playing for time, trying to create an opportunity. Hoping for any opportunity. "Why did Barrington *start* building bombs? Why do people set out to kill other people?"

"You've always thought there had to be a connection," Kahler said, a hint of mockery in the deep voice.

"Yes," she acknowledged.

He smiled, the small intriguing lines around his eyes moving, the top of his face shadowed and the lower highlighted by the light he held, still focused at Thorne Barrington.

"Was it because of Jenny?" Kate asked. Her voice was very low, but she was close to him now. So close. "Was Jenny the girl Hall Draper got pregnant?"

"Jenny?" Thorne said, his voice coming from behind her. She didn't turn at his comment, still watching Kahler, still waiting for a chance. And then Barrington said, not a question this time, but a realization. "Jenny Carpenter. My God, Jenny Carpenter." There were so many emotions trapped in the soft shock. Recognition. Remembrance. Regret?

"I'm surprised you even remember her," Kahler said. "She

was just a nobody. One of the hundreds of nobodies you dealt with through the years.''

"I never thought she was nobody," Thorne said.

"A cheap hooker. An addict. Of course you did. Did you even care what happened to her? Did you even know?"

"I knew."

"What happened?" Kate asked. She could not prevent the question. *The public's right to know* brushed through her consciousness, but *she* needed to know. *She* needed to understand what had set all this off.

"He put her in a cell, and she hanged herself."

The words were brutal, as cold and as horrible as the imagery they evoked.

"To him, she was scum," Kahler went on. "So he put her away, locked her up. Just to get her off the streets of the city his family practically owned. It didn't matter that someone had loved her. That she had once been someone's child, someone's—"

The sentence was broken, the pain it had revealed silenced, but in the darkness, Kate spoke the words he had left unspoken.

"Someone's sister," she finished for him, her voice almost as agonized as his.

"The bastards destroyed her. They *all* destroyed her."

"All those people had something to do with Jenny?" she asked. This was the heart of the mystery, the soul of the evil he'd perpetrated. A girl too young to die. A child in a black-and-white photograph. Innocent.

"They brought her to that cell. They all played a part in her destruction, so I found them. I hunted them down. All the steps on her journey to that place. It took me years, but I didn't care. I needed to understand what had happened. They all were guilty. They all killed Jenny."

"So you killed them," she said softly.

"Do you pity them, Kate? They used her. They corrupted her. From Hall Draper's teenage rutting to that bastard's sanctimonious judicial murder, they all were to blame for her death. First they taught her to use her body, a way to earn

affection. That was one of my mother's many boyfriends."
The word was bitter, still hating, still vindictive. "Jenny's father had deserted her. She just wanted someone to love her.
That's all she wanted, and he used that need. They all used
her."

"How did you find them?" she asked, so close to him now
she could have reached out and put her hand on the gun. *Just
keep him talking,* she thought. *Try to think of something to do.*

"The diaries," he said, a thread of amusement, gentle with
memory, in his tone. "She'd kept them. I had given her the
first one. She was maybe six or seven. A birthday present, one
of those little plastic things girls used to buy at the five-and-
dime. Hers were always pink. Even the last one was pink."

Kate could hear the memories in his voice. It had changed,
the accent of his youth stronger now. He was lost in the past,
a time when he had been the whole world to a little girl. When
he had bought her a birthday present, a simple thing she had
cherished, maybe because she had so little else.

"When she was dead, they sent all those diaries to my
mother. I found them when she died. Those pitiful childish
books were what Jenny had kept through the years, and everything I needed to know was there. The boyfriend. Draper.
The college boy who gave her her first hit. The people who
pushed her down when she tried to straighten out her life.
People who fired her from jobs, put her back on the streets
because she wasn't strong enough to leave the stuff alone. She
wasn't strong like you, Kate, but she didn't give up. She didn't
stop trying to make something of her life, trying to straighten
herself out…"

His voice stopped, controlling emotion that had crept in.
Not regret. Not even love, Kate thought. Hate? The need for
revenge had occupied Byron Kahler for so many years, long,
patient years of seeking those he believed had led Jenny to a
cell, to a cold and lonely dying. She was sorry for the lost
child Jenny Carpenter had been, but surely that was not reason
enough…

"He has to pay for his part, and then, finally, it's over,"
Kahler finished.

Did he really believe that? Was he so twisted by hate and his need for revenge that he thought this insanity made sense?

"And me, Kahler? What about me?" she whispered the unwanted thought aloud. She hadn't been mistaken about what he felt for her. She knew that he cared. Even as she was falling in love with Thorne Barrington, she had known that Kahler loved her. She had been sorry it was not a feeling she could ever return, that he was not the man she loved, but now she understood why.

"You were so strong. I admired that. Jenny was..."

Kate watched him swallow emotion, the movement of the muscles in his throat visible even in the shadowed darkness.

"You were so different. So determined to find the answer. I tried to keep you safe, Kate. I tried to warn you."

"That's what the confetti was—a warning?" she asked. "And then you sent me after Mays to take me away from the connection between Draper and Jenny."

"I didn't want you to be the one to figure it out. After I met you... I just wanted it to be over. I couldn't stop. Not until it was done. Until the debt was paid. You understand that. But when I met you, I wanted it to be over."

"That's why the timetable changed. Because of me?" she whispered. Hall Draper had died three months early because of her. Because of Kahler's growing feelings for her. *Just get it done.* The need to make everybody dead, so he had broken his own rigid schedule. He had gone against the pattern.

"I deserved something," Kahler said. "After all this time. Something for me. Was I wrong to want that, Kate? To want you?"

His gaze shifted for the first time from its competent, professional focus on Barrington. It moved to search her face. *Seeking acceptance of what he had done?* she wondered briefly before she realized he had given her the opening she needed.

She threw herself at the hand holding the revolver, hoping that if nothing else she might disrupt his aim enough to give Thorne a chance to run, to disappear into the darkness of the narrow hall behind him—if he were still capable of running.

Instead of the gun, it was the flashlight that fell. It bounced across the bare wooden boards of the hallway, and then began to roll, its light spiraling in revolving patterns along the wall.

Kahler grabbed her around the waist with the arm that had been occupied with holding the light. In the sudden darkness of the hall she could hear Thorne running. *Toward* them, she had time to realize. Toward them and not away as she had intended. He was reacting to the chance she had tried to give him by charging Kahler, again trying to protect her. Not trying to avoid Kahler's gun or the bullet, a bullet fired by a professional—calmly, coolly and accurately. Even in the darkness, the hallway was so narrow there was little chance Kahler would miss such a big target.

And of course, he hadn't. She knew that from the noise Thorne's body made as it fell against the wall and then heavily onto the wooden floor. With the realization that Barrington had been shot, she began to struggle again, fighting against Kahler's hold, writhing fiercely to free herself. Kahler took a step backwards, trying to control her, but she twisted her body from side to side, hating him. Needing to get to Thorne. A primitive urge to protect. She wasn't intellectually aware of all that was fueling her desperation to get away from the arms that held her. Arms that she didn't want around her. Arms she had never wanted there.

"Stop it, Kate," Kahler ordered, but it had no effect on the frenzy that possessed her. She dug her heels in, pushing backwards, turning and twisting in his hold. He moved again, dragging her arching body with him, fighting to control her. "It's all right," he said. "It's all over."

Insane, she thought. *He really is insane. Beneath all that cold control is only madness.*

The sound was subliminal. Like the crystal teardrops. Something she had heard before. Somewhere. Sometime. But she couldn't place it.

Not Barrington, she had time to realize with despair as the shadow launched itself out of the darkness at their struggling bodies, clearly outlined against the night sky behind them. The retriever hit with all the momentum of his sixty-five pounds.

Big enough and strong enough to push them through the doorway and out onto the top of the wooden stairs.

She was aware that Kahler's arm released her as they fell backward, the three of them falling together, her body sandwiched between the man and the muscled, silken frame of the dog.

The sound of splintering wood seemed to register on her consciousness simultaneously with the force of Kahler's palm against her back. He shoved hard, throwing her body toward the doorway, back toward the hallway where Thorne Barrington lay, and away from the rotten banister.

Unbalanced, hampered by the frightened dog who was struggling to find his own footing, Kate fell—forward and not back—to lie stunned over the threshold of the doorway. Kahler made no sound as he continued to fall, the impact of their bodies having shattered the railing behind him. But the noise as he struck the tiled roof of the portico three stories below was like nothing she had ever heard—dull and leaden and somehow, she knew, very final.

Kate lay a moment where she had fallen, her mind struggling to accept the fact she was still alive. The retriever had made it to his feet, apparently unhurt. He stood beside her now, whining, his cold nose examining her out-flung arm before he turned to disappear into the darkness of the hallway from which he had appeared like a miracle. Elliot's watchdog.

Charlie's bark, sharp and loud, came from the darkness down the hall. He was trying to arouse his master. Kate got to her knees, and then, using the frame of the doorway she had been thrown into, finally to her feet. She staggered, knees shaking, toward the light of Kahler's flashlight. It had all happened so quickly that the big, black handle was still rolling, moving slightly back and forth in an ever-decreasing arc, over the smooth wooden floor.

She picked it up and, more in control now, she ran down the hall toward Thorne's sprawled body. She pushed the dog out of her way and knelt beside the man. She put her hand against the side of his neck and felt the reassuring pulse of blood through the carotid artery. *Alive. Thank God, he was still alive.*

The bullet had struck his temple, and the wound was bleeding. Like all head wounds, it was bleeding a lot. There was a frighteningly large pool of blood already under his head, and she knew that she had to get help. Call 911. Call somebody. Find a phone. She stood up, and the dog looked up at her, trusting eyes following her movements.

"Stay with him," she said. "I'll be right back. I have to get help." He whined and then barked once, the noise echoing loudly in the narrow passage. "It's okay," she said, touching the retriever's head. "Everything's all right. He'll be all right."

She was reassuring a dog, she realized, when she should be getting help. Shock? Was that what was wrong with her? Was that why she was still standing here in the ruined house, trembling, fighting sobs that were pushing upward from her chest. What the hell was wrong with her?

"Stay with him," she whispered the command past the knot in her throat, and then she ran into the darkness to find someone who would help.

Chapter Fourteen

The media circus of the next four weeks was far worse than Kate could ever have imagined, and this time, of course she was in the center ring. The local news crews had arrived almost as soon as the police that night, camera lights providing graphic illumination for the work of the paramedics.

She had said too much in her panicked call for help. She should never had mentioned the Tripper bombings, never have said Thorne Barrington's name, too well-known to go unnoticed by those who avidly listened to the scanners. *The public's right to know,* she had to remind herself, but the phrase echoed in her heart with bitterness now.

News of Jack the Tripper's death had spread like the proverbial wildfire, attracting national attention. Of course, it had been a national story all along. Kahler's victims had been scattered across the country, connected only by the thread of the drifting, aimless life of a young prostitute, a life which had ended one night, virtually unnoticed, in a Georgia jail cell.

What had Jenny Carpenter been doing in Atlanta? Kate often wondered. Had she come here to find her brother? Had Kahler known she was in his city? Was that what had precipitated Jenny's tragic suicide—the fear that Kahler might find out what she'd become? Or the fear that she might embarrass the brother who, despite incredible odds, seemed to have transcended their tragic, broken beginnings?

The authorities were still studying the diaries they had found during their search of Kahler's apartment, but they had discovered no bomb-making paraphernalia there. The speculation was that the bombs had been put together elsewhere, somewhere safe and private—a small, lock-it-and-take-the-key storage building maybe, the necessary equipment concealed in strongboxes. All Kahler would need would be a folding table and chair, easily stored in the same building, maybe in another city, hundreds of miles away from the public life Detective Byron Kahler had lived.

Despite the publicity, no one had come forward claiming to have knowledge about such a rental. Just as no one had ever claimed to have seen him mail the packages through the years. He had been too smart for that. None of those accidental sightings, no bystander's intuition, would have brought Kahler down.

After Kate had told her story—at least half a dozen times, it seemed to her—the police had asked her to read through Lew's neatly labeled folder containing the material the paper had collected on Byron Kahler. They wanted to know what Garrison had found that had gotten him killed. Despite her feelings about all that had happened, Kate was surprised to find that she, too, still needed an answer to that question.

What she found in the folder wasn't even an interview, not like the other "hunter" files she had read the night she'd received the envelope. Kahler's file contained only two sheets of paper. One of them was a polite letter from the public information officer of the Atlanta PD, which explained that, due to the press of official business, Detective Kahler was forced to deny the request for an interview at this time.

But the helpful officer had supplied what small bit of information she could—something she obviously had not cleared with Kahler. She had sent the newspaper a photocopy of Kahler's employment application. Despite the detective's refusal to do an interview, the department had attempted to cooperate with Lew's request, to provide some background on the person who was carrying out the official investigation of the Atlanta bombing. Knowing Kahler, Kate suspected that this single sheet of paper was all the personal information the department had.

Kate scanned the lines of the form that had been neatly filled in more than fourteen years before, the ink faded, but Kahler's printing almost as meticulous as Lew's. Her eyes moved down the page to next of kin, and what she found was a little surprising. No name had been entered in the space.

She almost turned the form over without reading anything else on the front, but somehow a word caught her eye. Pennsylvania. It had almost jumped off the page at her, and then she looked at the town printed before it in Kahler's distinctive hand. Falls Bend. Place of birth. Falls Bend, Pennsylvania.

She knew immediately where she'd heard that name—during Jackie Draper's whispered narrative, but she also knew she had never transcribed her notes from that interview. She hadn't had time. Too much had happened and that task had been forgotten. So how would Lew have made the connection?

The cop to whom Kate made her request looked skeptical, but eventually he brought what she had asked for. She was right. None of the news releases in the file on Hall Draper mentioned his birthplace. Community activities in Tucson. Boy Scouts. Little League. Church. Nothing about his childhood, about where he had grown up, the tiny coal-mining community where he had known a girl named Jenny Carpenter, but probably, Kate realized, given the difference in their ages, not her older brother.

Hall Draper's death would have posed the greatest risk for Kahler, of course. There was always the possibility, however remote, that someone might make that connection. In remaining as reticent about his background as he had always been, Kahler had, before he'd ever embarked on his quest for revenge, unwittingly done everything that could be done to prevent any link to that past. And he had saved for last the two people who were connected to Falls Bend. One had been the old man in Austin, who, given his age, must have been his mother's boyfriend that Kahler had told her about, the one who had taught Jenny the dark lessons that had haunted her life. He might have had only a tenuous link to the town, a transient in all probability.

And the last victim, the strongest link to Kahler's past,

would have been Hall Draper. Lew couldn't have known the name of the town where both Kahler and Draper had been born, she finally concluded. The name wasn't anywhere in the Draper file. Only in her notes. Had Lew put it together on the very remote link provided by the state of Pennsylvania?

Maybe important. Maybe nothing. Lew wasn't stupid. He would never have let it slip to Kahler if he'd discovered he and Draper were from the same town, but maybe, just maybe, he'd mentioned Falls Bend, or mentioned that he'd been given Kahler's application form.

Maybe Kahler had heard something in Lew's voice. Maybe the thought that Kahler and Draper might have known each other had struck Lew in the middle of that conversation. He certainly had had access to the information that they had been born in the same state. She herself had told him about Draper. Would that have been enough to make an old journalist like Lew Garrison suspicious? Maybe, she thought. Maybe just enough.

No one would ever know exactly what had happened, but Lew had said or done something that had made Kahler afraid it was about to come unraveled. Maybe Kahler had realized if Lew had the application form, and if he were curious enough to check on the name of the town where Draper had been born, it was all over.

Then, after he had killed Lew, he had come to Kate's apartment to wait for her because, she had finally realized, he had to find out if Garrison had told her what he had discovered. While he was there, she had played Lew's message in his hearing—and in doing so, she had saved her own life.

Finally, only Thorne Barrington stood in the way of having it finished. *I wanted it to be over,* Kahler had told her. Because he had loved her. In his twisted, insane way he had paid that debt, too, when he had pushed her away from the splintering railing. There was no doubt in Kate's mind that had been deliberate, the last act of the man who had been Byron Kahler. And Jack the Tripper. In his insanity, he had collected Jenny's debt, but he had also paid his own. He had given Kate her life.

Experts all over the country were explaining what had made Byron Kahler tick, examining every detail of the painful past he had seemingly escaped, laying out all its dirty secrets for public scrutiny. All the things Kahler had hidden through the years—the grinding poverty, his stepfather's abuse, his mother's addictions—were now the property of a detail-hungry media.

The public's right to know.

Kate realized she had again been sitting, simply staring at her computer screen. Despite the managing editor's repeated requests that she write the conclusion for her series, she was probably the only journalist in the country who had not written one word on the death of Jack the Tripper. Interest would eventually have to fade, she thought, and maybe she wouldn't be forced to write the ending of the story she had lived. She had found that she had nothing to say about Kahler, nothing that could satisfactorily explain what had happened to the man who had at one time, she truly believed, been a good cop.

She took a deep breath and expelled it loudly enough to cause a couple of heads to turn, a couple of quick glances in her direction. No one asked what was wrong, probably because they already knew. It seemed that everything about her life was now public knowledge. There had been heated speculation—more than speculation in the tabloids—about the relationship between Kate August and the two men at the center of the Tripper bombings.

She had to admit that all the elements were there for a great story, begging to be sensationalized: the reclusive millionaire, the poor-boy-made-good cop who had gone so desperately wrong, and the woman between them. "The Eternal Triangle" one tabloid headline screamed. The grain of truth, Kate supposed, hidden in the mass of chaff that had been written about the case, about Kahler's death, and about Judge Barrington's injury.

She had waited through the hours of surgery that night and had breathed a prayer of thanksgiving when she had been told that he'd survived the operation, but that his prognosis was guarded. Whatever the hell that meant. The police, who had waited patiently for her statement, would wait no longer, and when she had returned to the hospital, it was to find that the same impenetrable security that had been imposed at the time of the first bombing was again in place.

She had been denied admittance to Barrington's hospital room—she and every other reporter. Nothing she had said or done in the intervening weeks had made any difference to that wall of silence. For some reason Greg Sandifer blamed her for what had happened—or at least for the media attention. He had made that clear in the one conversation they'd had. Kate had gotten news about Thorne's condition just like the rest of the world, through carefully phrased statements given by the hospital spokesman, always to the effect that "the judge was progressing as well as could be expected, given the seriousness of his injury."

There was no one living at the mansion, she knew. The gate was locked, and no one had answered the bell on any of her visits. She had no idea what had happened to Elliot or to Charlie. Even the unlisted telephone number had been disconnected. Greg Sandifer, with the help of Barton Phillips and his firm, had succeeded in keeping the press at bay, but what they hadn't taken into account was that their efforts had simply made the media more rabid to find out exactly what they were trying to hide.

She hadn't talked to the press, and she didn't intend to. Not about her relationship to Thorne Barrington. What had been her relationship, she amended. That wasn't and never would be public property. In the statement the paper had released on her behalf, she had told the truth, that Barrington had been shot trying to disarm Kahler, trying to save her life. That had only added fuel to the frenzy, the press turning Barrington into some kind of romantic figure: heroic, tragically wounded, and inaccessible.

She thought about how much he would hate that image, and she smiled. But the inaccessible part was certainly accurate. She found herself wondering, as she had a thousand times, if that were his choice. Or if that decision had been made for him because he was no longer capable of making his own decisions.

She closed her eyes, fighting emotion, fighting fear. When she finally reopened them, she had again found control, a control she had demanded of herself through these long weeks. But she might as well admit that she was wasting her time here. She wasn't working, and she didn't see much point in pretending.

She opened her bottom drawer, took out the black leather purse, and, offering no explanations, walked out of the newsroom. Maybe another day she could do this—satisfy the public's right to know. Maybe some day, but not today.

SHE HAD SPENT a long time soaking in water into which she'd thrown a handful of Shalimar-scented bath crystals, leaving behind in the small bathroom a cloud of fragrant steam when she'd finished. She put on shorts and a tank top and walked barefoot into the kitchen to try to think about something for dinner.

Eating had moved very low on her list of priorities, and it was beginning to show. She had probably lost six or seven pounds, and she was disgusted. Being too upset to eat was about as neurotic as you could get, and she was determined to put an end to that ridiculous behavior. It was time to get on with her life. Especially since she had been left no other choice.

She opened the refrigerator, automatically inventorying its contents. Eggs. A container of milk she wasn't real sure about. A small, hardening block of cheese. Some assorted condiments and a jar of pickles. An omelet or a cheese sandwich? she debated, fighting the urge to close the door and forget it.

The sound of the doorbell shouldn't have been unexpected. It had certainly happened often enough before. The police had put someone outside her complex for a few days after Kahler's death to keep the media in control. When the paper had released her statement, the press had been told that was all she intended to say. After that, the number of reporters awaiting her departures and arrivals had eventually begun to dwindle, but despite the passage of time they hadn't entirely given up. Even tonight she had walked by a couple, ignoring their questions and the microphone thrust at her face.

She knew she should just ignore the bell, too, but when it rang again, she felt her frustration boil over. *Damn it, weren't they ever going to let it go?* The flare of adrenaline sent her storming across the dark living room to slip the chain off and throw open the door.

"Look," she began, "I've told you guys—"

The man standing outside her door was literally the last person she expected to see there, his presence here a scenario she had never imagined in any of her fantasies.

"Hello, Kate," Thorne Barrington said.

Her heart jolted painfully, and she had to think about taking the next breath, the action no longer involuntary. Her eyes examined every detail of his appearance: dark glasses, a navy polo and worn jeans, the raven's-wing blackness of his hair, worn much shorter than she had ever seen it, short enough that it didn't quite hide the reddened line over his temple. The newer scar obscured the small white one she had noticed there before.

"What are you doing here?" she said. It wasn't what she wanted to say, but it was the logical question. *What are you doing showing up on my doorstep after putting me through absolute hell?*

"I thought we needed to talk."

"Talk?" she repeated carefully.

"Do you think I could come in? There are a couple of reporters outside, and I don't imagine it would do either of us any good if—"

"Okay," she interrupted, knowing he was right. The bidding would be sky-high for any picture of the two of them together.

When he was inside, she closed the door and led the way across the room to the facing sofa and love seat. She was aware that he took a look around the dark apartment before he sat down. She wondered with a touch of amusement if he were comparing her place to his. She sat down opposite him, the coffee table and the expanse of her small Oriental rug between them.

Neither of them said anything for a moment, the atmosphere growing uncomfortable. Whatever connection had existed between them had obviously disappeared. She found herself wishing he'd take off the glasses, so at least she could see his eyes. And then she remembered why he couldn't.

"Do you want me to cut off the kitchen light?" she asked.

He glanced toward the lighted kitchen and then back to her, shaking his head.

"It's all right," he said, dismissing her concern.

She didn't have the right to ask any of the questions she wanted to ask, and apparently he wasn't ready to reveal whatever it was that he had come here to talk about. The hope that he wanted to do more than talk was beginning to fade in the strain.

"Are you okay?" she asked. For an encore, she mocked herself mentally, she could ask him about the weather.

He looked up from the contemplation of his hands, the dark lenses a barrier to whatever he was thinking.

"I'm fine. Even Greg turned me loose."

She nodded again.

"I found out some things that I think you ought to know. About Kahler," he added. "And Jenny."

She wasn't sure she wanted to know any more. What she already knew had circled endlessly through her head night after night. Especially Hall Draper's death.

If Kahler hadn't fallen in love with her, if she had let him know at once that it wasn't going to happen for them, would Draper be alive today? Would someone have caught the Tripper before it was time for him to hit again? Was there any way she could have known how screwed up Kahler was? She was a reporter. Where were her instincts? She had always been so sure—

"He came to see her," Barrington said, breaking into the questions that had tormented her since the night he'd been shot.

"What?"

"Jenny. That night. Before she hanged herself. Kahler came to the jail. He signed the visitor's log."

"But he said…" She hesitated, trying to think exactly what he *had* said. He had given the impression that he hadn't known about Jenny's death until he'd found the diaries. And instead… She wasn't sure exactly what the instead was. "What does that mean? That he got the diaries then?"

"No. That part was apparently true. They *were* sent to his mother. Jenny's mother. Maybe he did find them later."

"But he knew about Jenny's death."

"He must have. It happened between the time he left and the next cell check. Since he was the last visitor, he would have been questioned."

"He came to visit her and when he left, she hanged herself?"

"Within minutes of his departure."

"But why? Why would she…"

Thorne didn't answer. The dark lenses were again focused downward toward his hands.

"What in the world could he have said to her?" Kate asked. The question was very soft, rhetorical, because she knew they would never know the answer.

"Whatever it was," Thorne said, "it was something she couldn't live with."

"*He* caused her death. Whatever he said that night. And he *knew* that. All those years, he knew it."

"But he couldn't accept that guilt."

"So eventually he decided that other people had to be to blame. You and all the others. He set out to get revenge for something *he* had done. God, he really *was* crazy," she said. "So damn crazy. She killed herself because of whatever he said to her that night, but he couldn't admit it. So everyone else had to be made to pay for Jenny's death."

He nodded.

"Does knowing that make it any easier?" she asked, remembering what he'd told her.

When he looked up, she realized he hadn't understood.

"To know that you had done nothing to deserve what he did to you? Is it any easier to know that?"

"I put her in that cell, Kate. Just like he said."

"That was your job. You were supposed to do that."

"Maybe. But maybe there might have been something…" He shook his head, the movement small and contained. Again he let the silence stretch before he broke it. "It was a sweep. Teenage hookers. Most of them runaways. Jenny Carpenter was picked up with the rest. She looked about sixteen, but she wasn't, of course, and she had a previous conviction. For possession." He took a breath, deep enough that the movement was visible in the dimness. "So instead of sending another kid home to her family, I sent her to jail. I knew she wouldn't be able to make bail…"

His words faded again and the silence was back. A different silence now. Full of cold and darkness, the lonely silence of a cell. The silence that must have remained after the words of her brother had stopped echoing through the darkness.

"There was something about her…" Thorne said softly. "Something in her eyes. Lost. Alone. She was the most alone person I'd ever met."

"It wasn't your fault," Kate whispered.

"You asked me once if there was anything about my life that I regretted."

Like Hall Draper, and like Kahler, Thorne, too, had been haunted by Jenny Carpenter.

"It wasn't your fault," she said again.

"But he was right. We all played a part. He was right at least about that."

"No," she denied. "Not even about that."

His mouth moved, the muscles tightening briefly, and then he nodded. "Thank you," he said.

She was aware that the ghost of the dark-haired child who had been Jenny Carpenter had not been laid to rest, but she didn't know what else to tell him.

They were quiet again for a long time until finally he said, "I kept thinking that you might…"

He let the sentence fade, and he looked back down at his

hands. He held them both palm upward in his lap, the right
one on top. She knew that mutilated hand would always be a
reminder of how one man's insanity had forever changed his
life.

"That I might what?"

"I thought you might come to the hospital," he said. He
was looking at her now, but she couldn't read his expression
because of the glasses.

"I *came* to the hospital," she said. "How the hell can you
think I wouldn't come? They wouldn't let me in. Your friend
Sandifer. All of them."

"I never knew you'd come, Kate."

"I was just another blood-sucking vampire of a reporter.
They made it pretty obvious I wasn't welcome, so eventually
I quit beating my head against that brick wall."

"I'm sorry," he said.

"Yeah. Me, too. It would have been nice to know whether
you were..." She stopped because she couldn't say out loud
the horrors she had imagined, all the things she had known
could result from a head injury. "Whether you were all right."

"I'm all right."

"Okay," she said.

Why was this so hard? The last thing she remembered saying to Thorne Barrington was to beg him to make love to her,
and now they couldn't even carry on a conversation.

"I guess I'd better go," he said finally. "I just wanted to
tell you about Jenny. I thought it might make you feel better
about Kahler's death."

He stood up, and she was aware again of how big he was.
She stood also and followed him to the door. He had simply
come to tell her about Jenny. It seemed there was nothing left
of whatever had been between them before. Violence and
death were barriers too hard to overcome, and all those deaths,
especially Jenny's, and even Byron Kahler's, lay between
them now.

They stood together by the door, as awkward as she and
Kahler had once been. She didn't want to open it. Despite the

strain, despite the awkwardness that seemed to be all that was left, she was reluctant to let him leave.

"Thanks for coming," she said.

"What are you crying for?" He raised his hand and brushed the tear off her cheek with the pad of his thumb. "There's nothing to cry about."

She hadn't even realized she'd been crying. Embarrassed, she rubbed at the place he'd touched with her fingertips.

"Why the hell didn't you call me? You could have let me know you were okay."

That had slipped out, just like the tears, past her control. She hated crying women. About as much as she figured he'd hate a nagging one. He had given her no right to question what he did. They had made no commitment. Except it had felt as if they had. A whole lot of commitment.

"For a while..." He began and then he hesitated. "I wasn't in any condition to make my own decisions. I didn't understand why you weren't there. I knew I wanted you there."

"I tried," she said.

He smiled at her tone. "Greg probably did what he thought was best. He read your press release. Maybe he thought..." Again he hesitated.

"That I shouldn't have told them anything? That I had only made it worse?"

"Maybe."

She shook her head, knowing that wasn't true. The security Sandifer had imposed around Thorne Barrington had ensured that the press would come after her. Her statement had been necessary, and she knew it. He should have known it. That was the way things were done.

"The fact that none of you guys would talk to them made it worse. I was the only one left. They would never have given up without something."

"I'm sorry you had to go through that," he said.

"And later? You could have called me later."

Why didn't she just tell him everything? she thought in disgust. Go ahead and confess the sleepless nights she'd spent worrying about him, her inability to work, the tears. Lay it all out there for him to smile at the next time he thought about her and her stupid obsession.

"There were some things I was learning to deal with," he said.

"What kind of things?" she asked, a small flutter of fear in her stomach.

"I haven't had another migraine. Not since that night."

She waited a moment, trying to think what that meant, what his tone meant. "And that's bad?" she asked, shaking her head. "You sound like that's bad."

He smiled at her, and his hand lifted to brush away another tear. "It probably means that they were right, that the headaches were..." He stopped and she could hear the breath he drew.

"Emotional," she said, finally understanding what he was thinking.

He nodded again.

"Do you think I care?" she asked. "Even if that were true, do you think I would care?"

"I think *I* would."

"Okay," she said. "*You* care. I don't. I'm glad they're gone."

He didn't say anything, and she reached up to put her fingers against the slash of the scar. He didn't avoid her touch.

"Maybe this had something to do with the headaches going away. Maybe it...rearranged whatever had been damaged before."

He laughed, and she smiled at the sound.

"It's a reasonable explanation to me," she said. "Are you telling me no one else thinks so?"

"Greg said it's possible."

"But you decided not to believe him because..."

He shook his head, the glasses again a barrier to reading his eyes. It didn't matter because she knew, of course, what he was thinking. He had already told her—that even the possibility that the bombing had affected him psychologically somehow made him something less than he had thought he was.

She *knew* the kind of person he was—the kind who would run toward a madman pointing a gun at him because she was in danger. And she didn't understand why the other would even matter.

"Is this some macho kind of crap?" she asked. "You get a bomb that blows off half your hand and damages your eyes and cracks your skull, and you think it's *not* supposed to make any kind of impact on your life?"

"Kate," he said.

"Is that what you think? You been reading your own press? You think you're a hero, Barrington? Is that what this is? You think you're different from the rest of us?"

"I don't think that—"

"That bastard put a little confetti in my bed, and I didn't sleep for a week. Does that make me a coward?"

"Of course not, but—"

"I think you're bright enough to figure this out. You're supposed to be so damn brilliant. Figure it out," she ordered.

"Kate."

"Don't 'Kate' me. Don't talk to me like I'm some kind of hysterical child. You don't have migraines anymore, and we should be celebrating, and instead we're standing here yelling at each other."

"I'm not yelling," he said.

"You go to hell, Thorne Barrington. You go back to that damn mausoleum where you holed up for three years and you hide in the dark. I don't give a damn if you do. If you think I give a damn, then you can just..."

"I wasn't hiding," he said.

"Yeah?" she said, derisively. "Except you can't have it both ways. And I don't care if you were. It doesn't matter. Why don't you understand that? I'm no bargain, Barrington. I'll probably not ever be able to hear a backfire without being scared spitless. Some nights I sleep with the lights on. Does that mean you don't want to sleep with me?"

"No," he said.

The single syllable took her breath. She didn't know how

his voice could be so different, but whatever had been there the night Kahler had interrupted them was back.

"It doesn't?" she asked, her mouth suddenly dry.

"No."

"Then I guess that means you do."

"I told you a long time ago I want to make love to you." She nodded.

"Nothing's changed about the way I feel."

She nodded again. And then she said it out loud. "Nothing's changed about how I feel about you either."

She didn't make a conscious decision to step into his arms, but they closed around her when she did. Closed and held her tightly enough to put to rest any doubts she might have had about whether he wanted her there. It felt so good being held. So good to be safe. She hadn't known until she was here that this was the only thing that would truly ever make her feel safe again—being held in Thorne Barrington's arms.

SHE WISHED she had cut the lights off in her bedroom. It was so bright, stark as daylight—not like the welcoming, moon-touched darkness of his that night. It hadn't been difficult then to undress, to expose her body for him. He had asked her and she had wanted to.

She stopped at the foot of the bed and turned around to find him still standing in the doorway, leaning against the frame. As she watched, he reached up and removed the dark glasses. He folded them and held them in his hand. His eyes were as dark as she had remembered. His gaze intense. Waiting. Too polite maybe to make the first move. She smiled at that thought.

His head tilted, questioning the smile.

"If the headaches are gone, why did you wear those?" she asked.

"Hiding from the guys outside, I guess."

She nodded. "It must have worked."

"And maybe because I'm not convinced the other is over."

"Maybe we ought to cut off the lights," she suggested.

He didn't say anything for a moment. "I'd rather leave them on," he said finally. "If you don't mind, of course."

"It's a little scary making love for the first time with the lights on," she admitted.

"I've been in the dark a long time, Kate."

A long time since he'd made love to anyone? she wondered. He had implied that before.

"And I'm…a little beat up," he added. "A few nicks and craters."

She smiled at him. "That's okay. I've got a few nicks of my own. Not bomb scars, of course. Life scars, I guess."

"I'd be more than willing to kiss them and make them better," he said softly. Whether it was the depth of his voice or the accent, she didn't know, but that didn't sound nearly as dumb as it should have. It sounded…interesting. Romantic. Old-fashioned and so damned romantic. Just like Barrington.

"I think I'd like that," she invited.

So he straightened and stepped into her room.

Epilogue

It was dark now. Some time during the long night through which he'd made love to her, Thorne had cut off the low lamp beside the bed. She had a memory of his long arm reaching upward, plunging the room into sudden darkness. And that wasn't, of course, the only memory she had.

She knew him intimately now. How his hands felt, both of them, tantalizing against her body, examining contours that had never to her seemed worthy of such a prolonged exploration. She knew his mouth and his tongue, trailing moisture over her shivering skin, caressing every guarded, secret place from which he could coax sensation. She knew the texture of his skin, even the scars he had warned her about, old and fading into paleness against his darkness or hidden by the thick hair on his chest.

She had wondered that night how his body would feel against hers, dark, hair-roughened skin moving over the wanting smoothness of her breasts, her nipples hardening under the gliding touch of his. She *had* wondered, but now she knew.

She knew so much about him. His strength. And his gentleness. His patience, she remembered with wonder. Infinitely patient. Taking an eternity over everything. Never hurrying. Learning the subtle differences in her needs, her responses. Enjoying her. She had known that because he had *wanted* her to know it.

He had taken pains to let her know that he delighted in every trembling breath he forced her to take, every uncontrolled movement, every sigh, every gasping word she whispered against his throat or his shoulder as he had moved above her. Patient. Endlessly patient with her pleasure.

There was definitely something to be said for making love with a Southern gentleman. The old regional analogies stole into her consciousness. Slow as molasses, hot as a summer's day, and as enduring as the land. Thorne Barrington was every bit as good as he was cracked up to be, she thought, her lips lifting into a small smile against the smooth, brown skin of his shoulder.

One long leg lay sprawled across one of hers. She bent the knee of her other leg to run the arch of her foot up his calf, the hair coarse and pleasant under her instep, the muscle firm. He shifted, his body moving over hers as it had so many times last night.

She felt the rush of moisture, anticipating his entry, wanting the now familiar invasion. He slipped his palms under her thighs, lifting, positioning her, and more than willing to obey, she wrapped her legs around his narrow hips, and felt him push into the slick, wet heat of her body.

She gasped, surprised as she had been before that her body could be so ready for him, so wanting, and yet he could fill her so strongly that it seemed he threatened the walls of her soul, the limits of what she was, of what she could ever be. Full and so deep. Entering and retreating, and then moving deeper still, past inhibitions and hesitations. Pushing toward the center of her desire that seemed to expand even as he moved within her. It had been this way from the beginning. As it had been with no one else. Ever.

She belonged to him. She had known it since she had seen the pictures. Obsessed with him. Obsessed now with this, with possessing him and being possessed.

His mouth was over hers, his tongue echoing the slow, deliberate movements of his body. Control. His was the control, and she was lost in it. He had given her permission to be lost in it. Making love to her. This was the reality of that oft-misused phrase—the reason it was new and different and so powerful. Thorne made love to her. And there were no demands except that she let him, that she accept what he wanted to give.

She could feel her body responding, lifting to meet his, to arch into the strength of each downward stroke, its power seeping into her body. Upward to make her heart pound and her breath a panting rhythm. Downward to tighten the muscles of her legs around his body, drawing him to her. Closer. Deeper. Always deeper and more powerful, moving within her. Forever. Endless. Until finally, after an eternity, she exploded, her frame rocking against him with the force of her release. She dug her nails into his back, unaware of what she was doing. On some level, she felt his skin moving against hers, wet and trembling, the heat of it burning against the sudden coldness of hers.

"Now," she said hoarsely. A request or permission. She didn't know, but she felt the response, hot and sudden within her arching body. She had wanted that. Together. Always together. As they were meant to be. As she had known from the first.

She lay exhausted in his arms. Somehow he had known that was important. To hold her. To keep her safe in the darkness. Once he had belonged to the darkness, and so long as she was with him there was nothing frightening about the night. Not any longer.

The sheets beneath her were damp and twisted. They should have been uncomfortable, but in the pleasant lethargy after his lovemaking, which left her body boneless and unmoving, there was only comfort and safety. Her breathing was beginning to even again, and her heart rate to slow.

He lifted away from her onto his elbows, dark eyes looking down at her face.

"I knew the first night you came to my house that I was going to make love to you," he said.

"Did you know it would be like this?" she asked.

"I knew I wanted it to be, but nothing has ever been like this."

"I thought—" she began and then realized that wasn't

something she should say to him, even after the intimacies they'd just shared.

"What did you think?" he asked when she didn't continue. He leaned down to brush his lips against her throat, his breath warm over the film of perspiration that had captured floating tendrils of her hair to curl against her neck.

"That you couldn't possibly live up to your reputation," she admitted, smiling again. She was glad he wasn't looking at her.

His mouth paused in its drifting caress, and after a long moment he lifted his head again. "What is that supposed to mean?" he asked.

"That the debutantes of Atlanta must have been feeling very deprived for the last few years, bless their little diamond-encrusted hearts."

"Debutantes?" The crease she had noticed before was between the dark brows.

"I had a picture of you—" she began, and then she realized for the first time what had become of that picture and all the others.

"How could you have a picture of me?"

"From the paper's files," she said, not really thinking about what he had asked. Thinking about Kahler, about Kahler's hands searching through her things, finding the folder with those pictures. Violated, she thought again. He had violated her privacy, and so he had known all along how she felt about Thorne Barrington.

"Kate?" Thorne asked.

"I had a collection of pictures. Pictures from before...before the bomb. He took them," she whispered, feeling sick despite the fact that Kahler was dead and Thorne was holding her.

"Took them?" he repeated, and then suddenly he understood. "*Kahler* took them?"

She nodded. "He must have taken them when he put the confetti—" *Into the bed they were sharing.*

"Don't," he whispered, and his arms tightened around her. "It's over. There's nothing to be afraid of."

He held her, and eventually there was a relaxation of the tension that had been in her body. And then he asked, his deep voice touched with the amusement she liked to hear there, more cherished perhaps because it was rare and often unexpected. "Tell me about the debutantes."

She laughed, remembering how many times she had looked at that picture. Envying those women because they knew him and she hadn't. "They were all looking at you," she said. She lifted her hand and ran her thumb along the line of his bottom lip. "Like they could eat you up with a spoon."

"And?" He caught her thumb in his mouth, holding it.

"That was all. Just looking at you. I used to look at that picture and wonder what you were really like."

"Now you know," he said. He had released her thumb, but he turned his head to press a kiss into her open palm.

"Not anything like I thought you'd be," she said. She put her hand over his cheek, the stubble rough against the smoothness of her skin.

"Disappointed?" he asked.

"No," she said. She moved her head against the damp sheets, side to side. "No," she said again, "I'm not disappointed."

"I just aim to please," he said softly. Another Southernism.

"Your aim's pretty good. Practice make you perfect?"

She regretted the question as soon as she asked it. She had no right. No rights at all where he was concerned. She had given herself to him freely, willingly, without any vows or commitments. That wasn't the way it was supposed to be, not the way she'd been raised, and now she knew why. It hurt too much to realize that he could go back to that life tomorrow. There was no reason now for him *not* to go back, she realized. Back to what he had been before.

He didn't say anything. There was a code about that, too. Gentlemen never discussed their conquests, no matter how numerous they were.

Deliberately she moved her gaze away from his. She focused on his mouth, as sensuous, she now knew, as it looked.

"Kate," he said, and she forced her eyes up.

"It's okay," she said. "I always knew that—"

"I love you. Don't you know that?"

She couldn't think of a single teasing answer. Men said that all the time. It didn't mean anything anymore. Just something they said. But still she took a breath, so hard it was almost a sob.

"How could you not know I love you?" he asked.

"Because you never told me. And then these last weeks, I didn't hear from you. How was I supposed—"

"You just know," he said. "You have to know. I love you, Kate August. Maybe I'm not much of a bargain, but—"

"I guess you haven't been reading your press. Or checking your bank balance," she said, smiling at him, beginning to believe him, maybe because she wanted to believe so much. Or because she recognized the doubt in his voice. It was one of the things she'd liked about him from the first—that he really didn't seem to know how attractive he was.

He didn't say anything, and she wondered if she had gone too far. "I didn't mean that. I don't care about that."

"I know," he said.

They were quiet for a while until then he said, "Tell me about the pictures."

She laughed. "I'll bet that's a real ego trip. To know I obsessed about you. Drooled over your pictures."

"Considering what I *thought* you thought about me."

"Now you know better."

"What exactly do I know?" he asked, the dark eyes smiling at her.

"That I love you. That I've loved you for a very long time, even before I knew you. That's why I came to find you."

"Into the darkness," he said softly.

She put her mouth against his, which turned, fitting over hers. Meant to fit. It seemed she had always known that.

Bless their little deprived hearts, she thought again, and then she smiled.

Gayle Wilson also writes for Harlequin
Historicals! Turn the page for an exciting preview
of her December, 1997 Historical (#393)...and
then find it in your local bookstore next month!

Prologue

April 1815

The chestnut gelding, fresh and eager for the promised run, resented the sedate pace to which his rider was relentlessly holding him. That resentment had been subtly demonstrated to the man who competently, and without conscious thought, controlled the horse's brief rebellion.

It was not until Lieutenant Colonel Lord Nicholas Stanton finally sighted the slender figure moving through the dappling shade provided by the ancient oaks that he allowed his mount his head, and only until they had closed the distance. Horse and rider sedately followed the strolling girl, until, apparently hearing them behind her, she turned to look over her shoulder.

Her blue eyes, shaded by the wide brim of a style of straw bonnet that would certainly not be seen in the fashionable city from which the Duke of Vail's younger son had just returned, openly considered the rider a moment. Her gaze then returned to concentrate on the path she had been following along the edge of the shadowed country lane.

The horseman's well-shaped lips tilted upward. Nick Stanton was unaccustomed to being snubbed, especially by women. Indeed, the adulation of the marriageable ladies of the ton during his recent visit to London would have been enough to turn the head of many a man. Not only was he nobly born and extremely well-fixed, but an acknowledged military hero as well.

It didn't hurt his standing with the fairer sex that his profile had, on more than one occasion, been compared to Adonis. The calm dismissal in the eyes of the girl in the outmoded straw bonnet was certainly not the reception Lord Stanton had recently been accorded by the London ton.

Perhaps in response to that obvious disdain, Nick touched his heels to the chestnut and guided him alongside the strolling figure. Again, blue eyes rose to his, their gaze far too direct for fashionable flirtation.

"Good afternoon," Stanton said, holding his mount to the pace the girl had set. A finger of sun touched briefly on his hair, turning it gold. The fair hair was darkened now with perspiration and slightly curling. His uniform jacket set off broad shoulders and a narrow waist, the tight pantaloons emphasizing the muscled strength of his long legs.

At his greeting, the girl's eyes lifted again, slowly appraising both horse and rider. Her upturned face was classically heart-shaped, but her mouth was too wide for the current fashion, her nose straight rather than retroussé, and there was nothing the least bit simpering in her manner. Her assessment was unflinching.

The sprigged muslin she wore was at least two years old, its skirt rucked up in the country style to protect the fragile material from briars, revealing underneath a plain white petticoat. Over her arm she carried a wicker basket almost half-full of red currants.

"My lord," she said simply, and then the blue eyes returned to the lane before them.

Again, that upward tilt disturbed the line of the rider's mouth. The silence lasted for several moments as they moved side by side.

"Berrying?" he asked finally, a ridiculous question, given the evidence in the bottom of the basket.

The girl's mouth, more used to laughter than to primness, flickered dangerously, almost losing its determined sternness. "Indeed," she agreed.

Again silence descended, broken only by the plodding hooves of the gelding.

"May I give you a ride?" Lord Stanton offered, holding out his hand. His fingers were long and deeply tanned, despite the months he'd spent in England away from his regiment. That had not been his choice, but the ball he had taken at Toulouse had proved to be far more troublesome than anyone had suspected. There had been talk that he might lose the leg, but thankfully that danger was past. Despite a slight, persistent stiffness in his right knee, Nick considered himself in fighting trim and that had been the point of his recent trip to London—to convince his superiors at the Horse Guards.

"Thank you, but no, my lord. I'm sure you're far too busy with your own affairs to bother with mine."

"I promise I should be delighted to assist a lady."

The girl's eyes rose to linger a moment on the handsome face. "But surely you can see," she said, "that I'm not—"

"A lady?" he interrupted, his mouth controlled and his face a politely inquiring mask.

"In need of assistance," she finished without apparent rancor at his insult. From her sleeve she removed a scrap of lace with which she touched the dew of perspiration on her upper lip.

"Making jam?" Stanton asked pleasantly, his eyes following the dabbing of the cloth along the beautiful bow of her lip.

The girl glanced at him, her dark lashes sweeping upward to reveal some emotion dancing in the depths of her eyes.

"Pies, I believe," she answered.

"For your sweetheart?"

"I have no sweetheart, my lord."

"For a lass so beautiful, I find that difficult to believe. Are all the men here blind?"

"Perhaps. To my charms, at least. It seems there are always...other pleasures that distract them."

"Then they're fools," Nick said softly.

"So I've often thought," she agreed. Then her gaze deliberately shifted from its focus on the man who rode beside her to the lane ahead.

"Do you have a name?" Stanton asked.

"Of course, my lord."

This time Nick lost the battle to control his amusement, and the smile that had charmed the feminine half of the *beau monde* was unleashed in full force. Remarkably, it seemed to have no effect on the girl.

"Might I know it?" he urged.

"You might," she said calmly, removing from her basket a berry which had apparently proved unworthy for the proposed pies. "And then, you might not."

"Has no one told you not to be pert with your betters?" Nick asked, laughing.

"No one but you, my lord. But I'm sure that was simply an oversight. My name is Mary Winters."

"Do you live here in the village, Mary?"

"With my father in the vicarage, my lord."

"The proverbial vicar's daughter?"

"Indeed, my lord."

"And have you finished gathering your berries, Mary Winters?"

"Oh, no, my lord. The very best spot, you see, is just through here."

As she spoke, the girl stepped off the apron of the road and, pulling aside a limb that had blocked a small footpath, she disappeared into the shadowed undergrowth.

Horse and rider were left alone in the sudden quietness of the lane. Stanton dismounted and, displacing the same branch, he led the gelding into the clearing into which the girl had vanished.

The man's gray eyes lifted to seek her. Surprisingly, she was standing on the gnarled trunk of an oak that had forked early in its existence. The basket rested on the grass. She had removed the straw hat, releasing a cascade of dark brown curls that seemed to lure all the leaf-diffused light to glint in their richness. She watched as Nick Stanton crossed the clearing.

"You appear to be limping, my lord," she said.

"I've just spent three days successfully *not* limping," he answered, smiling, "so I should think you might try to be less critical."

"A war wound, I suppose."

"An honorable one, I assure you. Taken in the front."

The girl's mouth quivered, almost a smile.

"And heroic, no doubt?" she asked tauntingly.

Smiling, Nick shook his head in denial, but his steps didn't falter. Inexorably, he continued his approach to the oak.

"And foolhardy? Incredibly brave?" she suggested.

"A matter of opinion, I should imagine," he said dismissively.

He stood now directly below her, his height enough that their eyes were almost on a level. Blue met gray and held a moment, and then she touched him. She had turned her hand so that her knuckles trailed against the golden hair at his temple. He put his left hand up to catch her fingers, bringing them to his lips.

His mouth drifted slowly over the slender fingers, stained at the tips with the juice of the berries she'd gathered. Nick released the hand he'd captured and, putting his on either side of her slim waist, he lifted her from her perch into his arms. There was no resistance. She melted against his body, arms clinging around his neck, her mouth automatically opening and lowering to his. Familiar and practiced, his tongue slipped inside, as intimate as a lover's. And as welcome.

The kiss was long and unhurried. Despite the limp with which he'd crossed the expanse between them, Stanton held her without effort, her body resting trustingly along the hard, masculine length of his. Slowly he lowered her until the toes of her kid slippers touched the ground, and still their mouths clung, cherishing one another. Finally she broke the kiss, her palms resting on either side of his face.

"Tell me that they refused you," she entreated.

Smiling, he shook his head. "You know better than that, Mary. The Beau needs every experienced officer, every veteran he can find. I told you that before I left."

"And you convinced them you were fit."

"To be truthful—"

"To be truthful, you lied about your leg," she accused.

"They were too glad of my offer to think of refusing," he said, still smiling down at her. "Don't be angry, Mary, my heart. That's where I belong. It's where my men will be. My regiment. It's where I want to be."

"Not again," she whispered. "I can't let you go to that hell again." There was no answer for that plea. No comfort. "How long?" she asked and watched his lips tighten.

"Three hours. Less…" His voice faded at the pain in her eyes, suddenly glazed with tears. "I came as fast as I could. But I have to be back in London to board the transport at dawn."

"You just arrived. Surely—"

"Three hours, Mary," he reminded, his mouth finding the small blue vein at her temple. "Shall we spend it arguing?"

"No," she whispered, her lips lifting to his, fingers tangling through the golden curls. "No," she said again as his mouth shifted over hers, turning to meld, to possess what was his. And always would be.

* * * * *

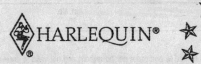

Take 4 bestselling love stories FREE

Plus get a FREE surprise gift!

DEBBIE MACOMBER

invites you to the

★ HEART OF TEXAS ★

Join Debbie Macomber as she brings you the lives
and loves of the folks in the ranching community
of Promise, Texas.

If you loved Midnight Sons—don't miss
Heart of Texas! A brand-new six-book series
from Debbie Macomber.

Available in February 1998
at your favorite retail store.

Heart of Texas by Debbie Macomber

Lonesome Cowboy	February '98
Texas Two-Step	March '98
Caroline's Child	April '98
Dr. Texas	May '98
Nell's Cowboy	June '98
Lone Star Baby	July '98

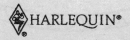

HARLEQUIN®

HPHRT1

WELCOME TO *Love Inspired* ™

A brand-new series of contemporary inspirational love stories.

Join men and women as they learn valuable lessons about facing the challenges of today's world and about life, love and faith.

Look for:

Promises
by Roger Elwood

A Will and a Wedding
by Lois Richer

An Old-Fashioned Love
by Arlene James

Available in retail outlets
in October 1997.

LIFT YOUR SPIRITS AND GLADDEN YOUR HEART with *Love Inspired* ™!

Steeple
Hill™

LI1197

Every month there's another title from one
of your favorite authors!

October 1997
Romeo in the Rain by Kasey Michaels
When Courtney Blackmun's daughter brought home Mr. Tall,
Dark and Handsome, Courtney wanted to send the young
matchmaker to her room! Of course, that meant the single
New Jersey mom would be left alone with the irresistibly
attractive Adam Richardson....

November 1997
Intrusive Man by Lass Small
Indiana's Hannah Calhoun had enough on her hands taking
care of her young son, and the last thing she needed was a
man complicating things—especially Max Simmons, the
gorgeous cop who had eased himself right into her little boy's
heart…and was making his way into hers.

December 1997
Crazy Like a Fox by Anne Stuart
Moving in with her deceased husband's—*eccentric*—family
in Louisiana meant a whole new life for Margaret Jaffrey and
her nine-year-old daughter. But the beautiful young widow
soon finds herself seduced by the slower pace and the much-
too-attractive cousin-in-law, Peter Andrew Jaffrey....

**BORN IN THE USA: Love, marriage—
and the pursuit of family!**

Available at your favorite retail outlet!

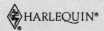 

**Harlequin Historicals presents
an exciting medieval collection**

THE KNIGHTS OF CHRISTMAS

With bestselling authors

Suzanne
BARCLAY

Margaret
MOORE

Debborah
SIMMONS

Available in October
wherever Harlequin Historicals are sold.

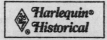

**Harlequin®
Historical**

As Seen on TV!

Free Gift Offer

With a Free Gift proof-of-purchase
from any Harlequin® book, you can receive
a beautiful cubic zirconia pendant.

This stunning marquise-shaped stone is a genuine cubic
zirconia—accented by an 18" gold tone necklace.
(Approximate retail value $19.95)

Send for yours today...
compliments of HARLEQUIN®

To receive your free gift, a cubic zirconia pendant, send us one original proof-of-purchase, photocopies not accepted, from the back of any Harlequin Romance®, Harlequin Presents®, Harlequin Temptation®, Harlequin Superromance®, Harlequin Intrigue®, Harlequin American Romance®, or Harlequin Historicals® title available at your favorite retail outlet, together with the Free Gift Certificate, plus a check or money order for $1.65 U.S./$2.15 CAN. (do not send cash) to cover postage and handling, payable to Harlequin Free Gift Offer. We will send you the specified gift. Allow 6 to 8 weeks for delivery. Offer good until December 31, 1997, or while quantities last. Offer valid in the U.S. and Canada only.

Free Gift Certificate

Name: _____

Address: _____   _____

City: _____ State/Province: _____ Zip/Postal Code: _____

Mail this certificate, one proof-of-purchase and a check or money order for postage and handling to: HARLEQUIN FREE GIFT OFFER 1997. In the U.S.: 3010 Walden Avenue, P.O. Box 9071, Buffalo NY 14269-9057. In Canada: P.O. Box 604, Fort Erie, Ontario L2Z 5X3.

084-KEZR